THE STILL PLACE

Greg F. Gifune
Sandy DeLuca

JOURNALSTONE
YOUR LINK TO ARTIST TALENT

ISBN: 978-1-68510-106-0 (trade paper)
ISBN: 978-1-68510-107-7 (ebook)
Library of Congress Catalog Number: 2023942086

First printing edition September 1, 2023
Published by JournalStone Publishing in the United States of America.
Cover Artwork and Design: Don Noble
Edited by Sean Leonard
Proofreading and Cover/Interior Layout by Scarlett R. Algee

JournalStone Publishing
3205 Sassafras Trail
Carbondale, Illinois 62901

JournalStone books may be ordered through booksellers or by contacting:
JournalStone | www.journalstone.com

For Rob Dunbar and Chas Hendricksen

"Paintings have a life of their own that derives from the painter's soul."
—Vincent van Gogh

THE STILL PLACE

CHAPTER ONE

~New York City, 2015~

Each time Klaus Riker did this, the more futile it seemed, the more hopeless it became. This useless, utter waste of time and resources was nothing short of torturous, but he kept at it, undeterred even after all these many frustrating, heartbreaking years. A sad and lonely, scarred old man chasing ghosts, forever lost on a quest for a Holy Grail he'd never find—that's all he was, all he'd ever be. He was sure of it. Yet he persisted, even now. Eighty years old, and like some poor desperate addlebrained miscreant chasing fairytales, a part of him still believed. He had to. How could he not? What was the alternative? His reality was and had long been one of suffering and longing, and only one thing could change that. He would either find what he had spent the last forty years searching for, or he wouldn't. Regardless, there would be no compromise. That was not an option. He would accomplish this task or die trying.

There could be no other way.

Somewhere in the distance, a car alarm blared, bringing him back. Klaus pulled his long wool coat in tighter around him, tucked chin to chest, and hobbled along the misty backstreet, pushing on through a light Manhattan rain. The cold made his bones and joints ache, and as he'd been walking all day and the sun would soon begin its descent, he knew his body wouldn't hold up much longer. But he was determined to make one more stop before heading home.

On the next corner he saw the small antique shop he'd come looking for. One of only a few he hadn't tried; like so many across the city and state, such places tended to blend one into the next. With a deep breath, Klaus approached the small building.

The front door was pitted wood with an etched glass center panel. Like the other establishments tucked away on this tiny side street, it had seen better days. Klaus pushed the door open, and an annoying little bell sounded from somewhere above him, announcing his arrival. Grunting

GREG F. GIFUNE & SANDY DELUCA

with disapproval, he closed the door behind him and was greeted by a burst of dry heat. He removed his fedora, smoothed what remained of his thinning gray hair with his fingers, and waited for his eyes to adjust to the dim light before venturing further.

Before him stood numerous archaic glass cases and dusty shelves housing an array of assorted bric-a-brac. Beyond, every inch of wall space was covered in paintings, old rugs, or vintage commercial signage. The uneven wood floors creaked as he stepped further into the narrow, cluttered shop, and near the back of the store he saw a woman only a few years his junior hunched over a counter.

With hawkish features and chalk-white hair, she glanced up from a crossword puzzle book clutched in her liver-spotted hands. Peering at him over half-glasses resting on the bridge of her nose, the woman arched an eyebrow then tried to mask her shock at Klaus' appearance by quickly forcing a warm smile and saying, "Good afternoon."

Klaus cleared his throat. He was used to such reactions. In fact, over the years he'd grown used to much worse. The deep scars along his throat and one side of his face were jarring to those who had never before encountered a burn victim such as himself. "And to you," he said with a curt nod.

"May I help you?" the woman asked, purposely looking past rather than directly at him. "Or would you rather just poke around some?"

"I am interested in any paintings you have."

The woman made a slow sweep of the area with one hand, indicating there were paintings all around him. "Anything in particular or…"

Klaus pulled a pair of eyeglasses from his jacket pocket and slipped them on. He looked around quickly, his eyes panning from one painting to the next. He knew what he was looking for, there was no need to scrutinize each one, he'd know the moment he—

"My *God*," he whispered, the words catching in his throat.

It felt as if he'd been hit across the chest with a baseball bat, and for a moment he was so overwhelmed he was sure he'd pass out. His mind simply couldn't comprehend what he was seeing. Not after all these years. It couldn't be, it—

"Are you all right, sir?" the woman asked, sliding out from behind the counter—as if she might be of some help when she looked to have enough trouble getting around herself. "Are you ill?"

With his mouth hung open and his tired glassy eyes wider and brighter than they'd been in decades, Klaus stood gazing at one painting on the back wall in particular. He was vaguely aware that the woman was speaking to him, but he'd already tuned her out. His complete focus and attention was leveled on the painting. Slowly, he moved closer to it, still unable to believe it. Forty years he'd searched. Forty *years*...and now...here it was. Here *she* was. He rubbed his eyes then kept them closed a moment. Could he be mistaken? He had to be certain. After all this time, what were the odds he'd found it now?

He opened his eyes.

There was no mistake. He'd spent decades dreaming of this moment, and now that it was actually happening, he couldn't get his mind around it. A tear rolled the length of his face. "That one," he said, pointing with a trembling finger. "I want that one."

"Certainly, I'll get it down and wrap it up for you. As for cost, that one is—"

"The price is immaterial. I'll take it."

"I was going to say it's quite reasonably priced," she said patiently. "No one's ever shown any interest in it but you."

"Do you know how it came to be in your shop?" Klaus asked, his entire body shaking now, his heart racing.

"I'm afraid I don't recall. It's been here for several years now." Her expression shifted. "I must say, your reaction to it is quite strong. Do you have some sort of *personal* connection with the work?"

Rather than answer, Klaus continued staring at the painting. It was a miracle. A goddamned miracle. Emotion throttled him, and he was suddenly worried he might faint. "May I sit down, please? I—"

"Of course," the woman said, taking him by the arm and helping him into a Gothic high-back antique chair displayed next to an assortment of very old books. "Are you sure you're all right? You look as though you've seen a ghost."

You have no idea...

"I'm fine," he assured her, still unable to take his eyes from the painting. "Thank you, I just need to sit a moment."

"I understand."

"Yes," he said, "I imagine you do."

If the woman found the response insulting, she gave no indication. Instead, she folded her arms across her chest and gazed at the painting along with him. "It is rather *different*, isn't it?"

"Unique," he answered evenly. "It is wholly and completely unique."

"Such an odd piece," she said as if she hadn't heard him. "Rather fascinating, though somewhat unsettling. It's certainly a conversation starter, that's for sure. What do you suppose they're doing, the people? Praying, perhaps?"

"Yes, in a way." The painting blurred through the tears filling Klaus' eyes. Ignoring his lightheadedness, he carefully pushed himself up and out of the chair, then reached for the painting. His fingers, still shaking, tenderly brushed the rough surface. "They're waiting. They've been waiting for a very long time."

"What do you imagine they've been waiting *for*, exactly?" the woman asked, clearly amused with his assessment.

For the first time in four decades, Klaus felt himself smile.

"Rescue…"

CHAPTER TWO

~Providence, Rhode Island, 2020~

Mina loved storms. During winter, especially when it snowed at night, she often went for walks after dark. And that night was no different. Snowsqualls blew about all around her, and the landscape, painted in hues of deep gray and black, reminded her of some of her own darker paintings. Dressed in ripped jeans, a sweatshirt, and a pair of worn boots, she was not dressed for such harsh weather, and the wet snow soaked through everything. As she shivered, the Atlantic stopped her in her tracks.

"I don't remember…"

Through the storm she glimpsed waves crashing shore. The ocean was churning and violent, and with the snow visibility was not good, but somewhere out there she thought she saw something bobbing along the waves. An ominous thing, it grew larger with each breath she took, and as she continued to peer through the snowy night, Mina became certain it was no trick of her mind. There was something there. Something…

She turned slowly, taking in the sky, the earth, the sea, and various nearby buildings. A bit farther from shore, she watched the dark trees with their bare branches bending in the winter wind. But those things were unfamiliar somehow. Even the heavens seemed different, littered with constellations she did not recognize; the moon unnaturally large and too close to Earth.

Everything was so strange that night, but then, how could it not be? She'd spent the evening drinking vodka and tequila and smoking weed. She even dropped some acid. Still, this seemed different than any trip she'd had before. Even in her mind-altered state, things seemed *off*.

Mina vaguely remembered leaving Salem's, a bar she frequented, with a man she'd never met before. They drove for a while and talked about the approaching blizzard. The man told her he didn't mind getting stranded with her and that his place was just up the road. But it wasn't near the sea. The coast was ten miles away.

What, then, was she doing here? And how had she come to be here, in this place?

That man, exactly when had she first met him? Had it been that night, or could it have been the night before? Mina thought about it a moment, and although everything remained jumbled and blurred, she was sure it had only happened a few hours ago. Hadn't it? Ralph would remember. He could almost always be found at Salem's on his off time, drinking and trying to recapture his youth. She remembered the disapproving look he'd flashed her when he spotted her leaving with the stranger. He'd scold her in the morning, and she'd pat his shoulder, tell him she was just blowing off steam the same way he had a long time ago and sometimes still did.

Ralph Deckard. Mina got a kick out of him almost as much as she loved him. His dyed hair was styled with the Barry Gibb grandeur of his youth, and his bar wardrobe was generally a peculiar combination of hippie and disco god. Mina often wondered if he purchased his clothing from thrift shops or had just never thrown anything away from his younger days. His apartment wall was strewn with photos of himself—circa 1975 through 1980—decked out in psychedelic jackets and shirts, wide bell-bottoms and platform shoes, posing with women he met at parties, mostly Janis Joplin and Patti Smith look-a-likes, all strung out on one thing or another. The rest were photos of him with his longtime boyfriend Clark, who he'd lost to cancer in the middle 1990s. Mina was certain Ralph had never been the same again. He'd had other relationships since, but nothing lasting or of any real depth.

"Where are you, Ralph? Can you come get me?" Mina slipped a hand into her pocket, trembling when she realized her phone wasn't there.

With her head pounding and the confusion mounting, she looked again to the ocean. The thing she had seen out there before had become one with that alien moon. It was so round and white, so enchanting. There was also something frightening about it—intimidating—but that didn't matter, because Mina found herself mesmerized by it as well, suspended there with such ethereal elegance above the ocean's fury.

More snow blew about, hitting her face like tiny needles and breaking her trance. Suddenly the flakes became so thick it was difficult to see the road above and the structures lining it. Standing there like aged sentinels, most of those houses had been built over one hundred years ago. Isn't that what the man had told her?

"How long have we been partying?" Mina shouted to the sea. "Dean or Duke, or whatever your name is? You have to get me home! Where'd you go, where are you?"

She gazed up at the row of buildings, searching for the guy's apartment building. He'd parked his truck outside, but there were no cars on that road, no signs of life.

And Dean or Duke or whatever the fuck his name was lived nowhere near the Atlantic. Isn't that what he'd told her?

Once more, through the haze of snow, her eyes scanned the houses along the bluff. With their aged and sagging porches, roofs slanted at odd angles, and general decay, they looked like something hastily sketched by some mad German Expressionist. All of them sat dark, like shadows.

As if in response, just for a moment, a dim light came to life in one window then just as quickly went off, followed by the brief flicker of a streetlight. And then all returned to darkness as a black and white world exploded around her, the only sounds those of an angry ocean and the solitary cry of a seabird.

Sadness filled her. Sadness laced with fear.

I'm lost, Mina thought. *I need to get out of here.*

But she knew she was far from home, far from everything and everyone she knew. She was lost, cut loose and drifting through this strange dark snowy night.

Mina looked to the inky water. The thing she saw before was closer now, and she realized it was actually a sail draped with snow and drenched with seawater flapping in the wind.

After a moment, a boat emerged from the darkness and chaos.

She rubbed her eyes and looked again.

The boat was not only really there, it was coming closer to shore, so close she was able to make out a grim-faced man with bone-white hands steering the vessel through the violent waves.

Despite her fear, Mina trudged closer to the water's edge.

The boat was just offshore now, and she could see the man's eyes. They were entirely void of life and white as the falling snow, as if covered with some strange glistening ivory film. His clothes—a rain slicker over a denim shirt and heavy workpants—were badly worn and tattered, as were his boots, as if he'd been wearing these things for ages. A faded bandana held his long stringy hair in place, and his face was covered in salt-and-pepper stubble.

Behind him, several others stood huddled on the deck, women and men both, resembling a ghostly rock band from decades before. Shabby velvet coats and halter tops hugged their bony frames, and their deathly pale lips parted to reveal teeth yellowed and brown with decay.

Slowly, the phantom ferryman raised a hand, pointed at Mina, and let out a deafening howl. The others joined him, their wails blending with the sounds of the storm and the continued screech of the lone seabird.

Mina knew she needed to run, but couldn't. Even when the boat finally reached shore and she could feel the coldness of death emanating from it and those aboard, she couldn't move. What struck her now was colder than the wind and the snow, colder than winter itself. Colder than anything Mina had experienced before.

This was a cold reserved for the darkest of graves.

"*Take my hand,*" the ferryman whispered, as if from inside her head. *"It's almost finished now—"*

All at once, the ringing of a cell phone, the smell of exhaust fumes, and the blare of a car horn startled Mina back into the present. As vague memories came to her of the previous night's date with Smirnoff Red and Tito's, too many dances with a guy name Dean or Duke (who lived in a shabby building on the south side of the city, the kind where you had to use the bathroom in the hall if you had to pee), and too many drugs, she took in her surroundings and remembered where she was.

She glanced at her phone: UNKNOWN NUMBER.

Probably a scam or a telemarketer, she thought, declining the call then crossing the street to the next block. A vague memory of falling asleep on a stained mattress the night before, only to awaken later sick to her stomach in the back of an Uber on her way home, danced across her mind's eye. As more memories worked their way through the fog in her head, Mina hurried through the hustle and bustle of city streets.

Once at home, she showered for a long time in an attempt to remove the remnants of her tryst. That much she remembered. That and how good that hot water felt on her skin. After a couple more shots of vodka, she collapsed into bed, only to have her phone alarm awaken her at dawn so she could get to work on time.

Now, standing in the sobering cold of morning, Mina took a hard pull on her cigarette then flicked if off into the gutter. Through plumes of breath and smoke, she took in the rundown campus where she worked. Here, in perhaps the worst neighborhood in the city, deep in the bowels of the decrepit building standing before her, she taught art to impoverished children. Her days mostly consisted of struggling from one class to the next, watching the clock while praising her students even when they drew crude figures and landscapes. Modern masters like Chagall and Beckmann, she reminded them, expressed their art from their hearts, tossing aside the need to prove that they could duplicate a tree, a building, or a person exactly as it or they appeared.

"Work with what you've got," she always told them. "Real art is what you *feel*."

Mina often questioned what tangible good her limited role in their lives actually accomplished though. Almost all of these poor kids were from broken families, many of them surviving day-to-day in foster homes or in government-run facilities where they remained wards of the state until they came of age and could be kicked to the curb. For most, art would never be anything more than a temporary distraction. It would not provide the escape or become the saving grace it was for Mina at their age, and that broke her heart. So despite the satisfaction she got from working with disadvantaged kids, she had to get away. Her own life was in turmoil. Her drinking and drug use was getting bad again and, as usual, that led to casual sex with strangers and often finding herself in dangerous situations. That wasn't the life Mina envisioned for herself, and not what she wanted, not really—it never had been—but she'd been unable to find anything else that could dull the pain of her own childhood, the string of foster homes, the abuse, the neglect. At the end of the day, she felt for these kids because she'd been one herself. But if she could barely keep herself together, what good could she be to them, what kind of example could she possibly set?

Besides, she told herself, *I'm getting too old for this, can't be on the run forever.*

Problem was, that's all Mina knew, all she'd ever known. This nowhere job was just one in a string of many. No security, no tenure, no real future. It was only a matter of time before she'd lose the ability to hold it together and they'd grow tired of her antics and her perpetually hungover ass and jettison her back into the street like all the others before them had. And with her background and history of jumping around and not being able to hold positions for long, it was getting harder to land teaching gigs. The point at which her opportunities ceased to exist altogether was closer than she liked to imagine.

Mina rubbed her temple, hoping to massage away the headache that was settling in, and then reached for the crumpled pack of cigarettes in her coat pocket, along with a lighter that was nearly empty. She'd have to stop at a bodega on the way home for a couple new ones. With a heavy sigh, she stabbed a fresh cigarette between her lips, but before she could light it her phone buzzed, indicating a voicemail message had been left.

Probably the fucking landlord looking for this month's rent, she thought.

Rather than listening to the voicemail, Mina hesitated just outside the building and pulled up the message in text form.

CONGRATULATIONS! THIS IS TO INFORM YOU THAT YOUR APPLICATION FOR RESIDENCY AT THE CROW'S CRY ARTIST COLLECTIVE HAS BEEN APPROVED. WE WILL BE EXPECTING YOU ON MONDAY AT NOON. SHOULD YOU HAVE ANY FURTHER QUESTIONS, OR IF YOU ARE UNABLE TO MAKE IT AT THAT TIME, PLEASE CONTACT PROFESSOR RIKER AT THE NUMBER AND EXTENSION PROVIDED.

"Holy shit," she muttered. "I got it, I— Are you kidding me? I fucking got it!"

Two older teachers passing by into the building looked her way and shook their heads disapprovingly. They all looked at her like that. Although most of her students loved her, to the other teachers and administrators she was a disgrace, always staggering into work, a weird and trippy young art teacher with issues aplenty and a foul mouth, not a serious educator. Far as they were concerned, she might as well have been there to teach recess.

Mina held the women's gazes, and through the phoniest smile she could muster said, "Good morning!"

They continued on without response.

"And kiss my ass," she added once they were out of earshot.

After one quick drag, Mina tossed the cigarette away and made her way into the building. She'd leave word with the office that she was done, then finish up the week and be on her way. This time she had a way out before she ended up without a job, strung out and homeless, and she planned to take it. She'd hit rock bottom before in her life, and she couldn't let that happen again.

Pushing open the steel door, she caught a glimpse of children in a classroom gathered in a circle, drawings in front of them, eyes so sad, kids that looked too tired to be six or seven. Just the way she used to be when—

"*Girl*, you could not possibly look worse and still be among the living."

Mina turned to see Ralph rounding the corner, his tweed jacket hanging from his slim frame, his faded jeans tapered, and his burgundy boots worn but polished. With a big grin and not even a hint of subtlety, he slowly looked her up and down. "Let me guess, that troglodyte you left Salem's with kept you up all night discussing great works of art and literature. Or did he opt for gracing you with a lengthy and no doubt devastatingly erudite dissertation on Postmodernism and its impact on—"

"Oh please, I'm too hungover for this right now." Mina waved a hand in the air between them. "Have mercy. Besides, I barely remember him. I was stoned as fuck."

"You think?"

"Whatever. Those nights are in the past for me now." She eyed him coyly. "Guess what? I got the residency."

"No you did not!"

"Yes I did too! And I am *out* of this shithole."

Ralph flashed a wide, toothy smile. "Are you serious? You got it?"

"Just found out this morning. Literally like a minute ago."

He stared at her, still gauging the situation. "You got it."

"I got it."

"You really got it?"

"Yes, Ralph, I *really* got it. Apparently I still have some value as an artist."

"Far more than you realize, my dear," he said softly.

This time she smiled. "Shut up."

"Sweetie, seriously, that's great news." He reached out and gave her shoulder a gentle squeeze. "Congratulations, I couldn't be happier for you or prouder of you."

"It's a minor, unknown residency," she said with a self-conscious shrug. "But—"

"Focus on the positives. This is going to be really good for you, wait and see."

"It has to be, right? I need to get away, have some solitude, focus on my painting, and try to get my shit together."

Ralph slid an arm around her and they slowly walked along the hallway together. "I'm sorry to see you go, but I was dealing with the same thing in the late 80s. I was spiraling down and completely out of control, you know? Only in my case, what rescued me was spending those six months in rehab."

"I get high and drunk with you all the time, Ralph, it obviously didn't take."

"Well not *totally*, you insufferable bitch," he said with a dramatic sigh. "But that's hardly the point."

They both laughed. Mina couldn't remember the last time she'd laughed sober, and it felt good. Ralph was the only thing she'd miss about this place. The kids too, she supposed; in her own way, she'd miss them too.

"This is going to work out great for you, doll. Mark my words. I know these things. It's a gift." A glint of sadness flickered in Ralph's eyes, but he covered it with a playful wink. "But you better keep in touch. Promise me, or I swear I'll hunt you down, move onto your couch, and become the thing that eats all your snacks and refuses to leave."

"It's in Massachusetts, Ralph, not the other side of the world," she explained. "Town called Crow's Cry. I've never been there before—never even heard of it—but I checked Google maps. It's less than two hours away, an hour and forty minutes or so."

"Fine, promise you'll keep in touch anyway."

"All right, all right," she said, chuckling. "I promise."

They wrapped each other in a big bear hug.

"Gonna miss you, kid."

"Then come visit me once I'm settled in."

"I may just do that. In the meantime, you watch yourself out there, you hear me?"

Mina nodded, and for just a moment longer, held on tight.

CHAPTER THREE

Mina stared at the glass. The vodka was long gone, and the ice had begun to melt. The flame from a candle in the center of the table reflected against it, flickering and dancing with a strangely beautiful motion in the otherwise dimly lit Chinese restaurant. All around her, people spoke in quiet voices as they ate their meals or enjoyed a wide range of exotic alcoholic drinks, and with the freezing temperatures outside, Mina found the warmth and atmosphere here not only welcoming, but soothing.

Although money was tight—wasn't it always?—Mina decided to celebrate the residency by treating herself to a nice meal before leaving town. She'd walked by the restaurant dozens of times and had always wanted to eat there. The place had a great reputation—and now she knew why—but it was also pricey. She couldn't afford it, but splurged anyway.

What the hell, she thought. *For the next six months I'll get to live rent free and have almost all my expenses paid by the residency program. It's not like a vodka-on-the-rocks and one overpriced entrée of spicy chicken and green beans with boiled rice is going to break me, right?*

"How was everything?"

Mina looked up to see her server, a young Chinese man in a white, button-down blouse and black slacks, smiling at her.

"Absolutely delicious, thanks."

He scooped up her plate that moments before had held her Yuen Yang Spicy Chicken. "Another drink?" he asked, indicating her glass.

"I'd love one, but I can't," Mina said. "Just the check, please, got a bus to catch."

As she waited, the awful cravings for a cigarette struck. She missed the days you could light up in restaurants and bars. *Just was well,* she thought. *I should quit anyway. Hardly anyone smokes cigarettes these days. Besides, this is the perfect time for new beginnings and a fresh start. Might as well kick the habit, it's long overdue.*

Five minutes later she was outside on the street lighting up and waiting for the Uber she'd ordered to drive her to the bus station. Due to a heavy rain that had been falling all day, the afternoon was so dark and overcast it more closely resembled early evening. Huddled beneath the awning in front of the restaurant, with her single suitcase, a large nylon portfolio tote housing numerous samples of her work, and a backpack full of art supplies slung over her shoulder, Mina watched the occasional car glide by and those unfortunate enough to be caught in the downpour on foot dashing through the rain.

For once, it felt nice to not be in a hurry.

She took a deep drag on her cigarette, and as she blew out a stream of smoke that mingled with a cloud of her breath in the frigid air, Mina felt herself relax to whatever extent she was still capable these days.

Part of her was going to miss Providence, but she was ready to go. It was time, and this residency program was one of the best opportunities she'd ever had. Over the years she hadn't gotten many breaks, and the few that had come her way she usually managed to squander. Mina knew this particular residency was relatively new, only about five years old, and quite modest—she'd never even heard of it until she came across the listing on a website that listed residencies nationwide—and that for many it would be of little interest. But to her, it was a genuine opportunity, and one that could very well be her last chance at truly accomplishing something meaningful and lasting as an artist. For the first time in her adult life, she wouldn't have to worry about living expenses, and that was huge. She could just focus on her art and hopefully produce her best work to date. A residency—even a small and obscure one like this—was something she'd hoped to land for years. Every chance she got, she applied for them all over the country, and she'd always been passed over. This time was different. This was her shot. They actually chose her from all the other applicants, and that meant they saw something in her the others hadn't. They believed in her, in her work, and that was a win, a big one.

Mina wasn't used to winning, but so far, it felt pretty damn good.

Now don't fuck it up, she told herself. *For once in your life, Mina, don't blow it.*

* * * *

Crow's Cry, an old mill town on the North Shore of Massachusetts, was nestled along the coast not far from the border with New Hampshire. Before English colonists arrived, the area was populated by Indigenous peoples known as the Pawtucket. While many surrounding areas were colonized prior, the first colony in what would eventually become Crow's Cry consisted of less than twenty people and was formed on its shores in 1650. Over the next one hundred years or so it grew not only in population, but scope.

The town of Crow's Cry was officially established in 1780, and continued to grow and evolve along with the times, the commonwealth, and the country. Though sawmills existed there as early as the late 1700s, by the early 1800s, the main source of income for the town was its textile mill. Not as big as mill towns like Lowell or Waltham, Crow's Cry was a modest but successful township that flourished until the late 1960s. In 1971, after years of steady decline, the mill finally shut down for good, and the impact was devastating. There were numerous attempts to reinvent the town by bringing in new forms of production and real estate investment, but none of those plans ever came to fruition, and the eventual result was a mass exodus of people and a high level of poverty among those that remained. Over the past fifty years, Crow's Cry had become a largely abandoned skeleton of a town, littered not only with the old dinosaur mill properties, but various empty rotting residences and condemned buildings throughout. A place that at one time housed a population of over six thousand residents now had only several hundred, and although the land itself had value, particularly along the stretch of beaches and Atlantic Ocean that bordered the town, the rest had become so rundown and largely forgotten that investors were hard to come by.

A minor resurgence had occurred in the late 1970s, when the original mill was converted into a giant retail shopping space, and due to its beach area and proximity to the ocean, a small artist community was formed. A playhouse and a series of small galleries opened, and it also became a draw for struggling writers. The retail shopping failed, as did other attempts at resurgence, but the artists remained. Rarely supported outside their own small community, they scraped by but had virtually no impact on the town financially. And now, all these years later, they and their handful of galleries were about all that was left of what had once been a busy and prosperous town.

In the summer months some still came for the beaches and swimming, but it was mostly transients, biker-types, and those who couldn't afford the pricier locales closer to and on Cape Cod, so it wasn't much in terms of a family destination. A handful of seasonal businesses near the ocean did fairly well—mostly bars, tacky souvenir shops, a sleazy adult club, a couple restaurants, and some palm reading joints—but by early fall, most were boarded up, and Crow's Cry was again forgotten as another long, dark, and desolate winter set in. All that remained were the year-round residents and the small community of artists.

Mina looked up from her phone. She'd spent the last half hour or so reading about the history of Crow's Cry on a website dedicated to former mill towns, and as the bus slowly made its way along the narrow main strip in town, her eyes focused on the bleakness beyond the windows. How even artists survived here was beyond her. The entire place looked like some post-apocalyptic ghost town. Almost everything was closed and dark, and when the bus finally reached the end of the strip and pulled up alongside an empty, weed-infested parking lot, the driver announced in a droning voice that they had arrived at the Crow's Cry stop.

The bus was only about half full, and its ultimate destination was Bangor, Maine, with several stops in Massachusetts and New Hampshire along the way, but when Mina stood and slung her backpack over her shoulder, she realized she was the only passenger de-boarding.

Figures, she thought. *Who the hell else would get off here?*

As she and the bus driver stepped out into the cold, he opened the luggage bin and pulled free her suitcase and portfolio tote. A short, rotund, middle-aged man with thinning hair the color of black shoe polish slicked straight back and away from his hawkish face, he looked around, then back at Mina with a questioning stare.

"You got somebody picking you up or something?"

"Yeah," she said through their clouds of breath. "I'll be fine, thanks."

The driver seemed unconvinced but gave a nod. "Okey-doke," he said, then waved wearily and climbed back into the bus.

As it pulled away, leaving her there in the empty lot, her suitcase and tote at her feet, Mina pulled her coat in tighter around her and waited. Someone was supposed to be meeting her here. She'd received a text explaining that once she'd confirmed her arrival time. But no one was around, and it was freezing out. Just over her shoulder, down beyond another smaller parking lot and some dunes, the Atlantic Ocean lapped the sandy shores of Crow's Cry, and an icy wind whipped in off the waves, cutting through her right to the bone with the precision of a razor.

In the other direction, across the street, everything was boarded up and dark except for a small boxy bar with a flat roof. A couple neon beer signs blinked in the curtained windows and a sign over the door read: TOPSY TURVEYS.

Mina lit a cigarette and smoked a while, contemplating slipping inside for a couple drinks. But then what if she missed her escort? If they were even still coming, that is. Besides, it didn't exactly look like the kind of place that was safe for a woman alone, so with her free hand she pulled up the contact information she had on her phone.

In the distance, a small black car turned onto the far end of the strip just as she was about to place the call. It was the only vehicle she'd seen since she got there, and as it roared closer, moving along the deserted street, Mina saw that it was an old beat-up Volkswagen Bug.

The car pulled over to the side of the road, just shy of the parking lot, perhaps thirty yards away. After a moment, the driver's side door opened with a loud creak, and though the car was still running, an older woman stepped out and stared at Mina with a guarded gaze. In a pair of loose jeans, rubber winter boots, a heavy wool coat, and a knit hat with a pompom on top, the woman moved cautiously around to the front of the VW and continued staring, but made no attempt to come any closer.

Not sure what else to do, Mina offered a timid wave.

"Are you Mina Vero?" the woman called out in a booming voice.

"Yes!" Mina shouted back, above the wind.

Pushing away from the Bug, the woman strode over to her with a slow, deliberate gate. She had a very subtle limp on the left side. While still a few feet away, she thrust a hand out and in the same gruff tone announced, "Frances Strengarden!"

Mina shook her hand once she was close enough to reach it. Ice cold, the skin along the woman's palm was taut and rough, her fingernails ridged, discolored, and cut nearly to the quick. At closer range the woman appeared to be somewhere in her early seventies, and despite her somewhat disheveled appearance, seemed to be in excellent shape. Wisps of chalk-white hair protruding from beneath her hat, a slight frame, and a long, angular face and pronounced chin conspired to give her the stern look of an old world spinster.

"Nice to meet you," Mina managed. "Thanks for picking me up, I—"

"Of course!" the woman barked, releasing Mina's hand and snatching up her suitcase. "Now let's neither dilly nor dally in this awful cold!"

Before Mina could say anything more, the woman was already headed back to her car, so she grabbed her portfolio tote and followed along as quickly as she could.

"What a rad old car," she said once they'd loaded her things into the front trunk.

Frances Strengarden slammed it shut, then put her hands on her hips and cocked her head as if baffled. "What does that mean?"

"Oh—you know—as in *radical*. It's just an expression. Like cool."

"I see," she said. "Of course that's because it's not one of those soulless newer models. It's an original, an older gal, much like I am. It has *character*, and a *history*, a story to tell if only one is willing to see it, appreciate it, and listen. It's become a lost art these days, listening. Do you agree?"

Mina smiled even though the woman was staring at her with a severe expression. "Yes, I—definitely—sure," she said, fumbling for some sort of appropriate response. "Nobody listens anymore—I—what's up with that anyway?"

"Come along," Frances said abruptly, walking around to the driver's side of the Bug. "It's time to get you to your new home."

* * * *

Unseen things rattled and shook as the VW rumbled along, the ride about as smooth as a bucking bronco. The interior, which looked like it hadn't been cleaned in ages, was in even worse shape than the exterior. Thankfully the heater still worked, but it also intensified a musty smell that permeated the car. An ancient radio in the dash, complete with knobs and pushbutton presets, was tuned to an NPR talk show, which played through tinny, scratchy speakers, but Mina concentrated on her surroundings instead.

Except for the occasional wind gust, the town was quiet and oddly still. They'd only traveled a few blocks, but Mina had yet to see anything but a few parked cars. Although it was a troubling thought, she easily could've believed she and Frances were alone here. It looked like the town had been deserted for years. There was also something unsettling and claustrophobic about the way the dark and largely empty buildings on either side of the narrow streets seemed to jut up into the gray sky like ghouls lording over them and their decrepit little car.

Her host hadn't said a word since they'd left the parking lot. Instead, the woman stared straight ahead through the smudged windshield, her back perfectly straight and her hands clutching the steering wheel at the ten and two o'clock positions.

"So," Mina finally said, "Mrs. Strengarden—"

"It's Ms., but you may call me Frances."

"Okay, *Frances*, do you work for the collective or are you an artist too?"

"Guilty on both counts," she said. "I'm a sculptor, but I also handle some of the administrative work for our little flock."

"A sculptor, that's awesome, I—"

"Awesome seems extreme in my case," Frances said with a frown.

"I just meant I've always admired sculptors, they—"

"Well, I don't consider myself anything special. You, on the other hand, we're all *very* impressed with. The samples of your work were quite promising. Suffice to say we're excited to have you here."

Mina was touched. "Thanks. I'm honored to—"

"Here we are!" Frances pulled over in front of an old two-story building that appeared to have once been a single-family home but that had at some point long ago been converted into apartments.

After taking in the dark old building a moment, Mina gave a quick look up and down the short side street. Again, nothing was moving, and there were no other people out. *Strange*, she thought.

"Is this town always so quiet?"

"You mean empty."

It wasn't a question, but Mina answered anyway. "I guess I do."

"Peace...quiet...isolation...*these* are an artist's friends."

Who am I to argue with that? Mina thought.

Frances shut off the engine. "Let's get your things."

* * * *

Once they passed through a small foyer and climbed the main stairs to the second floor, they arrived at the end of a dark hallway and a closed wooden door with a simple antiquated latch. Behind it lay a third set of stairs, these narrow and brief. With Frances leading the way, Mina followed her up and into an open loft-like studio apartment. With the slope of the walls and its slanted ceiling, it was obvious the space had been an attic at one time, but it was fairly good sized. The only windows were a tall twin set on the back wall that overlooked a small courtyard. Directly across, on the far side of the courtyard, was another dilapidated apartment building that was not quite as tall. Beyond its roof, Mina could see the ocean in the distance, including the lot where the bus had dropped her off.

"Not the brightest of rooms this time of year or in the evenings, but during daylight hours the windows help. Of course, when additional light is necessary, you have these." Frances hit a wall switch that activated a series of long fluorescent tube lights built into the ceiling. "And there are lamps there, and there."

As Mina's eyes adjusted to the bright light, she followed Frances' pointing finger to a lamp on a small nightstand next to the single bed on the far wall, and another on a table next to a modest counter area opposite it that housed a one-cup coffeemaker and a hotplate. On the floor alongside the counter sat an apartment-size refrigerator that reminded her of one she'd had in her dorm room in college. The area near the windows was empty except for an old easel leaned against the wall and a couple old rags spattered with long-dried paint lying on the floor. In the center of the room was an easy chair that looked comfortable despite having seen better days, and at the other end of the apartment another door was open just enough to reveal a toilet, a sink with a medicine cabinet above it, and a vintage cast-iron clawfoot bathtub.

"Your sleep area, food prep area, and work area," Frances said, indicating each with another stab of her finger. "And as you see, you've a private bath. No shower, but there is a lovely tub for long, hot, relaxing baths. We've stocked your refrigerator with coffee, milk, and a few snacks to get you started, but you'll need to purchase your own groceries, as stipulated in the contract, either from your own funds or from the monthly stipend we provide, up to you. There's a market, Sal's, a few blocks over."

"Okay, thanks." Mina leaned her portfolio tote next to the windows, dropped her backpack on the floor next to it, then looked around a bit more. There was no television or radio, but she was all right with that. She pictured herself working here—she could see it, sketching or painting in front of those beautiful windows—and spending evenings reading or playing on her phone or laptop.

"There is no landline," Frances explained.

"That's fine." Mina held up her phone. "What about Internet access?"

"Wireless WIFI is included for the duration of your stay here at no charge. The router is downstairs and shared by everyone in the building. It can be accessed through the use of the password. REMBRANDT, all caps."

"Cute."

If Frances shared her amusement, she gave no indication. "As you can see, the building is older and has radiators for heat. The oil furnace is in the basement. It's a bit loud, the tired old beast, but still functions satisfactorily." She motioned first to an ancient cast-iron unit to the left of the main door, then to a dated dial thermostat on the wall above it. "Each apartment regulates its own temperature. The thermostat is there."

"Is it all right if I smoke in here?" Mina asked.

Frances seemed mystified by the question. "I see no reason why not. Just be careful. You'll have to buy yourself an ashtray. The last resident was a nonsmoker."

"I'm planning on quitting soon, I—"

"Do you have any further questions?"

"No, I—"

"Then I take it you find the living arrangements acceptable?"

"Yes, it's a great little space," Mina said. "I love it."

Frances strode to the door, then stopped and looked back at her. "We thought you'd want to take your first day to get settled in, so nothing is planned for today. We have, however, arranged a meet-and-greet, as it were, with Professor Riker, the head of our community, and the rest of our members. Any other questions or concerns you may have can be addressed at that time. There is also some basic paperwork that needs to be filled out and signed, but we can deal with that in the morning as well. I'll be by to fetch you at precisely nine o'clock. Is that understood?"

"Sure," Mina said. "But I do have one more question, actually."

"Go ahead."

"The building, it's so quiet. How many people live here?"

"There is one apartment on the first floor and one on the second. The first floor apartment is occupied by a married couple, the one on the second by a single occupant. All three are members of our flock. You'll meet them soon enough."

"And the courtyard?" she asked.

"What about it?"

"Am I allowed to use it?"

"Few do these days, especially in the dead of winter. It's a shared property between this building and the one directly across from you." Frances' penetrating dark eyes locked on Mina. "But of course you're permitted to use it if you so desire. We're a collective of artists here, Mina. This is a community of like-minded souls, not a prison."

Mina wrapped her arms around herself as a sudden chill set in. The moment Frances was gone she planned to turn up the heat. "Thanks. I'm excited to be here."

"And we're pleased to have you," Frances said evenly. "But I have other things to attend to, so if there's nothing more I'll be on my way. I'll see you in the morning. Until then, should you have any immediate concerns or questions, simply call the contact number you received earlier and someone will assist you."

"Great, thanks for everything. I'm really appreciative of the opportunity to—"

"Yes, you're quite welcome." Frances extended her hand as she had when they first met, but this time to slip Mina a ring with two keys on it, one to the front door of the building and the other to her apartment. "I hope your stay with us here in Crow's Cry will be an enjoyable and productive one."

Mina felt the keys press into her palm as she closed her hand over them.

Outside, the wind picked up suddenly, sending a strong gust crashing into the old building. Startled, Mina looked to the windows, but there was nothing there. Had she expected there to be?

The building creaked and moaned against the onslaught, then fell quiet.

Too goddamn quiet, Mina thought, turning back to say goodbye to Frances.

But she was already gone.

CHAPTER FOUR

Mina dragged her suitcase and portfolio tote to the easy chair. Her muscles ached from sitting so long on the bus and she could feel a stress headache emerging. Pressing her fingertips to her temple, she flopped into the chair with a thud, something she'd done since she was a little girl. She laughed lightly to herself. Whenever she did it in front of Ralph, he'd say, "Why do you insist on plopping yourself into chairs like an enormous scoop of ice cream dropped from a rooftop?"

"I miss you already," she whispered. A bittersweet feeling struck her as she wondered if he was drinking at Salem's at that very moment. Probably flirting with the bartender, a heavily tattooed, muscular guy named Gus.

Be careful, Mina thought. Ralph sometimes got too drunk and let his guard down. He'd been jumped in the dark on his way home more than once. Unfortunately, despite all the strides society had made, there were still those closeted or repressed macho assholes out there eager to take their violent frustration and self-loathing out on an openly gay man. *He'll be okay,* she told herself. *Can't spend all my time worried about him just because I'm not around.*

A vision of them laughing together flooded her mind, and she felt herself smile.

He's probably sitting at Salem's right now thinking the same shit about me.

Mina took a deep breath and decided to get organized a bit, then maybe explore the neighborhood and pick up some food. Her head throbbed as she shifted position in the chair and slid back a bit, her fingers pressing into the cushy armrests. It was old but comfortable, the soft upholstery laced with a strong scent of lilac and a slightly more subtle odor of marijuana. Someone had obviously attempted to freshen it up with fabric spray. Slowly, her eyes panned across the room. Everything was clean—not a speck of dust on the counters, floor, or furniture. She looked up at a string of fluorescent lights. The twin windows would make the space bright for painting on sunny days, but at night or when it stormed, a painter needed more. The walls were white, except for a few splatters of orange and blue paint here and there.

Perfect. I'll do the best work of my life here.

Mina opened her suitcase, removed several plastic bags she'd laid on top of her clothes, and piled them on her lap. The first was filled with two old house painters' brushes, round brushes, liner brushes—filbert and shader brushes. Ink pens, erasers, pencils, a ruler, and charcoal had been loaded into another bag, along with several small pallet knives. Her gesso (a white paint mixture consisting of a binder mixed with chalk, gypsum, or pigment) and several tubes of acrylic paint—all primary colors—were in another. A small box contained tubes of Burnt Sienna, Indian Red, Burnt Umber, and two containers of white and black. She'd also stashed a couple small pieces of unstretched canvas beneath the bags, along with some bubble wrap and cardboard. And finally, she brought along several sketch books, her work clothes, a pair of paint-splattered jeans and a ripped AC/DC sweatshirt she liked to work in, and other assorted jeans, tops, a pair of flats, a pair of sneakers, and one pair of heels.

She'd need garbage bags, small containers, Ziploc bags, and paper towels too, but figured she could pick them up at any convenience or grocery store in town. As for additional art supplies, she could get them at the local art supply center.

Little by little she opened the plastic bags, laying the supplies on the floor in front of her.

"Should have brought a bigger tube of blue paint," she said through a sigh.

As she continued to unpack, she came across one of her favorite books, her bible, really—*The Elements of Color: A Treatise on the Color System*, by Johannes Itten. She'd also brought several smaller books featuring works by Chagall, Beckmann, and the German Expressionists. Inspiration in worn tomes she'd had and cherished since her freshman year of art school.

Just then, she remembered going to The Museum of Modern Art in New York for the first time while still a student, and being exposed to the work of Chagall, Picasso, Rothko, Francis Bacon, Pollock, and others. They were so free, these great artists, undaunted by what the eye could see, by what the brain recognized. They were faithful only to the whispers of their souls. That's when Mina first began to loosen up, forsaking painting a tree just like a tree, with every detail of its bark and all its leaves. The modern masters taught her that it was all right to purposely distort objects, to ignore the urge to make a work photo-real. It was all right to lay a canvas on the floor, dip a brush into a can of paint, and splatter it over the white sheet, allowing colors to drip and blend, to become a living piece of her soul.

"Before the camera was invented, artists wanted to paint as close to reality as possible," Ralph once told her. "Couldn't do it any other way, no other way to record the passage of time, I guess. But when the camera came onto the scene it threatened the manual creation of imagery. So, many started to paint in a way that *separated* them from photographic images. They painted what they felt, and then anything was possible, wasn't it? Imagination and the soul dominated. It's always been different for illustrators, of course, but that's not what we are. They essentially recreate someone else's vision. We paint and create our own."

Her eyes fell to the Chagall book, its cover sporting the famous *Blue Violinist*, which was a slightly abstract figure happily playing a tune as he floated over a city, a bird on his shoulder and another perched in his lap. In her mind, the birds' wings suddenly fluttered and the figure's smile became a scowl, but it was a just a flash. Mina shook her head. Why had her mind conjured such a thing? Or had her eyes actually played a trick on her?

Her stomach rumbled.

I'm starving, she thought.

Mina put the book aside and rubbed her eyes. The headache had dulled but was still there. Maybe a walk and some cold fresh air would help.

Time to explore…

* * * *

The grocery store, SAL'S FRESH FOODS, was nearly empty. Only one register was open, tended by a girl who looked about eighteen or so. Thin and pale, her eyes nervously darted to the entrance every few seconds, as if she was waiting for someone to show at any moment. Her face was devoid of makeup and her strawberry blonde hair hung limply over her shoulders. A name tag pinned to her faded sweatshirt read: Tiffany.

The girl's face brightened the moment she spotted Mina, as if the mere presence of another human being represented hope that there might be a respite from the boredom of the otherwise empty market. "Hey," she said in a self-consciously nervous voice. "You part of that artists' group?"

Mina selected a small basket from a stack next to the register. "Yeah," she said, hooking the basket over her arm. "I just got into town."

"I figured."

"You did, huh?" Mina gave a slight smile.

"Well, yeah, I mean, I've never seen you before and, you know, you look like one of them, except younger. That's not a bad thing, I'm just saying the younger ones come and go. It's the older artists that never seem to leave. I get it though. If you're old maybe this place is okay for the rest of however long you've got, but nobody younger wants to stay in Crow's Cry forever. Why would they? Especially if you have talent, right? A person could go anywhere. New York, LA, even other places in New England. Shit, better places in Mass they could go too."

The girl was awkward, but Mina couldn't help but be a bit charmed by her. "At least in my case you're not wrong. I'm doing a residency here, so I won't be—"

"Yeah, it's like a temporary thing, right?"

"Right," Mina answered, studying the girl's pale face. It reminded her of ghost portraits Ralph had done a few years ago, paintings he claimed were based on beings he'd seen in dreams or sometimes caught glimpses of in old buildings.

"See?" Tiffany said. "I knew it. Nobody else ever comes here. But, you know, welcome or whatever."

"Thanks. Do you like art?"

"I guess. I've been to the galleries before. Nothing much else to do in this town besides work, maybe catch a movie or get drunk and high as fuck." She smiled at Mina like they were sharing an inside joke. "I like to get really high and go to the galleries sometimes. At least it's something different, you know? And a lot of it's really, like, *dark*. That's fire."

Mina stared at her.

"*Fire*," Tiffany said again, and then, realizing Mina had no idea what she was talking about, added, "Dope."

Mina chuckled. "Okay, gotcha."

"I'm just saying like it isn't pretty stuff like flowers and kitties and shit like that. You know, like you see in somebody's house or in a restaurant or something." Tiffany lowered her eyes. "Sorry, I know I talk way too much. You need to shop, and I'm—"

"It's cool, don't worry about it."

Tiffany looked at her as if that were the nicest thing anyone had ever said to her. "Do you have any questions about where to find things in here or whatever?"

"I'd love to get some cold cuts, maybe some nice rolls?"

She pointed toward the back of the store. "Over there."

A small neon sign announcing freshly cut meats and prepared meals blinked over a glass case and counter area.

"And there's chips and stuff in aisle four," Tiffany added. "If you're looking to get your drink on, we don't sell liquor or beer—state law—but there's a package store two doors down, if you didn't already see it."

Mina had, but thanked her anyway.

"No problem. Need any help, just ask, only I don't slice deli meats, just so you know. Larry does that, but he's off tonight. He always does up a few packages before he leaves though, you know, in case anybody comes in later. There should be a few in the bin next to the counter."

"Thanks again," Mina said, her stomach grumbling and her headache still throbbing as she made her way to the deli. No one was behind the counter, but neatly piled in a refrigerated case were packages of cold cuts, ham, turkey, roast beef, just as Tiffany said. Alongside them were containers filled with assorted salads, including tuna, chicken, and egg. To the side of the case stood a rack of rolls and assorted artisan breads.

After Mina grabbed some roast beef, American cheese, a container of premade chicken salad, and a bag of Italian sandwich rolls, she took her time perusing the aisles. The lighting here seemed brighter than necessary, the smell of the place was antiseptic, and quiet classical music drifted about from hidden speakers in the ceiling. There was something strange about being the only shopper there, but in time she found mayonnaise, potato chips, some paper cups and plastic utensils, napkins, a plastic ashtray, and some paper plates, then headed back for the register.

Mina found a rack with some cheap lighters and several bottles of aspirin, so she added two of each to her order, then began stacking items on the short conveyer belt.

"Feels kinda sketchy, right?' Tiffany smiled and hooked a strand of hair behind her ear. "Being the only one shopping in here, I mean."

"It's different."

"Right?" She nodded knowingly.

"It can't always be like this, the place couldn't stay in business."

"No, but you'd be surprised. Some nights I can go my whole shift, and all I see is like two or three people. For real, the *whole* shift. Not gonna lie, it's creepy as fuck."

"I can see where it might be." Mina looked around. "Are you here by yourself?"

Tiffany leaned closer, and in a lower voice said, "There's a security dude, but he's like a million years old and mostly sleeps out back in the stockroom, so basically, yeah."

"Well, I guess it's better than—"

"Hell yeah, you got classic Lay's!" Tiffany held out a fist. "*Totally* my jam!"

Mina tapped Tiffany's fist with her own. "Just promise me we'll still be cool if I come back for some of those cheese-flavored pretzels."

They both laughed, and once she'd put Mina's items into a big brown paper bag, and Mina had paid her, the girl pointed to her nametag. "Anyways, I'm Tiffany."

"Mina."

"*Dude*, bad ass name!"

"Thanks," Mina said, laughing lightly again.

"I hope you come back. I mean, we got a couple bodegas in town, but this is the only real grocery store left in Crow's Cry. We're way better."

"I'm here a few months," Mina said. "I'll be back."

Getting too chummy with a *Normal* (Ralph's name for noncreative people) wasn't usually Mina's style, but she couldn't help but like Tiffany. She just wished she looked less like those ghostly girls Ralph had painted.

Undaunted, Tiffany grabbed a large fabric bag from a hook beside the register. "Here, take one of these for next time." She folded it, then stuffed it into the paper bag. "No charge for first-time customers. Ones I like anyway. Makes it easier to carry everything, you don't want your ass slipping and sliding all over the ice out there with a ton of bags in your arms, feel me?"

"Yeah, thanks, Tiffany."

"No worries, *Mina*." Her eyes nervously looked to the floor. "It's mad snowing again. Be careful out there."

"I will. See you later." The bag in her arm, Mina started for the exit.

"Hey," Tiffany said from behind her.

Mina slowed her pace and looked back over her shoulder. "Yeah?"

"Be *safe*."

* * * *

Snow and violent winds assaulted the ancient apartment building, rattling the windows and shaking the entire structure. In the distance, sounds of a turbulent ocean crashing shore echoed in the night, mixed with occasional unseen debris blowing about and scraping the pavement below.

A draft seeped in from the windows, and not long after the old radiator kicked on, hissing and rattling like the archaic instrument it was. Though loud and cantankerous, it brought heat to the room relatively quickly.

Earlier, Mina had swallowed a couple aspirin then wolfed down a chicken salad sandwich and nearly half the bag of potato chips. Now, with her headache gone, she poured a glass of Fucking Cool Vodka (an actual brand she'd found at the package store and bought three bottles of due to the name) and had a long sip. It wasn't her usual Russian vodka—this brand was distilled and bottled in Brooklyn, New York—but she found it pretty damn good.

Slowly, her nerves settled and she felt her body relax.

In darkness, she sat in the comfortable chair, sipped the drink, and gazed out the twin windows. The wind gusts caused the snow and ice to swirl about in an array of odd silvery patterns, which turned the night into an ominously beautiful haze of black and white.

Her eyes followed one particular swirl of snow as it twisted and turned before vanishing beneath the scope of the windows. As it did so, Mina found herself looking through the storm to the dilapidated apartment building across the way. The top floor was completely dark, but on the ground floor a light suddenly filled a large window facing the courtyard. Dim at first, it was followed by a string of overhead fluorescent lights that further brightened the room.

A lone figure walked toward the window.

Mina sat forward a bit and craned her neck. She still couldn't see enough of the first floor from her position, so she stood up.

The figure in the window below was a man. His was a thin but muscular build, and his hair was a bit long and unkempt. He was nude to the waist, wearing only a pair of baggy jeans, and he carried a drink of his own—brown fluid on ice, presumably whiskey or bourbon. He stared out at the night, at the courtyard, and sipped his drink, unaware that across the way and above him, Mina stood in the darkness of her apartment looking down at him.

She watched as the man turned from the window then set his drink down.

He considered something on the floor, standing over and gazing down at it. A blank white sheet of canvas lie spread out before him, several cans of house paint and a few large brushes surrounding it.

Mina pressed a finger against the glass as the man bent down, lifted a brush, dipped it into a can and began to paint. Wide, broad strokes followed as he moved around the canvas, stalking it like a predator. Suddenly, he threw down the brush, snatched up another, covered the bristles with bright orange paint, and began to spatter it across the canvas. He moved like some mad dancer, as if possessed. Through the curtain of swirling snow and distance separating them, Mina watched as the paint sprayed, exploding around the man and onto the canvas, spattering his chest and arms and neck in the process. The frenzy continued for a minute or two, and then his dance of sorts slowed, his movement became more fluid, his work more deliberate and precise.

Slowly, magically, an image formed on the canvas, abstract and haunting...

The sea, Mina thought. *He's painting the sea.*

He'd also painted a series of faces, pale and spattered with deep orange and dusty blues.

Slowly, the man crouched, holding his brush loosely and allowing paint to trickle over the canvas. The images dissolved into a layer of darker blue, intangible yet beautiful somehow, otherworldly. The painter's act of creation—his furious dance—was just as important, or maybe more so, than the final result. The way his hands moved, the way he stepped across the floor, turned, seeming to fly at times, as though he'd found his heart, his spirit evident within his movements.

The snow continued to swirl about in the night between them like some frantic muse as Mina brought her drink to her lips. Only then did she realize her hands were shaking.

The man stopped for a moment, paintbrush still dripping in his hand as he gazed at his creation. Suddenly he turned, as if distracted by something, and took a step closer to his window. He watched the snow a while, and then slowly...looked up.

She swore he was looking right at her. Heart racing, Mina took a step back from the window. But there were no lights on in her apartment, there was no way he could see her in the dark. It wasn't possible. Was it?

The man began to roll his head, like his neck was tight and he was loosening it up. He took up his drink, finished it in a single gulp, then turned back to his painting.

He didn't see me, Mina assured herself. *He just looked this way, that's all.*

The wind whistled, snow slapped against the windows, and Mina felt a strange sensation, something between excitement, arousal, and something more.

Fear...

Was it the storm, the vodka, her exhaustion? Or maybe spying on the man and intruding on his privacy was making her feel guilty and ratcheting up her anxiety.

Why should I feel like some creepy voyeur? What does he expect? He's working in plain view with his place lit up like a Christmas tree, so—

His apartment suddenly went dark.

"Jesus," she whispered. The heat was already rising in the room, but Mina felt herself shiver nonetheless. "That was fucking intense."

She threw back the rest of her drink, poured another, then powered that one down too. By the time she'd had her third, she was still standing at the windows and staring down at the now-dark apartment, but she'd begun to wonder if the mad dancing painter had ever really been there at all.

* * * *

The cast-iron bathtub was a treat. Mina couldn't remember the last time she'd soaked in a tub. When she was a kid maybe, in one foster home or another? But designer soap and plush towels were scarce—if not unheard of—when she was a kid, unlike the goodies she'd found in her new bathroom. Oddly, unlike the rest of the place, the bathroom had been well stocked with a few bottles of body wash, several packages of scented soap, bath oils and beads, expensive loofas, the nicest toilet tissue she'd ever seen, and an array of expensive thick towels.

Still reeling from the man in the window, Mina drew a hot bath, undressed, and slid in. The water was soothing and relaxed her aching muscles. She added a couple bath oil beads that were supposed to help relax her. They smelled of lavender.

"Check me out," she said quietly. "Pampering myself like a big shot."

A bottle of vodka—the *Fucking Cool* one—sat on the tub's edge. Every now and then she lifted it, unscrewed the top, took a pull then set it back down, carefully capping it. The last thing she needed was to spill it or break the bottle before she could get another. She slid lower, so that only her head was above water.

Miserable out there, she thought, *but nice and warm in here, bitches!*

Her thoughts turned again to the man she'd seen. He was older than she was, but not by much—maybe early forties—and Mina wondered if he was part of the *community*, as Frances had called it, that had brought her here, one of those few older artists Tiffany spoke of who never left. Whoever he was, he'd clearly been trained at a prestigious art school, Mina was certain of that. The man was obsessed with the abstract expressionists, with what had been coined *action painting*, and from what little she'd seen, he was very good.

Sexy too, with that mussed hair and lean, sculpted body.

With a grin, Mina told herself it was just the vodka.

Maybe she'd try to find out more about him.

"Maybe Tiffany knows him," she whispered.

Mina closed her eyes and imagined herself floating in the stranger's paint, her flesh the canvas, his hands the brushes, his breath hot and labored against her flesh as he moved around her in the darkness and the steam rising from the tub.

A loud thud snapped her out of it and sent her bolting upright. It sounded almost like someone had slammed a door. "Fuck was that?" she said aloud, water splashing around her. "Hello?"

Mina ran her hands across her face and sat up straighter. She listened.

The storm still raged, but that sound was closer, it—it sounded like it had come from inside the apartment, not out. She squinted through the sparse light—she'd only left a small nightlight on next to the sink when she'd gotten into the tub—and tried to see what she could. The bathroom door was ajar, just as she'd left it, but she couldn't make out much beyond it.

She'd almost convinced herself it was nothing when she heard what sounded like a slight creaking sound just beyond the bathroom doorway.

"Seriously?" she muttered, pushing herself up out of the water and onto her feet. "Hello? Is someone here?"

Shivering, she grabbed a nearby towel and wrapped it around herself. Had something dark, a shapeless shadow perhaps, just drifted by the threshold? Her heart smashing her chest, Mina carefully stepped out of the tub. She was lightheaded from the vodka, and in her wet bare feet she found little purchase on the tile floor.

I need a weapon.

Mina looked around frantically.

The bottle, it was all she had.

She grabbed the vodka. Even half-empty, if she hit someone in the head with the bottle they'd know it. Feeling the weight of it in her hand, Mina carefully padded over to the door.

"Hello?" she called again. "I already called the cops, so…is somebody here?"

Only the storm answered.

Slowly, Mina peeked out from behind the bathroom door. Standing there, trembling, she struggled to focus, peering through the darkness of the apartment. There didn't seem to be anyone there, no one she could see anyway, so she pushed the door open the rest of the way and stepped out of the bathroom.

Nothing. No one.

In seconds she had every light on, including the fluorescents, and the apartment was so bright she had to squint to focus, straining to see in one extreme to the next.

Mina hurried to the door. It was closed and locked, just as she'd left it. She could think of no other way anyone could get in here, but she checked the apartment thoroughly anyway. Every corner, under the bed, beneath the sink—she double-checked them all.

Too much fucking vodka, she told herself. *New place, long day, bad storm, that's all this is. You're fine. No one's in here. No one* was *in here.*

Relieved, she reached for a cigarette on the counter and one of the new lighters she purchased earlier. She lit up, took a deep drag, then made her way to the windows. There were no lights on in the building across the way. And, much to her disappointment, no painter either.

She'd look for him again. Maybe turn the lights on next time, give a little wave.

Or maybe she'd just watch him in the dark.

* * * *

The bed sheets were soft, the pillows just right. A handmade quilt with similar colors to the easy chair, and the same psychedelic pattern, was thick and warm. Mina had no doubt Frances and the others had done their best to make her comfortable, she just had to learn to accept it.

Childhood trauma had made trust difficult for her, and since she'd so rarely been treated well, she'd never grown accustomed to it. In those rare instances when it did occur, Mina usually neither believed it nor had any idea how to handle or process it.

Christ, she thought. *I can almost hear Ralph scolding me. I know, I know. I'm working on it, you pain in my ass.*

She pulled the quilt up to her chin and tried to relax. She listened to the storm, to the hiss of the old radiator, and to the sounds of her own breathing. Then, once more, she thought about the artist across the way. Was he a permanent fixture in Crow's Cry, or like her? A drifter, a ghost...

She heard Ralph's voice in her head. *Let me tell you about ghosts, doll. I swear I've seen them in abandoned buildings in Providence. Just a flash usually, moving in the corner of my eyes, or sometimes it's just cold air on my face. That's a clue that they're near, did you know that?*

"Goodnight, Ralph," she muttered.

It took a while, but eventually Mina drifted away and into the dark, where dreams of the sea and ghost girls flickered in her mind like an old movie reel.

Outside, the storm raged on.

CHAPTER FIVE

With the sun came a bright and clear morning, and for Mina, a renewed sense of purpose, opportunity, and resolve. Despite the snowy skies the night before, there wasn't much in the way of accumulation. The ground and rooftops were covered, but it was a dusting, nothing more. By dawn the storm had blown out to sea, taking the icy winds that throttled the old building all night along with it. In the hours since, the temperature had dropped, leaving the world beyond her windows iced over and still.

Mina had risen and gotten herself together early so she wouldn't be late. Now, as she waited for her ride, she stood before her apartment windows sipping a cup of coffee and watching a tiny black bird hop along the roof of the building across from her. It looked confused, poor thing, like it had lost its way in the storm the night before and was just now realizing where it was.

"I know the feeling, little guy."

Suddenly the bird took flight and shot out in the direction of the ocean, quickly becoming a tiny black dot swallowed by an endless expanse of gray sky.

Mina turned her attention to the apartment window below.

Still dark, no signs of life...

He's probably a late sleeper, she thought.

Memories of the man filled her mind: his lean but powerful body slick with perspiration as he leapt into the air like some crazed ballet dancer, paint spraying the—

Mina's phone buzzed. She hurried over to the kitchen counter where she'd left it earlier and glanced at the screen. The number was unfamiliar, but she answered anyway.

It was precisely nine o'clock.

"Hello?"

"Frances Strengarden here, I've just arrived."

"Hi, Frances, I'll be right—"

"I was under the impression you'd be waiting outside. It *is* nine o'clock, after all."

The abruptness of Frances' response felt like a slap in the face. "It's awfully cold out there," Mina said evenly. "I assumed you'd call and I'd come down."

"Assumptions are rarely wise. At any rate, hurry along."

Mina cringed. Subtlety and tact certainly weren't Frances' strong suits. Normally she would've pushed back. Having endured a childhood of abuse, Mina vowed no one would ever put her in a corner again, so as an adult she'd forced herself to fight back until it became natural to her. If anybody gave her shit, they got it right back, and then some.

But this time she let it go. What choice did she have?

New beginnings, remember? Don't screw this up.

"Sure," Mina said, as pleasantly as she could. "Be right down."

Although irritated, she told herself Frances didn't mean to be rude. She was just another eccentric artist, that's all. Mina was one herself, so maybe it was best to cut the old girl some slack and hope for the best when she met the rest of these people.

Mina had another swallow of coffee then quickly rinsed her mug out and put it in the sink. After a few deep breaths her anxiety began to settle. She was already nervous about the meet-and-greet; Frances and her bullshit was the last thing she needed.

You've got this. They chose you. Now get your ass in gear and go be fabulous.

With a defiant grin, Mina threw on her jacket, grabbed her purse, and headed out.

* * * *

The old VW was parked in the same spot. Frances sat razor-straight behind the wheel, dressed in clothes identical to those she'd worn the day before. If Mina hadn't known better, she'd have thought the woman spent the night in her car.

"Sorry if I kept you waiting," Mina said once she'd gotten in.

"I've always been of the belief that if one is on time, one is late." Frances dropped the car into gear then pulled away and drove to the corner where, after a quick look around, she turned and started down another street nearly indistinguishable from the last. "Thus, I always make it a point to be five to ten minutes earlier than the agreed upon time. I find this serves me well."

"I'll be sure to remember that," Mina said, buckling up.

They continued on through the mostly empty streets until they reached a small two-lane state road. To their right, Mina could see a long stretch of snow-covered beach and the ocean beyond, and it occurred to her that it was going to take some time to learn the lay of the land here. It all looked so maddeningly similar.

Same as the day before, there were only a few other cars on the road.

After a few minutes, Frances turned off onto a winding dirt road. Mina refrained from asking questions, thereby avoiding any curt responses, and instead enjoyed the heat blowing through the vents in the dashboard. There was no NPR on the radio this time, rather barely audible classical music that, despite its low volume, still managed to sound severe and rather ominous.

The unpaved road was bumpy and uneven. It hadn't been plowed, but there wasn't enough snow accumulation to warrant it. Even in such an old car, Frances had little trouble negotiating the road as it wound through the high-grass dunes that had suddenly appeared on either side of them. But as the road began to slant upward, the Bug struggled. Undeterred, Frances dropped the car into a lower gear then pressed the gas.

The VW jerked forward. Slowly, they continued up the incline.

It was then that Mina saw the house.

Seventy or eighty yards in the distance, their apparent destination, a large old Victorian built near a series of cliffs overlooking the Atlantic, came into view.

Sitting at the summit of their climb like a set piece from a gothic thriller, the three-story house was dark in color and enormous by modern standards. The closer they got, the more evident it became that the house's exterior upkeep, as well as that of the surrounding grounds, was not a priority, and hadn't been for a long time.

From the dark windows and snowy eaves, to a small widow's walk on the third story, to the nearby cliffs overlooking the ocean, the creepy old Victorian homestead made Mina feel as if she'd been transported into the pages of an Emily Brontë novel. She imagined a woman on the widow's walk gazing out at the sea, waiting for a ship and hoping for the return of the man she loved.

How ironic, Mina thought, that the house looked like something out of an old painting. As an artist, she could certainly appreciate the aesthetics of such a sight, as well as the scenarios it conjured in her creative mind, but the cold, bleak setting still left her vaguely uncomfortable.

Although a horse-drawn carriage would've looked more at home, a series of vehicles were parked outside the house instead. A Chrysler minivan, a Jeep Wrangler, a Volkswagen Jetta, a Land Rover, and a black 1975 Mercedes 300d four-door sedan in pristine condition all sat in a neat row at the end of the drive.

Frances parked alongside them. "This is the main house," she announced. "It is our headquarters, as it were, and also serves as Professor Riker's personal residence."

What Mina knew about Professor Riker was what she'd read about him on the Artists Collective website, where she applied for the residency program months before. She learned Riker headed the collective, and was originally from Germany. He was educated at the prestigious Berlin University of the Arts and, after graduating, spent the next few years teaching at different art schools across Europe. Eventually he returned to his native Germany, where he founded his own small school. Despite his unorthodox methods, Riker garnered a modest but fervent following. Both hailed and criticized for his wildly experimental and controversial philosophies—which included connecting the creation and study of art with alleged practices of mysticism—Riker and his wife Isa, an accomplished artist herself, opted to leave Germany for the United States in the 1970s. They found their way to San Francisco, where they established an artist commune which lasted until the late 1980s, when a fire destroyed their compound. Tragically, one member of the commune, a young woman, was killed, and Riker was badly burned and fell into a coma for several months before finally recovering. By then the group had disbanded, and with the compound destroyed, Riker traded the west coast for the east, settled in Crow's Cry, Massachusetts, and formed the collective. Over the last three decades it remained a modest group, and though it hadn't grown much in either size or stature since, it had survived and in some ways even thrived, albeit humbly. This eventually allowed them to begin offering a minor residency program for struggling artists. Each year, for the last five years, they'd chosen only one candidate to receive a six-month residency.

This year they'd chosen Mina.

Frances turned off the car. It rattled and sputtered before finally falling silent. "I'm sure you've done at least some cursory research into Professor Riker and his background," she said. "Just a word to the wise: when you meet him, do *not* mention his wife. It's a very sore subject."

"Okay, thanks for telling me. Is she deceased?"

"She's been quite ill for some time, bedridden, in fact. Her recovery is doubtful."

"I'm sorry to hear that."

"Yes, we all were. And while we do hold out hope, it is, to say the least, a delicate subject for Professor Riker. Therefore it's best if you simply do not mention her. Unless, of course, he does, which is highly unlikely, but there you have it. The other thing you should be aware of and prepare yourself for are Professor Riker's scars. He was badly injured in a fire many years ago."

"I read about that on your website."

"He suffered significant burns to large portions of his body."

"Poor man," Mina said, shuddering.

Frances stared at her as if unsure of Mina's sincerity. "At any rate, he has some rather disturbing scars along his neck and on one side of his face. Try not to stare at them, and do not speak of them unless he does. Understood?"

Mina sighed. "Yes, Frances, I understand."

"Good," she said, and then motioned to the house. "Shall we?"

With the old Victorian looming over them, Mina climbed out of the car.

* * * *

A foyer greeted them just inside the front door, along with the smell of lavender and a welcome rush of cozy dry heat. Soft classical music that sounded identical to what she'd heard in Frances' car played from unseen speakers, and a large staircase that looked to have once been rather ornate stood before them, winding up to a second-floor landing. Mina looked up. A faded but extravagant crystal chandelier hung from the ceiling above the staircase.

"I'll take your coat," Frances said.

"That's okay." Mina had worn a black leather jacket with a gray hoodie beneath, and decided to keep the jacket on. Despite the warm temperature in the house, she was still cold. "I'll hang onto it for now, if you don't mind."

With a scowl of disapproval, Frances strode over to a freestanding rack in the corner, pulled off her pompom hat, tucked it into the pocket of her coat, then removed that as well. After tossing it onto a hook, she motioned to the left of the staircase, indicating an open doorway that led to a much larger room. Within, several people milled about, but three in particular—two men and a woman—stood watching just inside the doorway.

The room was large, with a high ceiling and what appeared to be worn but original dark hardwood floors. The aromas of freshly brewed coffee and assorted baked goods greeted Mina and drew her attention to a long table against one wall, on which a coffeemaker, a pot of tea, and various donuts, croissants, and muffins were displayed. Near the front of the table were neatly folded cloth napkins alongside silverware, dessert plates, and matching teacups and saucers of fine china. There were no windows in the room, and unlike the foyer, the light here was limited to a series of candles burning in glass sconces strategically located along the walls. That, combined with the dark green Damask mural wallpaper, gave the room a shadowy Gothic look and feel that Mina found strangely unsettling.

The same classical music playing in the foyer could be heard here as well, and on the back wall, in an intricately carved wood frame, hung an enormous painting, a portrait of a young man and woman sitting side-by-side holding hands. Painted in a style Mina found reminiscent of Francis Bacon, dark hues surrounded the couple, engulfed them like deep shadows, the subjects' faces slightly distorted and ghostly, as if seen through a purposely blurred lens.

In a chair beneath the portrait sat an older man, but because there were others gathered around him, Mina couldn't make out much in the way of detail.

"Well now, this must be our new artist-in-residence, Mina Vero!"

One of the men stepped forward. He was holding a cup and saucer but offered her his free hand. His frame was slight, though he stood at least six feet, which made him significantly taller than Mina's five-foot-four inches. Clearly the oldest of the three, somewhere in his forties, his dark hair was slicked back and graying at the temples, and a thin mustache that looked like it had been drawn on sat above his top lip. His hazel eyes were bright and welcoming. Dressed in a blue blazer with a red silk ascot knotted around his neck, a crisp white shirt, and a pair of shiny penny loafers, he more closely resembled someone you'd find gallivanting on a yacht than in an art studio.

"Maurice Larocque," the man said with a slight bow before offering his hand.

"Hi," Mina said. It wouldn't have surprised her had he clicked his heels together, and although a bit embarrassed by his theatrics, she forced a smile and accepted his hand. It was warm, his grip delicate, barely noticeable.

"An absolute pleasure to meet you," he said.

"Thank you, it's great to be here."

"Allow me to introduce a couple other members of our little Crow's Cry coven," Maurice said with a mischievous wink, indicating the man and woman standing behind him. "Meet Jasmin Coyle, and this strapping young man next to her is David McGrath."

The woman shook Mina's hand first. About Mina's age, height, and build, she had a big floppy suede hat atop her head, long, curtain-straight brown hair, and was dressed in jeans, knee-high black leather boots, and a sweater with a huge sunflower on it. But it was the blue-tinted granny glasses resting on the bridge of her nose that caught Mina's attention. "Hey, Mina, welcome," she said in a dreamy, slightly slurred voice that sounded as if she'd only woken up a few minutes ago. "I dig the look, very Joan Jett."

"Thanks," she said through light, self-conscious laughter. "I like your style too."

Before she and Jasmin could speak further, the other man stepped closer and grabbed Mina's hand, pumping it with more enthusiasm than seemed necessary. "Hiya," he said, smiling to reveal uneven teeth with a big gap between the front two. "I'm Dave."

Short and stocky, with a thick neck and a powerful build, he looked to be in his early thirties. The nearby candlelight flickered across his shaved head, giving off a shiny glare, and in each ear were small, gold hoop earrings. Dressed in khakis and a sweatshirt, as they shook hands Mina noticed he was missing the ring finger on his right hand.

"Love what I saw of your work," he added. "Can't wait to see what you do once you're settled in."

"Thanks," Mina said, hoping he hadn't caught her staring at his missing finger. "That's nice of you to say."

"Not at all, we're all excited about you being here, trust me."

"Well, it's still nice to hear," she said as he continued shaking her hand.

"We're neighbors too," McGrath told her. "I live in the first-floor apartment with my wife Rita—she's here somewhere, you'll meet her in a second—and Jazzy's on the second floor all by her lonesome, ever our resident hippy-dippy bachelorette, this one."

Jasmin calmly flipped him the finger.

"Love you too, Jazz," McGrath cracked, chuckling before turning back to Mina. "So listen, if you need anything, seriously, we're around."

"Yeah," Jasmin said. "Definitely, just let us know, okay?"

Mina thanked them again, hopeful McGrath might let her hand go soon as his huge mitt had completely engulfed hers and his grip was becoming a bit painful.

"Come with me and I'll introduce you around," Maurice said, rescuing her as he slipped an arm around her shoulder and whisked her away from them and deeper into the room. "But first let's get you something warm to drink and maybe some nibbles, yes?"

It was all a bit overwhelming, but Mina did her best to maintain her composure. She wasn't used to people paying attention to her, much less fawning all over her, and she was already in desperate need of a cigarette.

At the table, Mina got herself a cup of coffee and a croissant instead. As she enjoyed both, several people approached and introduced themselves or were ushered over by Maurice. She counted eight people in addition to him, Frances, Jasmin, and McGrath. They all seemed nice and very pleased to meet her, and were all familiar with her work. It made her feel like a celebrity.

Mina had just finished her croissant when Maurice glided back across the room and leaned in close to her. "Now that you've met the flock," he said in a conspiratorial tone, "it's time to introduce you to the head of our program, Professor Riker."

"I'd like that."

As the others mingled and chatted, Maurice led Mina to the back of the room. Just below the huge portrait, an elderly man sat in a white, gold-trimmed, high-back chair that resembled a small throne. As the people that had been gathered around him moved aside, the man occupying the chair, clad in unassuming dark slacks and a wool sweater, gazed at Mina as if she were the most beautiful woman he had ever seen.

"Ah, Ms. Vero," he said, voice laced with a German accent. "There you are."

Mina realized he was the man in the portrait, sans scars, just a much older version, and the woman next to him was surely his wife. "You must be—"

"Klaus Riker."

"This is all so wonderful," Mina said. Was she blushing? She couldn't remember the last time that happened. Doing her best to ignore the scarring along his neck and the right side of his face, Mina smiled broadly. "I'm very happy to meet you. Thank you so much for this opportunity, Professor."

"Your work certainly warrants it. I only wish we could offer you more." Riker didn't stand, but held out a liver-spotted hand, the fingers bent with arthritis. "I cannot begin to tell you how happy we are to have you here, my dear. I know these initial meetings can be somewhat overwhelming. I hope we haven't made you uncomfortable."

"Not at all," Mina said, taking his hand. It was cold and bony, the skin paper-thin, but it was Riker's thinning silver hair and striking ice-blue eyes that drew her in. Even with the damage the fire had caused, the man possessed an undeniable presence at his advanced age, exuding an aura of serene confidence and gentle mystery. She imagined in his younger days Klaus Riker must've been quite dashing and, when it came to women, thoroughly disarming. The others seemed to shower him with a peculiarly exaggerated but genuine respect, almost as if he were some sort of deity, whispering and smiling and nudging each other as he and Mina chatted. "I'm just not used to this kind of attention, or any attention, really."

"That seems almost criminal." The old man continued to gaze at Mina, his attention focused on her and her alone. "Just know that we're not here to disrupt or bother you, but to help and support you in any way we can over these next few months."

"Thank you," Mina told him. "To be recognized this way by someone of your stature is—"

"You're too kind, Ms. Vero."

"Mina, please."

"Mina it is." As he let go of her hand, he held his own up, turning it over from back to palm, considering it as if he'd never seen it before. "Sadly, my painting days are long over. Time and age have taken that from me. But I continue to encourage and mentor others, and share my joy of art in whatever modest ways I'm able to. The residency is just one way we can help those *special* artists. Those that don't receive the consideration they should from the larger programs, those who otherwise might never have the chance to solely focus on their work without the day-to-day distractions that entangle us all. As I say, I wish it could be longer term and the accommodations more elegant, but we work with what we have. I'm sure you understand."

"It's fantastic," Mina assured him. "And I love the accommodations."

Riker smiled warmly, his eyes still locked on hers. "I'm pleased to hear that." He adjusted his position in the chair a bit, then crossed his legs at the knee. "And I take it our Frances has been of assistance to you?"

"Yes, she has, very much so."

"She's quite a character," Riker said with a knowing look. "But she has a good soul. That's what's important, our *souls*, and that which we conjure from deep within them. Don't you agree, Mina?"

She nodded. "Yes. Yes, I do."

His beautiful eyes revealed how pleased he was with her response. "Once you have yourself situated in your new apartment, if you can find an open evening, I'd love to have you join me here for lunch at some point."

"That sounds lovely, thank you."

"Just some good food and hopefully better conversation," he said, "if you'd be so kind as to indulge an old man."

"I'd be honored. In fact, I'd like very much to hear more about your work and history, and particularly your ideas regarding connections between art and mysticism."

"Is that so?" Riker arched an eyebrow. "Well, I'm happy to oblige, my dear."

"Do you have a strong interest in mysticism and spiritualism, Mina?"

She'd become so focused on Riker, the sound of someone else's voice startled her, breaking her concentration. Maurice, who had left them alone for a while, had returned.

"Somewhat," she said. "I'm far from an expert on that kind of thing, but I do find the concept of it relating to our art fascinating."

"Yes, it's quite…" Maurice frowned suddenly and fell silent.

Mina glanced at Riker. He was glaring at him with obvious irritation.

"Look at me, rattling on when I need another cup of tea," Maurice said, holding his empty teacup up as if in evidence. "Forgive the interruption. Excuse me."

As he moved away, Mina turned to Riker. "I hope I didn't say something wrong."

"Nothing could be further from the truth, Mina." Riker smiled, his intense stare again replaced by his previous warmth and disarming charm. "It's been delightful meeting you. I won't keep you, go ahead and mingle, enjoy yourself and get to know our community members better. Of course, please feel free to leave whenever you'd like. We try our best to make ourselves available to our artist-in-residence, but it's certainly not required or even expected that you spend time with us should you prefer to focus on your work. That is why you're here. However, if there's anything you need—anything at all—simply let me know, and if it's within my power to do so, I'll help as best I can."

"I will, and thanks again for such a kind and warm welcome." Mina shook his hand a second time. "You have a beautiful home."

Riker smiled but said nothing more. Sitting in his throne-like chair with the air of a displaced king lost in time, he gazed at her longingly.

The same as he had when he'd first laid eyes on her.

And in that startling, strangely intoxicating moment, with the shadows and secrets in that old house watching them both, Mina was certain they were the only two people left on Earth.

CHAPTER SIX

Mina tacked a sheet of white canvas to the wall, lined pieces of newspaper on the floor beneath it, then filled several paper cups with water. After scooping generous amounts of orange, white, black, and blue paint onto a paper plate, she dripped a large brush into the water, let it trickle into the blue paint, then stirred.

She paused a moment, gazing at the light, then brushed the watery paint onto the canvas, covering the entire surface. Aware of how fast acrylic paint dried, Mina repeated the process with the orange paint, but with a smaller brush, and this time making circular motions. Using her palette, she scooped up black paint, making jagged lines on the canvas, occasionally glancing outside at the bare wintery trees, and let the paint drip from her crude branches.

Mina rinsed the palette then painted a structure with the blue paint, an abstract rendition of the apartment building across the way, a dark figure seeming to float in one of the windows. *Him...*

As she added more paint to the canvas, she thought about the man. The raw passion in his movements as he painted was inherent, but there was something lonely about his wild dance too, something isolated. He was in agony.

"*My painting carries with it the message of pain,*" the great Frida Kahlo once said. Mina nodded absently, the quote drifting through her mind.

She'd always related to the idea of expressing her pain through her painting. In the end, she painted what she felt, so how could she not?

I paint what I feel.

"And right now I feel cold," she muttered, drifting away from her canvas long enough to turn up the thermostat. The ancient radiator hissed in response as she moved to the windows and looked down at the first-floor window across the way. *His window...*

The crumbling apartment building was dark, no signs of life within. No mad dancer, no streams of color spattered on muscled flesh, no masterpiece on white canvas spread on the floor.

Mina drifted back to her work-in-progress, but her thoughts had already shifted to the morning meet-and-greet at Klaus Riker's home, and how he and the others had discussed the modern art world. They certainly made no secret of their desire to remain unique amidst countless other artists and artist communities that gathered in places like Newport in neighboring Rhode Island, or other parts of New England—those setting up easels and straining to capture a landmark at a precise time of day, when shadow and light were this color or that, when the leaves were green in summer or yellow and orange in fall, when branches were stark and covered in ice and snow—that much was clear.

"Such nonsense," Riker said when Maurice had mentioned a painting he'd seen in Newport recently. "These people know nothing of the evolution of modern art, of artists like Kahlo and Bacon who painted *through* their pain. And I ask you, how can anyone call themselves an artist if they've never known true heartbreak?"

Mina had stood silently, listening rather than offering anything more.

"One must suffer true loss," Riker said. "One must dream of Hell, and not from a distance. Otherwise, what is the point?"

Maurice had nodded in agreement, but it was Jasmin who said, "Yeah, but some of the best art has been done by the modern primitives, man. Outside art, spiritual even. I've seen drawings done by people that spent their lives in mental institutions—even prisons—untainted by society or formal instruction—they just create from their hearts and minds' eye. There's something pure about that. Groovy, but profound, you know?"

"But then, that's exactly the point, my dear." Klaus' eyes twinkled. "Their pain, their madness, is precisely what they've tapped into. There can be great beauty in pain."

"I once spoke with a woman," Maurice said, "who had rendered a sunflower field on a farm near her home, somewhere or another in the western part of the state. At any rate, her contention was that she'd caught every petal perfectly. She waited until noon, you see, before mixing the perfect shades of yellow. Why not just take a photograph? She obviously had no interest in the depths of human passion."

"Nor human suffering," Riker added softly. "That requires digging deeper than whatever it is you see right in front of you. That which lies *beneath* is what matters."

"Painting is from the soul," Jasmin said. "It makes me high, like I'm touching God. I don't pay attention to what color a vase is, or the way the sun's setting over the ocean. I paint what I feel when I look at those things." She bowed her head a moment, then raised her eyes and smiled slightly at Mina before giving a sedate shrug of her shoulders. "But I get it. Most people don't give a shit about any of that. They don't want masterworks. They just want something pretty to hang over their couch."

"And there's more than enough so-called artists willing to give it to them," Dave added, chuckling. "Poor Mina, you must think we're all a bunch of snobs, huh?"

Mina took a moment before answering. "No, I do agree with Jasmin though. Not everyone's the same—and that's fine, good even—but for me, art is personal. Like she said, it makes me high. Sometimes it feels as if my soul's on fire."

"Mmmm," Riker said with a nearly lascivious moan. "And *there* is the spiritual connection to what we do. It's why your work will live on well beyond our days, Mina."

What do you feel when the hot sun burns your skin?

"I can only hope." Mina's eyes locked on his. "That's a very kind thing to say."

What do you feel when the wind stings you?

The longer she held the old man's gaze, the more the questions raced through her mind, as if he were somehow asking them from inside her head.

What do you imagine in the tall grass?

"I can't wait to see what you do first," Jasmin said dreamily.

Who do you run from, Mina?

"Thanks," Mina said, suddenly lightheaded. "I can't wait to start."

Who do you run to?

Now, in the silence of her apartment, as a light snow began to fall beyond the windows, Mina felt as if she'd absorbed the strange energy emanating from Riker and the other artists she'd met earlier. Their words, their inspiration—even their disdain for the commonplace—she felt it all surging through her like electrical current.

She wanted to be a part of it. She needed to paint.

She *had* to.

Mina returned to the canvas, the memories flooding her mind.

Paint and water spattered, time passed too quickly, and before she knew it night was approaching and turning the sky deeper shades of blue and gray. In the distance, the ocean churned, waves furiously crashing shore as a small flock of seabirds circled then scattered, disappearing into the gradually darkening horizon. Everything out there was a patchwork of blacks, deep grays, and blues, a stark and dismal scene really—bleak and agonizing and wildly unforgiving to every living thing trying to endure and survive it—and yet, Mina was able to see the beauty in it as well.

There can be great beauty in pain, Riker had told her.

She clicked on the overhead lights and considered her creation. Those trees—that building—so ethereal—haunting—so—

Maybe a dash of red here and there, she thought, yawning.

The buzzing of her phone snapped her back. Ralph's name appeared on the screen. She was surprised it had taken him this long to check up on her, and she missed him. But he'd have to wait for now. She needed to think more about the red paint, about tomorrow, about cleaning up her paint-caked hands, newspapers crumpled and stained with splotches of colors. Those cups of water and the brushes…

"Call you back soon, Ralphie," she mumbled, staring at the painting now.

No, she thought. *No red.*

Picking up one of the paper cups, she started for the sink then hesitated and looked out the windows again. His apartment was still dark.

Was it all in my head?

The entire building looked abandoned.

Were you *all in my head?*

Mina remembered Riker, how the old man had sat so still, listening intently to every word she said, and how his eyes—so beautiful and yet oddly unsettling—bore right through her. It was as if she'd been standing naked before him, able to hide nothing as those questions slithered through her mind in his soft, accented voice.

With a sigh, she tossed the water out, washed her hands, then gathered up and threw out the newspaper. Taking the bottle of vodka from the counter, and a cigarette from the pack beside it, she wandered back to her painting. Rolling a cigarette between her lips, she slipped a plastic lighter from her pocket and lit up.

The cigarette tasted good, smelled good, and immediately relaxed her, even though her lungs were probably filled with gunk from having been a smoker since she was a teen. That's what Ralph always told her anyway.

"Do you want your lungs to explode by the time you're fifty?" he'd often scold. "Because keep smoking those things and that's what you have to look forward to. The good news is lungs regenerate, did you know that? My doctor told me all about it. If you quit, over time they heal. Don't you want to live long enough to be a grandmother?"

"*Me*, a grandmother? Are you serious?"

"Stranger things have happened."

"Besides, you're one to talk. You've been smoking since you were twelve."

"Yes, socially, but I'm charmed so that doesn't count."

Mina shook her head. *Better call him back so he doesn't worry.*

She reached for the phone. Her gaze drifted from the canvas back to the windows as Ralph's number rang several times, then went to voicemail.

"This is Ralph. I'm unavailable at the moment. If you don't know how it works from here, there's really nothing I can do for you."

A tone sounded.

"Where are you, Ralphie boy? Busy with Bible study and having some milk and cookies before bed? Listen, sorry I missed your call. I'm fine, settled in safe and sound. Call me back when you get a sec, you maniac."

The light in the apartment below flickered to life.

And just like that, there he was...the crazed painter, standing perfectly still—almost too still—head bowed, arms at his side, paint speckled across his bare chest and on his jeans. His hair was damp, as though he'd just stepped from a shower. But he couldn't have, the paint would have washed away.

Mina disconnected her call and took a long drag on her cigarette, the smoke slithering around her like ghostly snakes.

So you are real.

The man remained motionless, as if he'd been frozen in time, a living statue. And his flesh appeared paler now, like white stone.

Moments later, he still hadn't moved. Mina hadn't either.

Masculine form, motionless—like George Segal's life-size sculptures of human figures set in environments like New York City's Port Authority, Mina thought, mind racing again. *Damn things always creeped me out, especially at night.*

A droplet of water fell from the man's hair, rolled the length of his neck, and dropped onto his chest. He remained unaffected; not a flinch, not a shiver.

What strange magic runs through your veins? Mina wondered.

She smoked her cigarette, unable to look away and unconcerned this time that the lights in her apartment were on, leaving her on full display were he to look up.

Who are you?

He definitely wasn't one of the community members because he hadn't been at the meet-and-greet. She'd have remembered him for sure.

Who do you run from, Mina?

Just another sad and lonely soul, lost in his painting, lost in the dark.

Who do you run to?

Visions from her nightmares filled her head.

A sail drenched in icy seawater flapping in the wind...

Mina suddenly felt lightheaded, the same as she had earlier at Riker's.

An old boat emerging from the darkness and chaos of an ocean storm at night...

She brought the cigarette to her lips, her hand shaking.

Coming closer and closer to shore, the grim-faced man with bone-white hands steering the vessel through violent waves...

Mina's arm dropped to her side, but her eyes remained on the man below, even as the nightmare visions continued.

The grim-faced man's eyes, completely white and glistening—alien, not human—his rain slicker and clothes badly worn, a faded bandana holding his long stringy hair in place...

Mina could hear herself breathing, each intake and exhale more harried than the last, her head floating now, as if her mind meant to shut this all down before—

Through the snowsqualls, with the boat rocking furiously, the ferryman reaching for her...

Despite the heat in the apartment pulsing off the old radiator, an ice-cold tremor throttled her.

Take my hand...it's almost finished now...

"No," Mina said aloud, her voice sounding odd to her—alien—as if it belonged to someone else. With her head a whirlwind, another strange sensation coursed through her body, pulsing and gradually synching with the rapid beat of her heart.

The room tilted and blurred, and in that strange moment she wanted nothing more than to give in to the sensation, the desire—the *need*—to move as the man below had the first time she saw him. Mina had enough experience with drugs and alcohol to know how similar this feeling was, but it was accompanied by a rush of warmth that shot through her body and made her feel nearly orgasmic. The beat of her heart was like a drum, luring her closer, but to what? She trembled as her need to spin and dance and literally throw herself headlong into the needs of her body grew stronger. A feral surge of pure abandon took hold of her, and like a wild animal that needed to run and ravage and devour everything in its path, she no longer felt wholly in control of her actions.

Fearing she might pass out, Mina placed a hand flat against the window to steady herself. The glass pane, cool to the touch, snapped her out of the spell she was under. The nightmare memories receded, the visions faded, and although her heart continued to slam her chest, the ravenous sensation was gone.

"Jesus," she said softly. "The hell is the matter with me?"

Confused and off-balance, Mina put the cigarette between her lips and left it there. Holding her hands up before her again, she made fists, clenching them tight until the shaking ceased.

Night had nearly fallen now, but the man below had still not moved. *Did you do that to me?*

Through a cloud of smoke slowly climbing toward the ceiling, Mina stared down at him. *Lift your head. Look at me. Let me see your face more clearly.*

As if in answer, the lights in the man's apartment were suddenly extinguished. The darkness swallowed him whole.

CHAPTER SEVEN

And so, she dreamed.

Moving slowly, she glides weightlessly just above the ground, the tall grass below sweeping past as she crosses an enormous field. The sun is bright and high in the sky, and Mina can feel its warmth against her back. In the distance, at the top of a small hill, amidst the tall grass swaying slowly back and forth in a gentle breeze, there stands a large tree. A squat oak, its branches thick with lush green leaves, the trunk forked and looking like giant gnarled fingers reaching up under the brush, it waits for her, a silent witness to her magic, her impossible flight.

It is magic. Isn't it?

"Black magic, Mina…"

Just as she reaches the tree, the world goes dark and night devours her. In a panic, she tries to get her bearings, but there is no up or down, left or right, no forward or back here, only thick, impenetrable darkness.

But then she hears something. It's very faint, but she can *hear it.*

Straining to listen more closely, Mina struggles to decipher the unintelligible murmurs into something recognizable.

Voices…

That's it, that's what she's hearing, voices speaking in unison. The cadence is repetitive, slow, and deliberately monotone. Chanting of some kind perhaps, or—

No, it's prayer. *A small group of people are praying, but not in English.*

Are they speaking German?

Suddenly, at the very limits of Mina's peripheral vision, the slightest flicker of flame catches her attention. Slowly, it carves its way through the darkness, growing stronger and brighter until the flicker becomes a flame, then a series of flames.

Mina sees torches burning, and as they slowly separate from the darkness, the figures in black hooded robes that hold them. She can see a group of them, but cannot make out any specifics. They could be male or female, young or old, human or even something else, something…more. Standing in a circle around the oak tree, which now looks more ominous than beautiful in the shadows cast from the fire, they recite their prayers to whatever god they serve, heads bowed and faces concealed.

Although she is no longer drifting across the field, Mina still feels weightless, as if she's floating in place. Nothing seems real, and yet she understands this is not entirely a dream either. She is suspended somewhere between the two.

The night opens wide, and the torches lower, come together to touch something on the ground. It explodes into a bonfire, shooting flames then sparks high into the night sky. The prayers continue, louder now, more urgent.

"Come to us, Mina," a voice whispers.

"I want to leave." She says it with all the desperation and terror she feels, but it comes out soft, dreamlike and slurred, as if she's been sedated. "I want to leave."

"The only way out is straight down," the disembodied voice tells her.

Mina looks to the ground around the bonfire, the tall grass pulled free in favor of dirt and small stones where slimy maggots wriggle and slither. And it is then that she sees a woman on her knees next to the fire, her hands bound before her and her head bowed. Her sweatshirt and jeans are worn and spattered with various colors of paint, and as she comes into clearer focus Mina sees she's roughly her age.

The woman looks up quickly, her mouth open and twisted in a silent scream.

She has no eyes, only raw empty sockets where her eyes once resided, the lids sliced free, two swaths of dark dried blood staining her sallow cheeks. Her head darts back and forth, as if trying to locate someone.

"Who's there?" she asks frantically. "Who is it?"

Mina wants to answer her but can't. She can feel the woman's fear, the evil of this night circling like wolves, but words refuse to come.

"He takes our eyes," the woman says. "So we can't find our way back."

The fire explodes again, and the woman vaults backward. As if seized by unseen hands, she is consumed by flames. Sparks fly, cascading to the ground in a shower of hideously beautiful embers.

The prayers intensify. Mina looks down. Her feet are not touching the ground.

It's not possible.

"Anything is possible in the dark," the voice whispers, reading her mind.

Mina can feel herself turning, slowly spinning and climbing higher into the night against her will. She kicks her legs in an attempt to slow her ascension, but her body floats higher, above the fire, above the tree.

"Mina, Hexen können fliegen…"

And though she doesn't speak German, somehow, amidst the screams of terror that can only be her own, she understands.

"Mina, witches can fly…"

* * * *

With the horribly helpless feeling of falling from a great height, Mina came awake kicking and gasping for breath, her arms straight out, hands clutching at air. She sat straight up, her eyes settling on the windows and the night beyond.

The apartment, I—I'm in the apartment—it's only a dream!

Her heartrate slowed, and as her mind began to make some sense of what was happening, what *had* happened, Mina realized she'd nodded off in the chair at some point. Her phone and a crumpled pack of cigarettes were in her lap, and on the floor next to her sat an ashtray filled with spent butts, an empty bottle of vodka, and a glass still about a quarter full. She glanced at her watch. It was just after eleven.

As her eyes found the painting she was working on earlier, she sighed. Reaching down, Mina scooped up the glass, swallowed what was left of the vodka, then put the glass back where she'd found it. As the liquor moved through her, she felt its warmth, and just as her nerves settled somewhat, her phone began buzzing.

Mina knew who it was before she looked at the screen. Only one person called this late. Come to think of it, other than scammers and telemarketers, only one person ever called period. "Hey, Ralph," she said, answering it.

"Hey, doll."

"You okay?"

"I was just about to ask you the same thing."

"It's been interesting."

"Interesting as in good interesting or bad interesting?"

"Mostly good," she said.

"You deserve to be there, remember that."

"It's just a lot to handle all at once, little overwhelming, you know?"

"You sound sleepy, I didn't wake you, did I? Please tell me the legendary party animal that *is* Mina Vero is not in bed at eleven o'clock. Lie to me if you have to. I'll buy it, don't worry. I've had several cocktails."

"I nodded off for a minute." Mina sat up and rubbed her eyes with her free hand. "Did you just get home?"

"More or less, you know I can only take so much of Salem's in a single sitting, especially without you there to look out for me."

"I think you've got that backward."

"Just go with it, I'm drunk," he said. "Okay, so spill. How is it?"

Mina told him about her new apartment, a little about how bleak and empty Crow's Call was, and finally, the meet-and-greet and those who had welcomed her there, including Klaus Riker. She almost told Ralph about the man across the way, but decided against it.

"The place sounds fairly morbid, but that can be inspirational. It only becomes a problem if you make it one. Use it instead."

"I plan to."

"The new digs sound cool," Ralph said. "And the meet-and-greet sounds lovely."

"It was very nice."

"Why do I sense an unspoken *but* here?"

"They're all very nice, but different, that's for sure. I dig it though."

"A colorful bunch, are they?"

"That would be an understatement."

"You didn't really expect anything less, did you? They're artists just like us, Mina. We're all nuts. It's just a matter of degrees."

"Speaking of which, I started a new painting tonight."

"Already? That's wonderful!"

"Maybe," Mina said, stifling a yawn. "It's a little early to tell if it's anything yet."

The sound of a match flaring was followed by the slow intake of breath. "You sound stressed," Ralph said, exhaling loudly. "You're telling me everything, right?"

Mina could hear one of Ralph's Shirley Bassey CDs playing in the background. "I was having a dream," she told him. "A nightmare, it— I've been having the *strangest* dreams lately."

"You and your nightmares," he said through a sigh of an exhale. "You've only been there a couple days and it's already a lot to take in, your mind's probably going in circles is all. What you need to do is smoke some of this weed I'm enjoying, zone the fuck out, and get some rest."

"I wish I had some."

"You do. Check your purse. I slipped three big fat joints in there for you."

Mina pushed herself up and out of the chair, went to the kitchen counter where she'd left her purse, and rummaged through it until she found three pre-rolled joints with filters in a small tin designed to hold cough drops. "Holy shit," she said. "You rule."

"Who am I to argue with such an astute observation? I scored them from the dispensary. Medical grade, don't you know. They'll do the trick, believe me."

After plucking one of the joints free, Mina snapped shut the tin and tossed it back into her purse. "I miss you, Ralph," she said softly.

He cleared his throat. "Miss you too, kid."

"When are you coming to visit?"

"I was thinking maybe next weekend."

"Why so long?"

"You need time to acclimate to your new situation, and the last thing you should be dealing with this soon is my magnificence distracting you from the task at hand."

Happy and excited as Mina was with the opportunity, she'd have traded it all at that very moment for an evening on Ralph's couch snuggling, sharing a big bowl of popcorn, and watching Turner Classic Movies. "Which is what again?"

"Taking full advantage of this residency," he said. "Be fabulous, and remember, when it comes to fabulousness, Ralph knows of what he speaks, child. You'll be fine, and this will be an amazing experience. You'll see. You just have to get over these initial jitters and your self-confidence issues and get nice and comfortable."

"Oh, is that all?"

"If you think it'll be difficult, it will be. Now manifest positivity, damn you."

Mina hesitated a moment before asking, "And what about you?"

"What about me, doll?"

"Are *you* all right?"

"Sweet Mina," he said fondly, almost whispering, "always so concerned for me."

"You're stoned."

"Yes, but I'm also drunk, darling," he reminded her. "And thus, closing in on a level of enlightenment one can only achieve through extreme measures of irresponsibility and debauchery, two of my specialties I plan on exploring to their fullest even at this late hour."

"Who are you kidding? You'll be asleep the minute we hang up."

He barked with laughter. "I know, it's pathetic, isn't it? Getting old *blows*, and not in a good way."

"I'm one to talk. I'm going to smoke a little of this and go right to bed too."

"Try to have some sweet dreams this time, okay?"

"You too," Mina said, moving back into the deeper shadows by the windows. The apartment below was dark. "And don't forget about me."

"Never, my love," he said. "Wait, wasn't that a song? The Association, I think. Hold on, I'll sing a few bars."

"Say goodnight, Ralph."

"Goodnight, Ralph."

* * * *

Follow us down, Mina. Let the night take the rest…

Although she only had a few hits of the joint, Mina slept soundly, the best she had since she'd arrived in Crow's Cry. This time, her sleep was dreamless. And if it wasn't, she had no memory of them. Hers was a deep and quiet sleep, and she awakened feeling unusually refreshed and alert.

She vaguely recalled the disembodied voice from her nightmare whispering to her again as she slept—or perhaps just as she came awake—but it was nothing she could bring into any kind of full thought or memory.

Just residual bullshit from the nightmare, she thought.

After a shower and a cup of coffee, she was about to return to her painting when someone knocked on the door. It startled her, and in a strange way delighted her. *My first visitor*, she thought. *I just hope it's not Frances.*

It wasn't. Mina opened the door to find Jasmin standing there dressed in tight bell-bottom jeans with multicolored flowers sewn all over them, a peasant blouse, and the same floppy hat she'd worn to the meet-and-greet. Over her arm was a heavy sheepskin jacket. Her razor-straight hair hung on either side of her nebulously attractive face, blue-tinted granny glasses resting on her nose. "Morning," she said through a lazy smile. "I'm not bothering you, am I?"

"Not at all," Mina said, stepping back and holding the door wide. "Come on in."

"Actually," she said, her dull eyes never leaving Mina's, "I was going to see if you wanted to go out for some breakfast. I know a groovy place a couple blocks over."

Mina hesitated.

"It's okay if you're busy working, no problem. We can do it another time."

"No, sounds good," Mina said. "I haven't had breakfast yet, and I'm hungry."

Jasmin beamed. "Copacetic."

"Um, yeah," Mina said, stifling a laugh. "Let me get my coat."

"Okay, far out."

As she threw on her leather jacket, Mina took the opportunity to glance out at the courtyard and the man's apartment. The snow the night before hadn't amounted to much, but it looked freezing out there.

Who do you run from, Mina?

"Is everything cool?" Jasmin asked from behind her.

Mina turned from the window, dismissing the strange things whispering through her mind, grabbed her purse and keys, and headed for the door. "Absolutely," she said, smiling in a way she hoped didn't look awkward. "Let's go get some breakfast."

CHAPTER EIGHT

"I know it's really cold but don't worry, it's not far, and I don't have a car anyway," Jasmin said as she led Mina along the otherwise quiet and empty street. "Plus the fresh air will do us good, and I need the exercise; been eating too much lately, my hips are getting humungo."

"Are you kidding? You look great."

"Aw, thanks, man." Jasmin smiled dreamily as they walked, their breath forming clouds in the cold air. "Come on."

Practically skipping, Jasmin moved ahead, showing the most energy Mina had seen out of her since they'd met. Despite the icy sidewalk, she moved with surprising grace, almost like a dancer.

Three streets over, they cut through a short alley and emerged onto a wider boulevard that Mina imagined, from the size and architecture alone, must've once been the hub of Crow's Cry. Almost all the buildings were empty now, except for a bar near the corner with a sign over the door that read: GINSBERG'S DINER. Other than a nearby bodega, it appeared to be the only thing still in business.

Mina looked up at the sign, and the array of crystals hanging from the awning.

"Yeah, it's a nod to the poet," Jasmin giggled, ducking through the door and setting off the chimes hung there and in the windows.

Never been a huge fan, Mina thought.

She followed Jasmin in, the odor of greasy, spicy foods greeting her along with a wave of heat. It had a basic layout, a bunch of tables scattered across an open area and an old-fashioned counter along the side wall. Vases holding big fake sunflowers sat in the center of each table, and posters of psychedelic mushrooms and old prints of Joplin, The Doors, Jimi Hendrix, and Alan Ginsberg covered the walls. Two waitresses worked the tables, dressed in bell-bottom jeans and tie-dyed shirts, one made to resemble Cher, the other, Mama Cass, while old rock tunes played from a jukebox at the rear of the diner.

"What a funky place," Mina said, taking it in as she followed Jasmin to a table.

"Isn't it cool? Good food too. You'll dig it."

There were only three other customers there, two older men and a woman, all of them at the counter. None seemed to notice or much care about their arrival, but as Mina and Jasmin sat down, the Mama Cass lookalike took their drink order. Jasmin got herbal tea, which she referred to as her "regular," and Mina asked for a large coffee.

"So," Mina said, taking up the laminated menu. "What's good here, any recommendations?"

"The steamed veggie plate with brown rice is amazing."

Mina frowned playfully. With her hangover she needed something more substantial than that, and far greasier. "I was thinking of something less healthy."

"Can't go wrong with the three-egg, bacon, sausage, and double cheese omelet," Jasmin said quietly, as if fearful someone might hear her. "It's just lately I'm all about lighter eating. Don't pay any attention to me though, get what you want. Be happy."

When Mama Cass returned with their drinks, Jasmin ordered her steamed vegetable and brown rice plate and Mina opted for the suggested omelet with a side of hash browns and a scoop of cottage cheese, just so she wouldn't feel too bad about herself.

"Did you know that they started eating tons of brown rice and stuff like alfalfa sprouts back in the 1960s?" Jasmin said. "Hippies started the whole health food craze. Before then, people ate steak and mashed potatoes more often than yogurt. I mean, doesn't it blow your mind that most people didn't even knew what tofu and tahini were before that?"

Jasmin was goofy at times, but Mina felt she had a good heart, and of all the people she'd met from the collective, she was the most comfortable with her. "I didn't know that actually. Apparently I've been too busy gorging on pork and cheese products."

"Hey, if it feels good, do it," Jasmin said with a laugh. "I'm not judging you, don't get me wrong. I'm not the type to harsh anybody's mellow. Enjoy."

"Oh, I will. I'll be riddled with guilt afterward, but whatever."

"Rock on." Jasmin raised her cup of tea as if to salute her, her eyes narrow and slightly glazed. "And fuck guilt."

"Yeah, fuck guilt."

"Hey," Jasmin said as if something had just occurred to her. "When we're done here, want to go to the collective's art supply store? Rita, Dave's wife, runs it. You remember her from the meet-and-greet?"

Mina did. "Yeah, definitely, she's gorgeous."

"Rita's awesome."

"Is it nearby?"

"Sunshine, everything's nearby in Crow's Cry."

"Sounds like a plan."

"There's some heavy shit there, totally groovy. It's a great store, you'll see."

Mina couldn't help but be enchanted by Jasmin's hippie routine. In most it would've come off annoying, but with Jasmin it was entirely sincere, and there was something disarmingly charming about it. "Tell me something, Jazz. Are you always so cool to your artists-in-resident?"

"Depends on the resident, I guess. I took to you at the meet-and-greet, what can I say? I got this really good vibe from you, so I figured I'd see if you wanted to be friends. I mean, I'm always there if somebody needs help, but doing breakfast and shopping trips with resident artists isn't normally on my schedule."

"Well, I'm glad this time it is, "Mina said, feeling more and more comfortable with Jasmin. She hadn't had a female friend in a while. Ralph was the only person she let loose with these days, and she could just imagine how much fun the three of them would have.

Mina sipped her coffee. "Can I ask you something?"

"Ask me anything."

"Who had the residency before me? Are they still around?"

Mama Cass arrived with their food, and Jasmin didn't answer until she moved away. "Dude named Robert Sanders, went by Bobby." She scooped up some rice with her fork. "Very talented, painted a lot of big abstract pieces. His style was a lot like Klaus' when he was younger and could still paint. In his day, Klaus was better though."

"Did this guy Sanders stick around?"

Jasmin looked confused. "He went back to Los Angeles, that's where he was from. He was going in with some other dude on a gallery in West Hollywood. Not sure how he made out. I wasn't that close to him, so I haven't heard from him since, but I know a couple others did reach out to him and never heard back. Residents come and go, and when they go, they tend to stay gone, you know? They move on to whatever. We all try not to take it personally. Like Klaus always says, it's about the work and helping them get to whatever next step they're looking to take. Still, I think it's always a mistake to forget the importance of places. People too, you know?"

"Well, I'm already indebted. Trust me. I won't forget any of you or this place."

"That's sweet."

"I mean it," Mina said, taking a bite of omelet.

"You're special, Mina." Jasmin smiled again, but this time with a hint of melancholy. "You really are, always remember that."

"Thanks. You sound like my friend Ralph. He's always saying things like that."

"I hope you listen."

Images of the mad painter danced through Mina's head. "I do my best to believe in myself, but it's not always easy."

"It's *never* easy." Jasmin ate a little more, then asked, "Why'd you want to know about the last guy?"

Mina wasn't sure she should get into it. "I saw a guy," she said hesitantly. "A painter in the building across from my place, he was—"

"The collective owns that building too," Jasmin said with a look of concern.

"He was an action painter, reminded me of films I saw of Pollock when I was studying abstract painting back in school. Do you know who he is by any chance? I'd love to learn more about his work."

Jasmin's concern morphed into bafflement. "Wait, you mean the building across from the courtyard, right?"

"Yes, the first-floor apartment."

"Mina, that can't be. Nobody lives in that dump. Nobody's lived there in years. The wiring's funky as fuck, the plumbing is nonexistent now, and I heard there's really bad mold, awful shit that can make you sick. Nobody even sets foot in the place these days. Can't sell it as is— nobody's buying real estate in Crow's Cry—and it'd cost too much to renovate and rent out, so we use it as a tax write-off for the collective. Frances knows more about that financial stuff than me, though, and how it all works."

Mina put her fork down. "Jazz, I saw a man in there painting. It was at night, and the place was filled with light."

"There's no electricity." She pursed her lips. "Whoever it was had to bring light with him. I mean, Jesus, I wonder if there's somebody squatting in there. I'll let Dave know, have him check it out. You never know today."

"I hope I don't end up wasting his time." Mina felt awkward and regretted mentioning it now. "Maybe I dreamed it, I—I don't know, the whole thing was strange."

Jasmin reached across the small table and gave Mina's hand a gentle pat. "Maybe what you saw was a ghost."

At first Mina thought she was teasing her, but Jasmin's expression was serious. "I'm already feeling foolish and delusional enough, thanks," Mina said with a sigh.

"No reason to feel that way. These things happen all the time, Mina."

"Sure, at this point I might as well throw a ghost in the mix too, why not?"

"I'm serious." Jasmin took another bite of her meal. "There are ghosts in Crow's Cry, trust me, girl. This is ancient land, Mina, lots of spirits here. We even had some of those ghost hunters from TV in town a couple years ago. Klaus said they were clowns and charlatans and told us to stay away from them, so we all did, but I saw the episode once and they said they found paranormal activity in the old mill buildings, and even more stuff down by the ocean."

"Did they happen to see a sexy ghostly painter by any chance?" Mina joked.

"He was sexy too? Don't leave that part out." Jasmin winked. "But hey, who knows, right? Like I said, I'll have Dave check the place out. He likes to do the whole macho thing, probably go in there with all the subtlety of a charging bull. If there's a squatter in there, Dave will throw him out."

"I wouldn't want anyone hurt."

"Don't worry. Dave just thinks he's a tough guy." Jasmin rolled her eyes playfully. "He'll just yell and puff his chest up and hope for the best."

"Could the last guy—*Bobby*, was it?—could he have come back for some reason?"

Maybe he's running from something…

"Even if he did, he was in the same apartment you've got. All the residents use that one. Why would he go to the other building? It's awful, and besides, he'd have to break in and he wouldn't do that." Jasmin shook her head. "He's gone, it must be somebody else. If you really *did* see someone, it's got to be a squatter or something. Don't worry, we'll figure it out."

Who do you run from, Mina?

Mina remembered how pale the man's skin was, how still he was the second time she saw him, and how the darkness had come suddenly, devouring him.

"I hope it's a ghost."

"Why do you say that?" Mina asked, eating more of her breakfast.

"Hardly anything exciting ever happens around here. Ghosts are cool."

"I'd rather have peace and quiet, a total no-ghost zone, if you don't mind."

Jasmin sipped her tea, and with her dreamy smile said, "Like Klaus says, it's about the work. So ghosts or no ghosts, I promise we can offer you peace and quiet here, and the chance to do great work." And then, in a near-whisper, she added, "And we *always* keep our promises."

* * * *

Like Ginsberg's, the artist collective's shop had an array of crystals dangling from its awning—purple, green, and turquoise pieces reflecting on glass, on the snow—and displayed in the front window were various books on art technique and history, mostly tomes about Pollock, Helen Frankenthaler, and Robert Motherwell, all masters of the abstract.

Jasmin pushed on the door, allowing the smells of old books, candle wax, and various scented herbs to waft forward. Displays of numerous paints—acrylic, oil, and watercolor—lined the entrance, and there were shelves upon shelves of art papers, pencils, charcoal, and sculpting tools. Rolls of un-stretched canvas hung on the walls—some primed with gesso, others raw linen—waiting to be primed and stretched by an artist.

Wooden stretchers of all sizes, and how-to books on making them by hand, were featured in another area, along with premade canvases in an array of different sizes, most in standard shapes. But there were some in unusual shapes too—pieces that looked like coffins, others round, and still others heart-shaped.

Toward the back of the store were cases filled with jars. Mina read a few of the labels, the descriptions filling her head and making her feel like she'd wandered onto the outskirts of another crazy waking dream.

Aconite, for the cleansing of tools...

Calea (smoke before bed for sweet dreams)...

Mugwort, for astral travel...

Alder, for Divination and rituals of death and dying...

And others labeled *Witch's Sweets, Bat's Head Root, Belladonna,* and a flagon of *Dragon's Blood porter (for raising the dead)...*

Before Mina could read any more, Jasmin took her by the arm and said, "Come on, let's talk to Rita!"

"That stuff for real?" Mina whispered as Jasmin led her deeper into the shop.

"Oh, the herbs and shit?" she asked. "Just stuff Rita's into and likes to sell. Tourists eat it up. She's really into it though. Her mother was Caribbean, and blended all kinds of religions together. Rita's a great artist but she's a witch too. Don't freak, she's a good one. She's studied Tarot and astrology, knows all that shit. It's really far out, I dig it a lot. Anyway, when her mom died, she left her a bunch of so-called spell books. Handwritten shit that goes way back, passed down through generations, probably worth a lot of money."

"A witch, huh?"

"She's really spiritual. We all are here. Spiritual, I mean. You know how Klaus teaches us how important the connections between art and the spirit are. And besides, we've got to make money however we can in this dead town. Selling art doesn't pay as much as it should, but people go nuts for this kind of stuff. Rita's got a collection of spell candles in another room downstairs here too, and a book section that's amazing. Shit by Laurie Cabot and Raymond Buckland are mixed in with color formula books and how-to books on preparing canvas. It's fucking trippy."

"I don't know those names," Mina said. "Sorry, should I?"

"Famous witches."

"I went to Salem once for Halloween years ago, but that's about it, I—"

"Here she is, the foxiest chick in Crow's Cry," Jasmin said, spinning Mina around in the opposite direction.

And there was Rita, standing behind a counter where piles of drawings, color sample books, and boxes of pastel sticks were stacked high. A black cat was sprawled across a copy of *The Dying Swan* by Vladimir Tretchikoff. "What other crazy things is Jazzy filling your head with now?" Rita asked through a bright smile. She was stunning amidst the clutter, blue-black hair hanging past her shoulders, braided with colorful ribbons and fitted with multi-colored beads. In a low-cut, blue silk dress that contrasted nicely with her ebony skin, a necklace of cowrie shells and dangling earrings to match, she had the beauty and presence of a great movie star. Her dark eyes twinkled beneath the bright fluorescent lights, and she raised a hand in a casual wave as Mina and Jasmin approached, bangle bracelets on his wrist jingling.

"Nice to see you again," Mina said.

Rita wore a ring on every finger—butterflies, dragonflies, moons, and stars. She literally shimmered in the silk dress, and her beauty was natural. She wore no makeup, except for some blue liner around her eyes. She made her way out from behind the counter, held out her arms, and waited for Jasmin to fall into them. As they hugged she said something softly to her that Mina couldn't quite hear.

Once they released each other, Rita held a hand out. Mina took it, and before she knew it she was wrapped in a hug as well. The silk dress was cool, and she smelled of violet and other pleasant scents Mina couldn't identify.

Rita let her go, then looked directly into Mina's eyes. "Even though we live in the same building now, I didn't want to bother you, so I'm happy to see you here."

"You and Dave are on the first floor, right?"

"Yes, but as I say, I didn't want to intrude."

"Not at all, come on up and say hi anytime."

"I will," Rita said, eyes sparkling. "I wish we'd had more time to talk at the meet-and-greet, but it's difficult when everyone's clamoring for your time. We've all been talking though. You made a wonderful impression on all of us. You're *perfect*."

"Trust me, I'm nowhere near perfect, but thanks." Mina felt self-conscious and sloppy in her cracked and worn black leather jacket, ripped jeans, and AC/DC shirt. Her hair looked like it hadn't been combed in days, done on purpose, but pale in comparison to those beautiful braids. She also knew her lips were chapped and there were probably big dark circles under her eyes. And now she felt enormous after that breakfast, not slender and elegant like Rita.

"Mina's curious about the herb containers," Jasmin said suddenly. "I told her that it's mostly a tourist thing, not sure if you—"

"No need to sugarcoat what goes on with me," Rita interrupted. "Lots of it is what you might call *sympathetic* magic. Graham Collier said it best, and my description is nowhere as sophisticated as his. It's like you get into the soul of another person, creature, *thing*, and you feel close to it. Because of that feeling, well, magic happens."

"I don't know a lot about magic," Mina confessed. "But that sounds—"

"Far out," Jasmin finished for her.

Rita gave her a quick, noncommittal sideways glance but otherwise kept her eyes on Mina. "They say prehistoric peoples practiced the first magic with crude paintings in caves. The animals were probably painted before a hunt—and it's thought they believed there was a kind of magic there, a ritual, and by extension, in the motion, the *creation* of their art. Yeah, Collier said something about human consciousness causing us to believe in manifestation—or magic—because of the connection to a person—to anything you desire, really."

"Groovy concept," Jasmin said, running her fingers through her hair.

Mina wasn't entirely sure what Rita was talking about but nodded and smiled anyway. "Yeah," she said, searching for a better response as she noticed a bottle of Witch's Sweets on the counter. "Maybe everything and everyone is spiritual. We just have to tap into it."

"Nothing *maybe* about it," Rita told her gently, then pointed to her forehead. "It's all right here. You just have to set the stage, in a sense; get your props lined up, and your subconscious does all the so-called magic. Sometimes I burn candles, incense, and herbs to conjure my muse right before I start to paint. Klaus teaches us the connection must be made if we're going to do any work that's really important."

Mina knew they all respected Klaus a great deal and meant well, but the way everyone in the collective sometimes spoke of him, it reminded her of cult members praising their leader. "I tend to just drink too much vodka or smoke a joint, or both," she said with light nervous laughter. "Maybe I should try it your way."

"Maybe not the healthiest approach for everyone, but different things work for different souls. Just *never* censor your process." As Rita reached behind the messy counter, the cat meowed then rolled over on his back. Jasmin gave his belly a little rub while Rita lifted a canvas out from behind the counter. Three-feet wide and two-feet tall, it was beautifully primed with some sort of shiny gesso, the wood stretchers dark and sturdy. "This is for you, Mina."

"Oh no, I couldn't. You guys have done so much for me already, I—"

"Don't be silly." Rita's gaze darted to Jasmin then back to Mina. "I do it for all the residents. I made it when I knew they'd selected you. The stretchers are made from Black Limba. They say you can repel dark magic with it, or even cast your own hexes if somebody…well…if someone angers you." She grinned slightly. "I mixed a little pokeroot in the gesso when I primed the canvas too."

"What does that do?" Mina asked, noting a subtle but musky smell coming from the canvas.

"Puts you in touch with your spirit guides, or whatever you're comfortable calling them. It helps to make the connection that Klaus teaches is essential, between our work and the spirit world. It actually opens your subconscious to all kinds of creativity. Think of it as your altar, a place where you can do your own kind of magic, a place where you can reach into time and space, where your soul shares communion with your hands and mind as you work. The same way priests perform their rituals on actual altars, it acts that way for the artist." Rita pressed the canvas into Mina's hands and smiled. "Or so they say."

Mina was filled with a sudden feeling of warmth, and the odd smell from the canvas grew stronger, filling her nostrils and causing a tingling sensation behind her eyes.

"Thank you," she said, looking through a window on the wall behind the counter. It had started to snow again. A light snow, the flakes danced as wind scattered roots and twigs and other debris about.

"Come back any time. But for now, go paint." Rita put her hands on Mina's shoulders and gently squeezed. "Paint with your soul, and take a small red candle with you. Red's good for passion, for what we do. Paint until that candle burns down to the quick. You just have to believe, Mina. That's the most important part. *Believe.*"

Rita looked to Jasmin, and then followed Mina's gaze, which had returned to the window behind the counter.

"Snowing again," Jasmin said pensively.

"*Believe*," Rita said again, whispering it this time.

Mina nodded, absently watching the sea of flakes beyond the window now as if they'd mesmerized her without her consent. The tingling behind her eyes grew stronger.

Believe...

CHAPTER NINE

A gentle snow fell, the flakes catching the wind off the water and dancing about in tumbling swirls. Despite the cold, Mina thought there was something majestic about the beach in winter. As she and Jasmin walked the sand together, waves lapped the shore, the tall grass of the nearby dunes swayed gracefully, and the sounds and smells of the ocean filled the air. It was still early afternoon, and after a heavy breakfast and the visit to Rita's shop, it felt good to be outside for a while, strolling and taking in the crisp fresh air. She and Jasmin stopped by the apartment and dropped off the canvas and other things Rita had given her, and then ventured down to the beach for a walk together. It had been a while since Mina had felt icy ocean winds against her face for any extended period, and though they chilled her to the bone, they also reminded her she was alive and how magical life could sometimes be.

"Rita's so cool," Mina said. "That was really nice of her to give me that canvas and the candle and—"

"She's the best. I just love her. Everyone does."

"And she's married to Dave, huh?" Mina asked hesitantly.

"I know, right? Nobody's ever been able to figure that out."

"Love's a crazy thing sometimes."

"Dave's not a bad guy, he's just—well—he's just *Dave*."

"He seems nice too. They're just an odd couple."

"Oh, he is, he's just—I don't know—not subtle."

When Jasmin laughed, Mina figured it was all right if she did too. "I shouldn't have said anything, I'm sorry. It's none of my business."

"It's not like you're the first person to notice. I could hang with Rita all day, she's fascinating and smart and sweet. Dave I have to take in smaller doses. Who knows what she sees in him. But they've been together for years, so whatever it is, it works."

"Hey, good for them then, right?"

"Definitely," Jasmin said.

Mina shivered as another burst of wind struck. "God, it's cold."

"It *is* cold out here on the sand, but it's peaceful too." The wind whipped about, mussing the otherwise perfectly straight curtains of hair hanging from beneath either side of Jasmin's floppy hat. "I dig it in summer too, but winter's my favorite time to come to the beach. Sometimes I walk along the shore for as long as I can stand it. I get so cold, but it's like, when that happens I know I'm alive and then everything's okay, you know? Not just okay, but I feel *powerful* in a way, like I'm a part of it all, me and nature as one, points on the same circle."

"I'm freezing though!"

"Me too, but it's groovy if you let it be!" Jasmin took hold of Mina and they continued on, arm-in-arm. "Sometimes when I'm here alone it all seems so surreal. I mean, I'm alive on planet Earth, right? But in winter the beach looks so different, almost like an alien landscape or something. Not in a bad or scary way, it's more like I'm alone on this whole other planet, a planet of my very own. It sounds stupid, but—"

"No, it doesn't actually, not to me."

Jasmin gazed at her thoughtfully. "Really?"

Although Mina was badly craving a cigarette, she'd never be able to light it with the wind, so she did her best to ignore it. "In some ways, to do what we do, we have to go somewhere else to a certain extent."

"For sure," Jasmin said, gently resting her head on Mina's shoulder as they walked. "I knew you'd understand."

"And wherever it is we go in ourselves, it's not like anywhere else. We see the world differently than other people. All artists do. It's not better or worse, necessarily, just different, and it can take us places no one else ever goes. Even somewhere like this, a beach where so many people come and go, we can still see and feel it in a totally different way than anyone else does. We see it from a different angle, I think, a different perspective, and that opens our eyes and minds—our souls—to other things."

"Wow, you said that so perfectly," Jasmin said. "Hey, maybe that's what happened with that guy you saw, the sexy painter in the apartment across from yours. Maybe it was like an artistic vision! That'd be so far out!"

Mina shrugged. "I don't know, maybe."

"That kind of thing happens sometimes, Mina. It's almost like we're under a spell or hypnotized or something. You know what I mean, I know you do. Almost anything's possible when an artist is in that state. That's a big part of what we mean when we talk about connections between art, artists, and the spirit world."

"It's not like I'm unaware of those connections," Mina said. "I've felt the same way for most of my life, but until now I never put it in the same context you guys do. I've always known it isn't fantasy or playacting. It's as real as anything else for me. It's definitely a state of being, like you said. He just seemed so real, so grounded in reality."

"But wasn't there an ethereal feel to the whole experience too?"

"Yes, there was."

"It's possible then."

"Who knows? I *do* know one thing for sure though. I could walk this beach and feel the same things you described. I'm kind of feeling them right now to be honest."

Jasmin gave Mina's arm a little squeeze. "Are you flirting with me?"

"No," Mina said, her eyes tearing in the cold. "Maybe, I don't know."

"Okay, well I'm totally flirting with you," Jasmin said. "I just suck at it."

Mina laughed.

"I'm teasing," Jasmin added.

Mina stopped and turned toward her, causing Jasmin to lift her head. "It's okay, Jazz, I—"

"You like guys, I get it. I'm into guys too. I just don't limit my feelings to—"

"I'm not saying I wouldn't—or couldn't—or haven't. It's just—"

"It's cool." Jasmin unhooked her arm from Mina's. "I was just being silly."

Mina reached out and tenderly placed a gloved hand flat against Jasmin's cheek. "You don't have to explain yourself to me, Jasmin. We're fine."

"Sorry, I tend to feel things really intensely. I have so much love flowing through me, sometimes I just—"

"Don't apologize. You're a beautiful soul and you did nothing wrong. I feel a connection too, okay? I'm just more about being friends right now. Is that cool?"

"Of course," Jasmin said through a big smile. "I didn't mean to freak you out."

"Stop, you did no such thing." Mina turned and walked on, hopeful Jasmin would follow. When she did, Mina was relieved.

"Well *that* was awkward," Jasmin said a moment later.

Mina took Jasmin's hand and they began walking arm-in-arm again, staying quiet for a while this time.

Sounds of the ocean filled the silence.

"I'm really glad you came here, Mina," Jasmin finally said.

Mina looked out at the ocean as they walked. The choppy waves, the dark water, the gray sky, it all looked so oddly perfect and completely chaotic—like it had been conjured in the mind of a painter in the throes of exactly what they'd just been talking about—and although that irony was in no way lost on her, in that moment Mina felt the most comfortable she had since she'd arrived in Crow's Cry. "Me too," she said softly.

Eventually they reached a long stone jetty that jutted out into the turbulent ocean and marked the end of the beach. Had they continued on, they would've crossed a small dirt parking lot, and then there was nothing but forest.

"We should head home," Jasmin said.

She didn't know why, but as Mina looked out at the water again, she suddenly had the urge to tell Jasmin about her nightmares, about the boat and the ferryman and the strange and frightening lost souls.

"Mina?" Jasmin asked, gazing at her. "Are you okay?"

Mina shook off the nightmare, dismissing the idea of mentioning it. "Yeah, fine."

Jasmin seemed unconvinced. "Are you sure?"

"Addiction calls," she said, managing a quick smile. "If I don't smoke a cigarette soon my head's gonna explode."

"Yikes!" Jasmin said, eyes widening in faux terror. "Come on then, we better split and get you some nicotine."

Together, still arm-in-arm, they turned and headed back along the sand in the direction they'd come.

* * * *

In the relative warmth of her apartment, with each exhale, Mina watched ribbons of smoke slowly curl and glide around her. Leaned against the kitchen counter, she smoked in silence, and despite the odor of cigarette smoke filling the air, she was still able to smell the wonderful and strange fragrances from the new canvas Rita gave her, which she'd propped over by the windows.

She pictured Jasmin in the apartment beneath hers, and how she'd seemed disappointed when Mina politely declined an invite to come in for tea, opting instead to get some work done, but promising to take her up on it next time.

She's down there all alone. I wonder if she's sipping herbal tea and thinking about alternate realities and artistic visions. Or are darker things filling her mind? Is there necessarily a difference, and if there is, would she even realize it or identify it as such? Is she inspired to paint like I am right now, or lost in some dreamy cocoon?

Having grown up as she had, Mina learned to recognize predators early on in life. Jasmin was not anything along those lines, she was sure of it. In fact, Jasmin was innocent and sweet, almost childlike at times to the point of often appearing utterly clueless. Yet like everyone else here, there was something *off* about her, something Mina couldn't put her finger on but sensed in a way she could only define as instinctual. From the moment she'd arrived in Crow's Cry, she felt like she was lost in a lucid dream where everything and everyone was slightly askew and nothing was entirely what it seemed. She realized it could simply be that she was overwhelmed and off-balance due to all the recent changes. That, coupled with the pressure she'd placed on herself being the new resident artist amidst a collective of people she'd never before met and still felt somewhat unworthy of.

Something deep within her insisted there was more to it than that.

Pushing away from the counter, Mina moved over to the windows. The painting she started the day before wasn't coming together the way she'd hoped. Maybe she'd put it aside for now and try something with the new canvas. The cigarette dangling from her lips, she watched the blank canvas a moment, the odd smells from it even stronger now.

She closed her eyes, embraced first the scents circling her, then the visions of the strange painter leaping and spinning about, paint spraying his canvas with both crazed abandon and precise focus.

Maybe it was *a ghost.*

When Mina's eyes opened, she was standing in front of the windows and looking down at the dark first-floor apartment.

Maybe he was an artistic vision.

Grabbing the plastic ashtray she'd purchased, she took a couple quick drags then stubbed out the cigarette.

There are ghosts in Crow's Cry, trust me, girl.

Mina put the ashtray aside and folded her arms across her chest. She could feel her heart beating, the rhythm of it pulsing in her ears.

This is ancient land, lots of spirits here.

"Leave it alone, Mina," she said aloud.

But she wasn't sure she could.

You just got back, it's nice and warm and safe and you're inspired to paint—it's what you want right now, what you need. Do it. Focus on that, lose yourself in it, forget the rest of this shit and do what you came here to do.

"I know what I saw," she muttered, still staring at the apartment.

The snowsqualls had stopped, but it was even colder out there now, and the temperature would continue to plummet as daylight crept closer to darkness. Mina tore herself from the windows.

Her leather jacket was draped across the chair where she'd thrown it. She eyed it a while, aware that there was no point in attempting to dissuade herself from what had already become inevitable.

"Fuck it."

Snatching up her jacket, Mina headed out the door.

* * * *

Carefully and quietly as she could, Mina moved along the stairs, passing first Jasmin's second-floor apartment, and then Rita and Dave's on the ground floor. She knew Jasmin was home and that Rita was at work, but couldn't be sure about Dave. Given the time of day, and assuming he had some sort of day job, she assumed he likely wasn't home, but she didn't want to risk being wrong, so she moved stealthily through the foyer, this time following it to a door on the side wall rather than going out the front.

The door stuck at first, but opened when she gave it a tug. Slowly opening it the rest of the way, and cringing when it made a loud squeaking noise, Mina hesitated a moment to see if anyone stirred in the first-floor apartment or if any sounds came from Jasmin's apartment above her. The building remained quiet, so she stepped out into the courtyard and gently closed the door behind her, making sure it was secure before venturing any further.

As the cold air hit her, she pulled her jacket in tighter around her and took a few steps into the courtyard. The paver stones between the buildings, quite beautiful once, were now old, many of them cracked and stained and damaged, as was a small cement bench, the remains of some old birdfeeders, and a fountain that obviously hadn't been used in years. Remnants of the snow dusting and natural debris littered the area, and a mischievous looking stone cherub perhaps two feet tall crouched over the fountain, chips missing from its eyes, face, and body.

Mina looked up and realized that all three apartments in her building had the big double windows on the courtyard side, which meant if Jasmin was anywhere near hers, she'd be able to see Mina standing out there. But daylight glare made it impossible to know for sure if anyone was in the windows, so she'd just have to risk it.

Slowly, she crossed the courtyard, trying to appear nonchalant just in case anyone *did* see her. The building across from hers was much closer now, the big window where she'd seen the man just a few feet away, but whatever lay beyond it was obscured by glare as well. To the left of the window, there was a door identical to the one she'd used to enter the courtyard. She grabbed hold of the black knob and, to her surprise, the door opened rather easily.

After stealing a quick glance over her shoulder, Mina stepped inside.

She pulled the door closed behind her but left it slightly ajar so the light could at least partially illuminate a narrow hallway which led to a foyer quite similar to the one in her building. It smelled musty here. The floors were uneven and badly damaged, the walls scarred and the ceiling cracked and stained with water damage. An old light fixture dangled from a frayed wire overhead, looking as if someone had yanked it down and tried to rip it free but had fallen short. The staircase that led to the other floors was unusable, many of the steps broken and open, the entire thing littered with debris and garbage.

To her right was the door to the first-floor apartment. *His apartment...*

A board had been nailed across the door at some previous point, a large padlock fastened to it and the doorframe, but both had been torn free, and now the board lay against the wall, the padlock dangling free.

Whoever broke such a heavy-duty lock went to a lot of trouble, Mina thought.

She reached out and tried the door. It came away from the frame easily, so she opened it but remained where she was. A horrible stench wafted out that was so strong she covered her nose and mouth with a hand. There was plenty of light from the large window facing the courtyard, but the apartment was otherwise draped in shadow.

She could see it was filthy and cluttered with debris, broken pieces of furniture, and various fixtures; even pieces of appliances and chunks of what appeared to be porcelain were scattered across the floor.

As Mina stepped through the doorway, she felt a sudden sense of dread. Something deep within her wanted her to leave this place, and to do so immediately, but she ignored it and crossed the main room anyway, her boots crunching trash and debris.

The apartment had the same layout hers had: kitchenette area to the left, a main room in the center, and a bathroom in the back. The only difference was instead of two windows there was only one, and rather than being located on the back wall, it was on the front. But the place was in shambles. What she could see of the sink beyond the garbage thrown into it was stained black with some sort of grime or mold-like substance, which also covered good portions of the walls and ceiling, both of which were damaged with several holes that appeared to have been made by punches or kicks, while those along the ceiling looked more gnawed. The sea of rodent droppings all over the floor amidst the other garbage explained those.

Mina moved across the main room carefully, stepping over the remains of what had once been a chair and a rusted, old, bare box spring. The chair looked like it had been disassembled with an axe, perhaps a sledgehammer.

Standing in front of the window, Mina looked out at the courtyard and then up at her apartment. The window was filthy and smudged on the inside, so everything beyond appeared distorted and blurred.

This is impossible. He was standing right here.

Mina ran a hand through her hair and sighed.

He was painting right in this spot.

She looked down at the floor again. There was barely any room to move with all the garbage and debris at her feet, much less leap and dance as he'd done. And there certainly wasn't enough of an area to accommodate the large canvas he'd been working with, not with the place in this condition.

"The fuck," Mina mumbled, her breath hitting the cold air and misting around her.

She took her hand from her face, but the stench was still awful. A musty smell mixed with the stink of animal waste and rotting garbage, it was literally making her eyes water. Or maybe the cold was doing that, she couldn't be sure at that point and didn't much care; her head was reeling and she just wanted to get the hell out of there.

As she turned from the window, Mina saw the door to the bathroom had been ripped from its hinges at some point and was lying on the floor. Carefully negotiating her way around the trash, she tested the door to make sure she wouldn't go right through it, then stepped onto it and peeked into the bathroom.

It was empty except for an old medicine cabinet that had been partially pulled off the wall and now dangled there, the door removed and on the floor beneath it reduced to shards of broken and filthy glass.

Mina had no sense of anyone or anything here. It had been so long since anyone lived here, all traces were gone, any residual energy long extinguished. And yet the feeling of dread remained. She'd felt something similar as a child when she entered certain foster homes, but nothing this strong. Something had happened here. Not just something bad, but something horrible, something evil. Long ago, perhaps, but it was all that survived in this awful and forgotten place.

"What am I doing?" she said, shaking her head. "I need to get out of here."

She was about to leave when something in the far corner of the bathroom caught her eye, a small bit of color amidst the shadows along the floor. Hesitantly, Mina crept into the bathroom and crouched before what appeared to be the remains of a candle. Burned to the base, the lump of mutilated red wax sat before her. Melted to the tile floor, a relic of some earlier moment lost in time, it was as forgotten and discarded as the rest of this place.

But it frightened her like the ghost it was.

I burn candles, incense, and herbs to conjure my muse right before I start to paint.

Isn't that what Rita had said?

Paint with your soul, and take a small red candle with you.

Mina stood up.

Red's good for passion, for what we do.

She took a step back.

Paint until that candle burns down to the quick.

A shiver shook her, a chill slithering up her between her shoulder blades and fanning out across the back of her neck.

"Who were you?" Mina said softly. "What happened to you here?"

She hugged herself, shrugging off the cold.

Okay, calm down, this is making you crazy. It's just an old candle. Lots of people burn candles, and red is a common color. Maybe whoever lived here even bought it from Rita. So what? The collective's been here for years, right? Besides, it wouldn't necessarily mean—

Something moved behind her, out in the main room.

Mina whirled around, not sure what to do. She was cornered.

"Hey!" a male voice called. "Is there somebody in here?"

Breathing quietly through her mouth, Mina stayed as still as she could.

"I'm not playing around!" the man growled. "If there's somebody in here you better come out, it'll be better than if I have to come get you, believe that!"

That voice sounds familiar.

"Look, I won't call the cops if you just come out, okay? You can't be in here."

Mina stepped through the doorway and saw Dave standing just inside the entrance to the apartment, a baseball bat in his hands. "It's just me."

"Mina?" He squinted as if he couldn't see her clearly.

"Yeah," she said. "Sorry, I—"

"Jesus," he said, breathing heavily and slumping with relief against the doorframe, his free hand over his heart. Then, realizing what he'd done, he quickly straightened up and assumed a more aggressive posture. "Jazz told me you thought you saw someone in here the other night, I told her I'd check it out. Figured it was some nutty homeless guy hiding in here or something. Thought I was gonna have to kick some ass."

"Nope, just me," Mina said meekly.

"What the hell are you doing in here, girl?"

"I just— I'm really sorry. I wasn't sure if I saw somebody the other night, so—"

"You didn't break that lock, did you?" he asked, jerking a thumb toward the door.

"No," she said. "I would never do that, I—"

"I didn't think so. Probably was a homeless person then."

"Yeah, the lock was already broken, so I just—"

"We don't have too many homeless around here, more in the summer months. But in winter there's a few that stick around. It's not unheard of for them to break into places that are abandoned like this, especially this time of year. Hell, you can't blame them, it *is* freezing out. Jesus Christ, it stinks in here, wow."

"I didn't mean to do anything wrong, Dave, I shouldn't have—"

"You okay?" He took another step into the apartment. "You didn't hurt yourself or anything, did you?"

"No, I'm all right."

"Condition this place is in, it's a wonder you didn't. See that shit?" He pointed to the black gunk along the ceiling. "That's mold. It can make you really sick. Hell, it can even kill you if you breathe in enough of it."

Mina nodded awkwardly. "I don't know what I was thinking. I'm really sorry."

He seemed to think about her response a moment, and then shrugged. "You don't have to apologize, Mina, I'm just trying to figure out what would possess you to be here in the first place."

"It was stupid, I thought I saw someone in here the other night, and when Jasmin said nobody has lived here for years, I decided to come take a look, that's all. Not a wise decision, obviously. I won't do it again."

"Well that's good to hear, because I don't want to have to come back into this shithole any time soon. Place gives me the creeps, you want to know the truth." Dave smiled. "Speaking of which, I hope I didn't scare you before when I first came in all badass and whatnot."

"Little bit." Mina moved toward the door. Dave didn't move out of her way. She smiled at him but she was trembling. "You sounded pretty serious."

Dave puffed up his chest as Jasmin said he would. "I can kick butt when I have to. It's not something I like doing, you understand, it's not like I'm one of those Neanderthal types that go looking for it—I'm an artist, same as you—but if it's necessary I can get it done, know what I mean?"

"I do," Mina said. "Again, I'm really sorry."

"No harm, no foul. You didn't do anything wrong necessarily, just not the smartest move in terms of safety and wellbeing. Do me a favor, stay out of here from now on, okay? It's really dangerous."

"I will, I promise. I'm so embarrassed, I shouldn't have—"

"Don't worry about it. We'll keep the whole thing between us, no reason not to." "Thanks."

"Hey, we all go places we shouldn't sometimes, right?"

"Sure," she said softly.

"Just remember, curiosity killed the cat. Isn't that what they say?"

Mina couldn't read Dave's expression. Was he being kind or threatening?

"I'm just messing with you," he said suddenly, laughing and slapping his thigh. "I guess I don't know you well enough to bust balls like that yet, my bad."

"It's okay," Mina said, forcing a light laugh. "I probably had it coming."

Dave finally slid out of the way and let Mina pass. As she did, he followed her out into the hallway and closed the door behind them. "I better head over to the hardware store and grab another lock, get this door secured again. Want to come along?"

"I would, but I want to get some work done this afternoon," Mina said as she drifted out into the courtyard. "And I already wasted enough time with this stupid shit."

"I get it. That's more important anyway." He watched as Mina fumbled her cigarettes from her jacket pocket and quickly lit one. "Hey, heard you and Jazzy went to Rita's shop today, huh?"

"Yeah, what a cool place, loved it." Mina drew the smoke deep into her lungs then let it out. Her nerves began to settle a bit. "And Rita's awesome."

"She has her moments," Dave said with a wink.

"Definitely," Mina said, starting back across the courtyard to her building. "I'll see you later, Dave."

"You bet," he said from behind her. "Behave yourself now, you hear?"

"I'll do my best."

"Just joshing, see you later!"

With a quick wave, Mina hurried back into the building.

The cold followed.

CHAPTER TEN

With the heat going in her apartment and a blanket over her shoulders, Mina still couldn't seem to get warm. A cigarette in one hand and a glass of vodka in the other, she sat in the chair, her phone on speaker and resting in her lap.

"Okay, hold on, let me get this straight," Ralph said. "So you're saying the apartment was *that* much of a disaster?"

"No one's lived there in a long time, Ralph. Just rodents, if the shit all over the floor's any indication. But somebody broke that lock, so probably a homeless person's passed through too. I've seen some big rats, but never one that could break a padlock."

"That's only because you've never lived in New York City. Christ, the ones in my apartment back in the day were huge. Some of them drove cars."

Mina laughed a little, she couldn't help it.

"Now didn't that feel good?" Ralph said. "Take a couple deep breaths, doll."

"It's just, my head's spinning, you know?"

"So this man you think you saw, he—"

"I either saw him or I'm losing my fucking mind."

"Believe it or not, there are other options."

Mina took a big gulp of her drink and continued manically smoking her cigarette. "I'm all ears."

"Couldn't it be possible that you were stoned, tired, maybe drunk, and—"

"Ralph, I saw him twice."

"But, however ill-advised it may have been, you went into that apartment and saw for yourself that not only was no one living there, it wasn't possible for this man to have been doing what you thought you saw him doing, yes?"

Mina pressed the glass against her forehead. She was getting that strange tingling behind her eyes again. "Yes," she said. "There wasn't enough room, too much garbage."

"Then why don't we look at the most logical explanation, how's that sound?"

"Like you're patronizing me."

He stayed quiet a moment, and all she could hear was Ralph's breathing.

"I'm sorry," Mina said softly. "I don't mean to be so…"

"I think *unbearable* is the word you're looking for." Ralph sighed. "I'm not trying to patronize you, Mina. I'm trying to help, okay?"

She crushed her cigarette in the ashtray and blew out her final drag. "Okay."

"Things happen. We all see things sometimes that we misinterpret or think we saw one way or another, when in reality, we didn't. The mind's a tricky thing. It's very complex, and like anything else, sometimes there can be glitches."

"Right, so there's a glitch. In other words, I'm losing my mind."

"Not at all, it's just a strange situation. People see things in dream states all the time. They swear they're awake, because in a way they are, but they're in the throes of a waking dream, or something similar. It's like how we hypnotize ourselves without even realizing it. Ever been driving and then suddenly it feels like you just came to and you have no idea what you've been doing or thinking for the last few seconds? You were driving and functioning the whole time, you just don't remember it. That's the human mind at work, kid. Granted, in ways we may not fully understand, but still, it's not illness, it's actually so commonplace it's practically mundane."

Mina thought about it a moment. "I know what you're saying, but I've never experienced anything like this, something that seemed *so* real."

"Look, if we're under tremendous pressure or stressed out of our minds, these things can happen. Or when we're frightened, even when we're sleepy and not fully seeing or experiencing things as we normally do. It can lead to all sorts of things that may not be easily explainable. But that doesn't mean you're mentally ill. This kind of thing happens more than most people realize. Maybe it was some sort of hallucination. Who knows?"

"If I'm sober and hallucinating then I *am* nuts."

"Are you under the impression that only insane people hallucinate?"

"Well, I wasn't under the impression that sane people do."

"They do, all the time." Ralph cleared his throat. "Look, kiddo, you're in a new place and into a new experience the likes of which you've never dealt with before. Knowing you as I do, I'm sure you're putting a ridiculous amount of pressure on yourself because you don't feel worthy of having been selected for this residency. I'd also bet my bottom dollar you're not sleeping well, drinking too much, and not smoking nearly enough dope. You've likely been wound tighter than a drum from the moment you got there, so you're stressed out of your mind and exhausted. That can lead to many unpleasant things, substantial confusion being just one of them. Get it? Are you picking up what the great and powerful Ralph is putting down here?"

Ralph had come to know her so well, sometimes it was maddening. "Yes, I'm confused and stressed and seeing things that aren't there. Awesome!"

"It beats being psychotic."

"Well that's reassuring."

"Hey, I'm a fucking art teacher, not a psychologist. I'm doing my best here."

"And that red candle I found burned down in the bathroom?" she said. "That really freaked me out."

"Gimme a sec, I'm turning on." The sound of a lighter igniting was followed by a slow intake of breath and then a slow exhale. "I get how the whole candle thing could set you off, but think about it. Is it so unusual for people to have candles, even red ones?"

"No."

"Well, there you go. Your mind was already going to strange places because of the confusion over the visions—or whatever they were—of this sexy painter jumping around, and when you saw what was left of some old red candle, you immediately made a connection where there isn't one, to this Rita woman and the candle she gave you."

"I want to believe you."

"Why wouldn't you? I'm brilliant. Mina, listen to me. Unless you've left something out, from everything you've told me so far these people seem lovely, and like they've gone out of their way to welcome you and make you feel comfortable. Christ, from the sounds they're *celebrating* you."

"I know."

"All right, then are you telling me you now have some reason to suspect they might want to harm you?"

"No, of course not," Mina said through a heavy sigh. "They're eccentric and a little strange, but what artists aren't? We're weird too."

GREG F. GIFUNE & SANDY DELUCA

"Fabulously so, but yes, I see your point." Ice cubes clinked against glass, and then came the sound of liquid pouring. "All right, so if you don't feel these folks are a threat to you, and I see no reason why they would be, then there's no need to make connections supporting that they are. Is there?"

"No. I wasn't trying to do that exactly, I..." Mina swallowed the remainder of her drink then shook her head in frustration. "Shit, I—I don't know what I was trying to do, I—"

"You said yourself last time we talked that you've been having disturbing and strange nightmares too. I'm sure they're not helping. From the sounds, Crow's Cry is a little strange, kind of deserted and dark, yes? Use that, kid. Don't let it drag you under."

"Can I ask you something?"

"Anything, you know that."

"You've always told me there were ghosts in Providence, and that you've seen them in the windows of old abandoned buildings—faces—remember?"

It took Ralph a few seconds to answer, but when he did his tone was more serious. "Yes, I remember."

"Are *they* real?"

"I don't know. That's part of their mystery, I suppose. I'm not sure it matters."

"Maybe I saw something similar? Jasmin, the one I was telling you about—"

"Little Miss Trippy Dippy Hippie?"

"Yeah, remember the Muppets? The hippie chick on there, she—"

"Janice."

"Of course you'd know her name. She kind of looks like her."

"I love her already. Please tell me she has the hat."

"She does. Anyway, she said maybe I saw a ghost or experienced some sort of haunting. Couldn't that be possible too, that I really *did* see him, the same way you see those faces sometimes?"

"Honey, if my twenty-nine years on this planet have taught me anything—"

"You missed a couple decades there."

"*Such* a cunt," he said under his breath. "Fine, my *thirty-nine* years, I—"

"You're getting warmer."

"What was I saying about you being unbearable?"

"Go ahead."

"Could you have seen a ghost? Sure, why not? Anything's possible. Happy?"

"That's it?"

"That's all I've got. For Christ's sake, let me get stoned in peace, will you?"

"I'm serious, do you think—"

"Don't sabotage this opportunity, Mina. I know a part of you wants to."

She nodded even though he couldn't see her.

"Besides, I'm coming to visit soon."

"Promise?" she asked, her mood brightening a bit.

"Cross my heart, so don't go mucking up my plans." Ralph swallowed loudly, then crunched some ice. "Now, have you gotten any work done or have you been too busy with all this Nancy Drew business?"

"I've gotten a little done."

"That means hardly anything, doesn't it?"

"God, you never let me get away with anything. It's *so* annoying."

"I've told you repeatedly to call me Ralph. *His Eminence* works too, but even for me, *God's* a little over the top, don't you think?"

"If you could see me right now, you'd realize I'm flipping you off."

"That's my girl."

"Thanks for putting up with me."

"Right back at you," Ralph said. "Now, try to focus on your work, and maybe even enjoy yourself a little. Whatever you saw, it didn't hurt you, and it won't interfere with why you're there unless you let it. You experienced it, fine. Go with it as best you can, don't turn it into a negative if it doesn't have to be. Was it real? Sure, in some sense, but like the things I've seen over the years, the how and why of it doesn't matter as much as what we do with the experience itself. Focus on the task at hand and keep everything else in perspective. Maybe it's simply one more piece of the overall experience. So let it be that. Are we mad? To some extent, of course, we're artists. Comes with the territory, yes? It's why I call everyone else *Normals*, because we aren't. Just do your best to remember that this is a great opportunity, doll. Focus on that. The rest is all—forgive the pun—window-dressing. I know this is a modest residency, but there's no telling where it might lead."

Mina thought about it a moment. "I wonder if any of the other recipients have amounted to anything since they left here and went back to the real world. There are only five of us, been one a year for the last five years."

"I'm sure some have done well. It'd be easy enough to find out."

"The guy before me, his name was Robert Sanders," Mina explained. "Jasmin told me he was from Los Angeles and went back there to open his own gallery."

"Well, there's your answer then."

"Sure, if it actually happened."

"Do you have reason to believe it didn't?"

"No, but Jasmin said they hadn't heard from him since he went back home. That was the plan though, to open a gallery in LA. I don't know about any of the others."

"What's his name again?"

"Robert Sanders, he was awarded the residency last year."

"I'm jotting it down."

"Why?"

"If you promise to get some sleep, clear your head, and get a little work done, I'll see what I can find out about what Mr. Sanders is up to these days. Maybe his story will further inspire you."

"You don't have to. I can just as easily Google the guy, Ralph, I—"

"Yes, but you'll be too busy relaxing, clearing your mind, forgetting about sexy phantom dancers, getting some sleep, and creating amazing work, remember? Now say I win. Say it."

Mina smiled. "You win."

"Good, I have to scoot. This joint's gone, and I've nearly achieved maximum chill, so it's movie time. I'm streaming *Gentlemen Prefer Blondes* tonight. It's been a harrowing day—somebody still has to teach those little fuckers, you know—and I'm in serious need of the shenanigans only Marilyn Monroe and Jane Russell can provide."

"Have fun," she said, wishing she could be there with him. "And thanks, Ralph."

"Did you smoke those joints I gave you?"

"Just one," she said. "Still got two left."

"Good, go smoke another one and see if you can get some work done. Let it flow, Mina, don't question it. Fall into it, see where it takes you."

She knew exactly what he meant. "Okay."

"Just do me one favor, yes?"

"Sure. What?"

"Don't look out the fucking windows."

* * * *

Night had fallen, and the old radiator rattled and hissed as Mina turned the heat way up to combat her chill. It, like most of the bottle of vodka she'd opened earlier, was soon gone, so she stripped down to a pair of panties and a half t-shirt from a

Mötley Crüe concert she'd gone to years before, then put aside the painting she'd started previously and focused instead on the blank canvas Rita gave her. It took its place near the windows and beneath the glow of fluorescent lights, the strange aroma wafting from it mixing with the smell of pot smoke filling the room. What remained of the joint—about half— dangled from Mina's lips as she slipped her headphones on and padded barefoot across the room, her body moving in time with the slowly rising electronic beats of Donna Summer's disco classic "I Feel Love." She'd always been more of a rock and roll girl, but there was something about that song in particular that moved her, affected her in ways few others did, especially when she was drinking or high, so she often threw it on when she was painting and lost herself in the driving, otherworldly beat. On this night, she used headphones so as not to disturb her neighbors, but once they were in place she turned the volume as high as she could without blowing them out.

The music blaring and as intoxicating as the booze and weed, Mina stared at the canvas, her mind a whirlwind of thoughts and visions—light and dark—fantasies and memories and nightmares, they all blended together like the smells drifting around her as she danced. Mina moved slowly at first, strutting back and forth like a tiger walking its cage, contemplating, planning, feeling, being—*stalking*—the blank canvas. She spun, twirling round and round on the balls of her feet, her arms out on either side of her and undulating like serpents to the music, her head bouncing, swaying in time as all inhibition left her, releasing her into her process on this night, her desire, her *need*.

Mina closed her eyes. The music, her movements, it was all so liberating. She was there, and aware of herself, but no longer fully in control, and there was phenomenal power in that. She belonged to the music now, the beat, the movements of her body, and the concepts slinking through her mind, gradually taking form and shape before she even tried to bring them to life on canvas.

Let it flow, Mina, don't question it.

Whirling to a stop, she opened her eyes, still bouncing to the beat, feeling it exploding through her in waves like an orgasm—the vodka, the weed, the dancing, all of it setting her free.

Fall into it.

She ran her hands up and down her body as she danced, feeling the electricity.

Reaching for a brush, she picked it up without interrupting the beat, dancing closer to the canvas now—smelling it, seeing it, *feeling* it—and like a living thing awaiting her touch, Mina swore she saw it move—breathe—pulsating to the rhythm along with her.

See where it takes you.

Dropping the brush, she grabbed the paint—one tube and then another—squeezing them into her hands and running them over her body as she twirled. Streaks of red—like bloody wounds—slashed her face and torso, her legs. And then greens and blues and blacks covered her as well, smeared across her flesh, her own touch sending waves of fear and pleasure surging through her, as if she were being touched by someone—some*thing*—else. Falling into whatever was happening to her, she spun and danced harder, her bare feet slapping the floor, her back arched, breasts bouncing, nipples straining against the thin t-shirt.

With abandon, Mina threw herself deeper into it, smearing the canvas with what remained on her hands and between her fingers—moist and fluid, like blood, like cum—and grabbed the brush again. As she danced, jerking about more violently to the beat and feeling the wetness between her legs, the heat, she moved back and forth between her body and the canvas, spraying both in turn with paint. Eyes wide and feral, mouth open and chest heaving, she watched it spatter against the canvas, *felt* it hit her face and neck and body as the music continued to pound through the headphones, forcefully pushing her, enveloping her, *consuming* her.

Mina dropped the brush with no concern, spun over to the chair, and snatched the bottle of vodka from the floor. Dancing back to the canvas, she took a long pull from the bottle, emptying what was left of it before dropping it back to the floor and pressing her hands flat against the canvas. She could feel the power coming from it, and it was like nothing she'd experienced before.

It was alive. *She* was alive.

Covered in paint, she spun away, letting the music take her.

As her eyes opened, the room tilted. She was high and drunk and God knows what else. It didn't matter. Nothing did. All she wanted was for that music and this feeling to never end. The paint felt like another skin against her own, concealing her in a cocoon of many colors, her body and the canvas the same now.

Darkness closed in, as if someone had suddenly thrown a huge black tarp over her. She felt herself sinking, falling while the music seemed to grow even louder, pulsing and pounding in her head, as if it were fucking her with each crazed thrust.

As she made her way up and out of the darkness, back to the bright fluorescent lights, the canvas, and her tiny apartment, Mina continued to dance, spinning and spinning and spinning, even though she realized then she was no longer alone.

Something told her to stop, but she couldn't.

As the room swept past, blurred and whirling as if she were on some rapid carnival ride, she saw them—all of them—standing beyond the light, in the shadows, watching her, smiling demonically with approval and glee.

Maurice Larocque, with his dark hair grayed at the temples, blue blazer and ascot and penny loafers, grinning maniacally at her…Frances Strengarden scowling…Dave McGrath in the corner, licking his lips, his eyes wild with lust…Rita, serene and distant, expressionless but laser-focused…Jasmin bopping in place, eyes closed and lost in the music…the others from the meet-and-greet huddled in the shadows of the kitchen…and finally, Klaus Riker, his scars moving, gliding across his neck and face as if alive.

Near the ceiling, in the corner, peering down and impossibly crouched there, suspended like some hideous cross between human and insect, he gazed at her with wild eyes and a hideous grin, his flesh pale, white as chalk, bloodless.

"S-Stop," Mina heard herself say. Or had she only thought it?

Scream it, Mina.

"Stop!" she screeched, the music and the spinning, the light and the dark alternating, blinking, dizzying as the flashes of ghouls continued.

That's it, scream for us, Mina.

"This isn't happening!"

Do you have a strong interest in mysticism and spiritualism, Mina?

The music began to fade, the electronic beat sounding as if it were slowly moving away from her, into the shadows with the others. She knew Riker had spoken, but she never saw his lips move. She heard him from *inside* her head.

And then, there came pain.

She felt something moving through her, as if it were being absorbed into her skin then hardening somehow inside her, cracking her bones and ripping her flesh.

"You're killing me!" she gasped, realizing now that she was flat on her back and they were all standing over her, around her. "You're *killing* me!"

"No, Mina," a voice whispered. "It's only a new kind of life..."

She thrashed about, tried to stand, but couldn't get up. "I'm dreaming," she said. "This is a nightmare, it's not real!"

Nightmares are the only things that are real, Mina.

A finger moved along her cheek, spreading paint as it went, following it down along her throat, between her breasts, across her stomach, and between her legs.

From somewhere deep within the shadows, Mina heard breathing. Heavy, lascivious and evil, like the panting of a ravenous beast, she felt it against her face and neck in quick, warm intervals.

And then, as the last pulses of music died, the fluorescent lights extinguished and the world was plunged into darkness; she was alone again.

Snowflakes began to fall from the night sky above, tumbling and twirling toward her with grace and beauty.

Her terror subsided. Mina felt nothing.

Nothing at all...

CHAPTER ELEVEN

"Look, another one!"

A summer a couple years before...a hot late afternoon on the shoreline, Mina stands in the wet sand, watching Ralph as he holds up another shell he's found.

"What a beauty!" he says proudly. "Look at the colors!"

Are they stoned? Were they? Mina can't remember for sure, but it feels that way.

Ralph drops the shell into a large McDonald's cup and, high-stepping comically, runs on along the sand in search of more. "I'm coming to get you, my pretties!"

"Who cares about shells?" Mina says, wondering if she said it loud enough for him to hear. "We've got to pull your Jeep out of the sand or we'll never get out of here."

He looks back at her and smiles mischievously. "Enjoy the high, Mina. Enjoy the goddamn moment for once in your fucking life, would you? Stop being a downer."

"Fuck you!" she shouts, feeling the coolness of bedsheets beneath her.

But I'm not in bed...

She stands on the beach beside Ralph's Jeep Wrangler. The tires are beginning to sink in the wet sand. He swore he could drive it onto the beach with no trouble, but now he's running around out there and his Jeep looks like it is being devoured.

"What are your thoughts on this one?" Ralph calls to her, holding up another shell he's found. "I'm on the fence, honestly, could take it or leave it. Sort of like Renée Zellweger."

"Do you have roadside service?" Mina asks, pointing to the Jeep. "The tide's coming in, Ralph, we need to get out of here."

"Fine, fuck this little asshole then." He tosses the shell into the ocean.

Mina touches her forehead, feels the subtle pulsing of veins, the warmth of her flesh, and smells the faint odor from Rita's canvas.

"We're not really here, are we, Ralph?" Mina says, slurring her words. "This already happened."

"What you're experiencing, doll, is a hypnopompic hallucination," Ralph says, standing there with his cup of shells, his bare feet sunken in the wet sand, jeans rolled halfway up his calves. "However, that should not be confused with a hypnagogic hallucination, because that is a totally different thing. See, now hypnopompic *hallucinations—like you're having at the moment—happen in the morning when you're waking up."* He cocks his head, seems to notice his Jeep for the first time. *"Stop worrying about my Wrangler. It's a Jeep for a reason. It would have to be completely buried under the sand in Narraganset Bay before it got stuck. It's designed for off-roading and all sorts of other badass, allegedly big-dick shit. Being the seething macho asshole I am, I know all about this kind of thing, baby, so don't worry your pretty little head over it! Or, you know, something obnoxious like those extreme bros or whatever they're called say."*

Mina wants to laugh, but can't manage it. She feels so dizzy and disoriented.

"Oh wow," Ralph says, squatting and plucking a shell from the sand. "Here's a nice one, bitches!"

"I'm afraid, Ralph," Mina tells him. "What's happening?"

He drops the shell into the cup and stands. "You're happening, Mina."

"I'm not really here, am I?"

"You better wake up now, love." Ralph shakes his cup, the shells rattling within. "Go ahead, it'll be okay. Quick like a bunny now, wake up. It's time to open your eyes."

The image of Ralph staring at her, rattling that cup of seashells, faded, vanishing into an otherwise dark void as her eyes slowly opened, bringing the bedroom into soft focus. The back of her head was pounding, her throat dry and sore. She remembered drinking a lot the night before and smoking a joint, but had no memory of going to bed. What she *did* remember was a strangely erotic and terrifying dream in which she danced and painted as if possessed by some crazed spirit. And there were people. Here, in her apartment. But all she could remember was shadows and otherworldly eyes watching her from within them.

Mina yawned and looked down at the sheets. They were tangled around her as if she'd been thrashing about all night.

Jesus, is that blood?

She bolted upright, frantically pulling the sheets away from her for a better look at the long red splotches on her bedding. There were smears of it everywhere, from the sheets to the floor next to her bed.

"Oh my God," she said, realizing it was just paint.

Flashes blinked across her mind's eye, paint smearing, covering her.

Mina threw back the covers, realizing then that her hands were stained with the same paint. Her half t-shirt and panties were smeared with it as well. But this was not like some of her jeans, which were covered with old paint stains, indelible markings of years of creativity, scars from her hard work. These stains were fresh.

She swung her bare feet around to the cold floor. A few feet away lay the canvas Rita had given her. A painting now—Mina's painting—a piece she had no real memory creating; it had become a figure, a woman dressed in red, her face white because she'd apparently left that part mostly unpainted, the white canvas untouched but for black slits for eyes, the nose a slash of gray and the pale lips sewn shut with the same acrylic hues. And those hands—long, pale, with red claws extending from the fingers—were a hideous blend of human and wild animal. The piece was dark and semi-abstract, unlike anything she'd done before. Figurative work didn't click with her, even after several semesters of life-drawing and painting. Once, she'd wanted to be like Francis Bacon, painting through the terror and pain of life, using pictorial deformation and relying on vagueness. But the landscape became her favorite theme, images that manifested in her mind, formed with feelings that rippled through her life. *That* had been her forte, at least until last night, evidently.

Still slumped on the edge of the bed, Mina leaned forward, taking in more of the painting on the floor. It hadn't been made from layers of acrylic glazes prior to heavier paint being added to the canvas. It was constructed with thick layers of color, left to dry overnight, causing the paint to crack in several places but adding to the strange allure of the piece. It was done in what was known as the *Impasto Style*, something she'd learned in school.

Mina had always preferred building her pieces by working with layers of thin acrylics instead. Yet somehow, she'd painted this woman, a figure.

Maybe it was the pokeroot, the booze, the music, the weed. Whatever the culprit, the painting perfectly captured the mood and feel of Crow's Cry beyond anything she could've imagined.

Unbelievable, Mina thought. *That may be the best thing I've ever painted.*

Vague dream fragments of dancing through showers of red, streaks of black, threads of gray hues—as if her soul had caught fire and the paint was extinguishing it, penetrating her flesh and churning within her like a living organism.

But that was all a dream.

Wasn't it?

Her little plastic ashtray was filled with cigarette butts and ash, her last cigarette, burned nearly to the filter, still pressed into the lip of the ashtray, the filter smeared with red. Her lighter was on the floor next to it, spattered with paint. Mina popped the butt between her lips and lit it while studying the painting.

What the hell was I doing, channeling someone?

Her phone began to buzz, and it took a moment but she eventually realized the sound was emanating from beneath one of her pillows. Managing one more puff from the butt, and feeling the warmth in her chest, she rummaged around beneath her pillows until she'd located her iPhone.

The number was unfamiliar, Massachusetts area code. She answered anyway.

"Hello?"

"Good morning, Mina, this is Leonard, remember me? I hope I didn't wake you."

Leonard?

Mina searched her mind, and soon remembered a young guy at the meet-and-greet. "Hey," she said, clearing her throat. "No, I've been up a while."

"Not sure if you remember me specifically," he said sheepishly. "We met at the meet-and-greet. I drive for Klaus, among other things. Lenny, remember? Korean dude, long hair?"

"I do remember, yes," she said, recalling a thin man with soulful eyes, long dark hair to his shoulders, and a kind smile. There was a rawness to him, like some of the boys that were in foster care with her who ran away and ended up on the streets young, still boys that, if lucky enough to survive, became hardened men with a faraway look and pain etched into each crevice on their faces. They always came out one way or the other: humbled, tortured, self-reflective, and sweet as puppies, or destroyed, aggressive, cruel, and full of rage.

Lenny, she remembered, was the former, and had an unconscious sensuousness to him, the way he moved and spoke or just stood there looking at you. If she remembered correctly, he'd worn jeans and a sweatshirt, a heavy coat with a faux fur collar, and winter boots. She also remembered a scar on his neck, likely courtesy of some asshole on the street.

Mina absently touched her cheek just below her left eye with her free hand, her fingers finding the small scar of her own there. Flashes of Mrs. Denholm came to her just then. A rotund and sadistic old woman with a penchant for house dresses and sandals, Mina had lived with her for about a year when she was seven years old. One day she taught Mina about being careful around stoves by pressing her face against the handle of a hot cast-iron skillet and holding it there even as Mina screamed and cried, her flesh burning. She never forgot the horrific pain, or that awful smell.

And she never forgot Mrs. Denholm.

You tell the hospital you were being a bad girl and playing near the stove after I told you not to and ran right into it and burned yourself.

Mina clenched shut her eyes, trembling at the memory, rage building inside her along with terror.

Understand me, you little bitch?

"How's it going?" Lenny asked.

She dropped her hand and pushed the horrors back into the dark where they belonged, remembering instead when she'd first met Lenny.

"Pleasure," he'd said, taking Mina's hand.

His palm was warm, despite the fact that he'd come in from the cold just moments before. And on his left wrist was a tattoo of a serpent eating its tail, the Ouroboros.

"He's our gallery guru," Jasmin told her. "He hangs every show. He's got a genius eye for making everything look amazing!"

Lenny blushed. "I don't know about that, but—"

"And a knack for not leaving walls marred with holes!"

He smiled at Jasmin and then at Mina. "I'm also skilled with putty and touch-up paint."

"Good to know," Mina said.

"So nice to meet you, Mina, we're all thrilled you're here."

They'd talked a little more about nothing of consequence then he'd moved away.

Mina didn't recall speaking to him again before she left, yet now she felt oddly exposed, as if Lenny could see her right through the phone. Her mind raced. Had she done something wrong? She was covered in paint. The apartment was a mess. And her bed was a total disaster. She'd have to get everything cleaned, then spend some time scrubbing the floor before anyone found out as, thankfully, acrylic paint often peeled off hard surfaces, unlike on fabrics.

"Mina?" Lenny asked with concern in his voice. "Are you there?"

"Yes, sorry, I—I was up late painting last night, little out of it."

"Great! Well, on the painting part anyway, sorry to hear you're wiped out. But listen, Klaus has invited you to lunch at the house today if you'd like to join him."

"Today?" she asked, glancing around at the mess.

"If today's no good I can let him know you're not up for it. I'm sure we can reschedule."

Lunch with Klaus Riker, she really couldn't turn that down. She wouldn't want him to think she was being rude or blowing him off, and besides, it would probably be fascinating. What would they talk about? The spirit world as it relates to art?

"No," she said. "No, today's fine. Will it just be the two of us?"

"I think so, but honestly I'm not sure."

"Okay, what time?"

"I can pick you up in a couple hours."

Mina snatched her watch from the nightstand. It was almost eleven o'clock. She'd nearly slept all morning. Christ. "That works. I'll be outside at one, cool?"

"Most cool!" Lenny said. "See you then."

As she disconnected the call and tossed her phone back on the bed, Mina once again focused on the painting on the floor. It was so red...like blood...and the face, haunting and caught somewhere between human and beast, night and day, ecstasy and agony, Heaven and Hell.

Where did you come from?

The face seemed to stare back.

You can't make me holy again...

Mina shook her head. What the fuck were these insane thoughts coursing through her head?

Who are you? Did I conjure you, or is it the other way around?

Only the sound of melting snow dripping outside her window answered.

As she rose from bed, still a bit unsteady and her headache throbbing along the back of her skull, Mina noticed something else. Over on the windowsill were the remnants of the red candle, the one Rita gave her. It was burned down to the base.

Mina had no memory of lighting it.

In fact, she couldn't remember much at all.

* * * *

Lenny pulled up in Klaus' black 1975 Mercedes, the same one she'd seen at his house. It was in pristine condition, and the interior was spotless, mostly tan with a black steering wheel. Although it was old, it had a new car smell.

"What a gorgeous car," Mina said as she got in. "I'd be afraid to drive it."

"Yeah, it's a beauty, isn't it?" Lenny's dark eyes welcomed her, his hair pulled back into a ponytail. "It's belonged to Klaus for years. He loves this car. It sits in his garage for months at times, but hooked up to a charger so the battery won't die. I was set to come get you in my old pickup, but Klaus insisted I take the Benz, so here I am."

"That was nice of him, but the pickup would've been fine."

"Klaus is a great man," Lenny said without a hint of irony.

Following suit, "You Put a Spell on Me" by Screamin' Jay Hawkins began playing on the radio.

"Love these old songs," Lenny said. "Did you know that the original version of this song was banned? It had too many grunts and groans, they said—whoever *they* are—so radio stations wouldn't play it until it was edited."

"I didn't know that actually." Mina gazed out the window. They were traveling by a seawall and a string of old, mostly closed taverns and inns. She didn't remember any of that the first time she'd gone to Klaus's home. "Nothing looks familiar," she said. "Are we going a different way?"

"Klaus wanted me to make a quick stop before lunch. Okay?"

"Sure," Mina said, a bit uncomfortable as they pulled onto a street that looked like it had once been a commercial hub, though most of the buildings sat empty now. "Where are we stopping?"

"Right here," he said, slowing the car then easing into a parking space in front of a small building with massive storefront windows. And in those windows were paintings, large, colorful pieces, some clearly inspired by Picasso—others inspired by Pollock, Grace Hartigan, and Lee Krasner—but all with an original take. "It's our gallery."

"Oh, cool," Mina said, relaxing.

"Klaus felt you should've already seen it by now, so he asked me to bring you by before lunch real quick." Lenny put the Mercedes in Park. "Come on, I want to show you your wall space. We want to make sure you're completely satisfied with everything."

Mina stared at the windows, feeling a bit overwhelmed by the brilliance on display. How could she ever compare?

Before she knew it, Lenny was opening her door. Once she stepped out into the cold air, he quickly led her inside. The smell of roots and herbs wafted forward when he opened the door—pokeroot was dominant, but she was starting to get used to the smell.

Mina stood in the midst of these genius works, realizing that soon her own work would be a part of it.

"Check this out," Lenny said excitedly, walking her quickly past walls filled with amazing art, mostly abstract or semi-abstract. "The work of past residents mixed in with people from our group."

They stopped in front of a blank white wall on the left side of the gallery, a massive space, and Lenny asked, "Is this spot all right?"

Mina's mouth dropped open. "You mean for me?"

"If it's not, there's no problem, we can move some paintings around and get you a space you like better. We do it all the time."

"No, I—Jesus—This is awesome, are you kidding? It's great!"

Lenny put a finger to his chin. "You can probably fit half a dozen large paintings here—more if you've got smaller pieces too—or you can mix it up. Just do your thing and we'll figure it out, okay? We want your opening night to be something special."

"Opening night?" she asked.

"Of course, everybody has an opening night before they leave their Crow's Cry residency. It's the least we can do for all your hard work."

Mina was speechless, gazing at the space. As she glanced around, just beyond a small steel spiral staircase in the corner that led to a second floor she couldn't see, she noticed another painting displayed by itself on a large wall and lighted from above. As she focused on it, she trembled.

"Is something wrong?" Lenny asked.

She pointed at the distant wall. "That painting…"

It was all there right before her eyes, the ship from her dreams surrounded by rough seas at night, a violent storm raging. All that was missing was the ferryman with the white eyes and the others behind him like phantoms watching and waiting.

"Stunning, isn't it?" Lenny said. "That's a special piece. It tends to impact people rather severely. You're not the first person to have such a strong reaction to it."

I dreamed it, Mina wanted to say. *I saw this in my dreams*. But she simply nodded and said, "It's very powerful."

"Sure is."

"What is it trying to convey?" Mina asked.

"You'll have to ask the artist over lunch. Klaus painted it years ago, when he could still work. In fact, it was done at a time when many believe he was at the height of his power." Lenny winked, grinning at her. "So to speak, as they say."

Heart racing, Mina turned away from the painting, her mind a jumble. Her hangover was still throttling her, and now this. "It's astounding," she said.

"Like I said, Klaus is a great man."

Mina was unsure of how else to respond.

"Come on," Lenny said, taking her by the arm. "Let's not keep him waiting."

* * * *

The dining room was dim. No windows flanked the walls, only wine-colored wallpaper decked with small painted landscapes—the ocean, mill houses, people walking on the shore, all rendered with purposeful distortion and shades of blues and grays, monochromatic pieces, moody, reminiscent of night, of deep winter, of sorrow—and a single large portrait alone on one wall in a beautiful frame. The subject was a woman of perhaps thirty or so that Mina assumed was Isa, Riker's wife. Unlike the portrait of Riker and the same woman Mina had seen when she first met him, which was done in a style reminiscent of Francis Bacon, the faces somewhat distorted, this one was a bit more traditional, though still abstract, looking more along the lines of a Max Beckmann piece.

Dressed in a sheer white gown, her dark eyes were reserved and quiet, looking down at them with a sereneness Mina envied. The woman's skin was the color of porcelain, her lips ruby red, and her long black hair cascaded down across her shoulders with a subtle elegance. She was beautiful.

Mina sat at one end of a large dining room table, Klaus across from her at the other. From the moment she arrived and saw him, flashes from her dark dreams the night before came to her, quick snippets of the old man crawling into a corner near the ceiling in her apartment like some giant spider, watching her from the shadows.

Stop it, she thought, forcing it all away. She already felt shaky, her hangover was doing enough of a number on her system, the last thing she needed was frightening and nonsensical visions of Klaus Riker climbing the walls in her nightmares, especially while the kindly old man was seated a few feet away from her.

"I noticed you eyeing the portrait just now," Klaus said.

"Yes," Mina said carefully, remembering what Frances had told her about how Klaus' wife was a sore subject and not to bring it up unless he did.

"My beloved wife, Isa," he said, gazing up at the painting.

"She's astonishingly beautiful."

"Yes, she is," Klaus said softly. "To me, as beautiful today as she was when she sat for that portrait all those years ago. Maurice painted it as a gift to us. Isa and I have been together for many years. I'd love for you to meet her, you two would get along marvelously, I'm sure of it, but unfortunately she's extremely ill."

"I'm so sorry," Mina told him.

"Thank you. She's been sick for a number of years now, but we continue to pray for her recovery. My beautiful bride has been bedridden for so long it's often difficult to remember her any other way."

Mina pictured a much older version of the woman in the portrait, confined to bed in one of the many rooms in the large old house, probably a bedroom above them. She wondered what was wrong with Isa, but didn't want to delve any deeper than Klaus was willing to go on the subject.

"One of these days she'll come back to me."

"That would be wonderful," Mina said.

"Yes." Klaus' striking blue eyes blinked slowly, then panned down from the portrait and settled on Mina. "On to happier things," he said, indicating the table between them with a slow sweep of his hand. Assorted rolls and fresh-baked breads sat in a large wooden bowl in the center of it, and lovely vintage dishware had been set out, some of it mismatched. Same with the silverware, as there were knives, forks, and spoons with various patterns and subtly different styles. There were also bottles of white and red wine, two crystal glasses beside them. A couple red tapered candles in small silver holders burned on either side of the bread bowl, flames fluttering, rising and falling, and for a moment, Mina became transfixed, watching the fire intensely.

Come to us, Mina.

"The silverware," Klaus said, breaking the spell, "Wallace Hotel, Mepra Dolce, Oneida Wordsworth, and so many more. And the dinnerware is Mid-Century Modern, Neoclassical, Art Deco. Isn't it beautiful?"

"Yes, lovely."

Dressed in a black shirt, black slacks, and black slip-on shoes, even at such an advanced age, his charisma was unavoidable, his presence larger-than-life. And it wasn't a one-time occurrence, Mina now realized. Klaus had this aura consistently. There was nothing facile about him, he was intelligent and erudite, and possessed deep wisdom on a great many things. It was evident. "I've lived a long life, Mina, and sadly, much of life is loss. But I believe that when one loses something, when something is damaged, one should replace it. When something is lost, something else should come forward to take its place. It's a law of the universe really, except for those times when something is irreplaceable, of course. But then, those are very rare instances, don't you agree?"

"I do, yes," Mina said. "Most things are replaceable, you're right. We live in a throwaway society where almost everything is disposable. So when those things come along that aren't, they're all the more special."

"And all the more tragic when lost," Klaus added sadly. He looked away, as if even speaking the words had hurt him. "So over time, I've learned to cherish things that truly have deep, intrinsic meaning, and I've come to the conclusion that perhaps even they could be replaced in some way. Nothing is impossible in this existence, Mina."

Nothing is impossible in the dark.

"That can be a little frightening, I suppose, depending upon how one looks at it." Klaus smiled warmly. "But it's also quite beautiful, that proposition."

"Go on," Mina said, fascinated. "Please."

"For example, I love old things, as you can see. Some might call it extravagant, and as time goes on, sometimes I think perhaps it's time to sell some of my treasures and live a simpler life. Just the money from the sale of this old house alone could do so much good." He drew a slow, deep breath. "In the end, *things* are not what life is about. It's the fire in our souls that's important. Who we love, and how we love. Faced with the power of love and true devotion, how much value does some silly spoon or dish or piece of furniture or car or house truly have in the overall scheme of things, however lovely they may be? Alas, not much, I'm afraid. Because our spirits are free to go to either the light or the darkness. The choice is, and always has been, ours. And ours alone."

"I'll take the light," Mina said.

"Indeed. Though to get to the light, one must sometimes cross through a great deal of darkness."

Mina nodded.

Klaus stared across the table at her, his beautiful ice-blue eyes twinkling and catching the light from two candles burning in the center of the table. Just as he was about to add something more, Lenny, who had left them alone the moment they'd sat down, burst through a door to Klaus' right, pushing a serving cart.

"Lunch is served!"

"I'm afraid subtlety is something young Leonard has yet to master," Klaus said playfully. "But he has a wonderful soul."

"Hope you like baked scrod!" Lenny said, pushing the cart up alongside the table. "And we've got garlic, oven-roasted potatoes and a Caesar salad."

It smelled delicious, as Lenny swiftly placed their plates before them, and then motioned to the wine. "As I'm sure you know, white goes with fish normally," he said to Mina. "But we've got both. We also have white zin on ice in the kitchen, if you'd—"

"The white's fine, thanks," she said, even though she would've preferred the red.

Lenny pulled the cork and served them both a glass of white wine.

"Pour one for you as well," Klaus told Lenny. "I'd like to make a toast."

After quickly retrieving another glass, Lenny rejoined them.

"To Mina," Klaus said, raising his glass. "May your spirit merge with the essence of the work we do here, and may you create, live, and love as you do so. It is my sincere hope that you see, through the importance of your work and presence here in Crow's Cry, how vital you are to your future as well as ours. Your muse watches and waits for you, guides you with each brushstroke; may you find peace and release in your sacrifice, not only for your art, but for others."

Mina felt her face flush. "Thank you, Klaus. That was beautiful."

"Enjoy your lunches," Lenny said, and then turning to Mina added, "I'll see you later on the ride back."

"Thank you, Leonard," Klaus said evenly.

"Of course," he said, pushing the cart back through the door.

Mina watched as Lenny made his way out, and then she looked to the food, her stomach rumbling. "Everything looks delicious. Do you have a chef?"

"Leonard has many talents as an artist," Klaus said. "Fortunately for an old coot like me, who can't boil water if his life depends upon it, culinary skills are among them."

Mina laughed politely and took bite of fish. "Wow, this is amazing."

"If you have the time and desire, I hope you can join us on Friday, Mina. We have a group dinner every Friday evening, it's a tradition."

"I'd like that," she said, feeling welcome and important in ways she never had before. But there was something else too; something she was struggling to keep below the surface despite how much effort Klaus had obviously gone to in assuring theirs was an exquisite lunch. Fear and uncertainty—visions of a phantom painter...the painting at the gallery...the painting she'd done even though she had no memory of having created it—she couldn't simply shrug it off. She was trying, but something deep inside her kept trying to convince her she shouldn't.

"I wanted us to have lunch together, just the two of us, I hope you don't mind." Klaus ate delicately, taking tiny bits of fish and potato and salad into his mouth and chewing for what seemed prolonged periods. "I wanted to get to know you better outside of the group, and I've found over time, with other residency artists, that get-togethers like this are the best way to achieve that. I can't express to you how appreciative I am that you accepted my invitation."

Mina let her worries drift. "Of course, I—I mean, thank *you*, this is wonderful."

He sipped his wine. "I understand Jasmin took you by to see Rita and her shop."

"Yes."

"And that she gave you one of her *special* canvases."

"She did, and a candle too. She's very kind."

Klaus' eyes twinkled again. "Isn't she?"

"Everyone's been so nice. I can't thank you all enough."

"We should be thanking you, my dear."

"That's kind of you to say, Professor Riker."

"If you're comfortable doing so, please call me Klaus," he said, taking a bite of fish. "Tell me, have you started painting on that canvas yet?"

For a moment, the flames from the candles caught Mina's eye, bringing back images of the crazed dream she'd had, of paint raining down on her and burning into her flesh. In that moment, she could've sworn Klaus somehow already knew the answer to his question. "Yes, I have," she said.

"And how is that coming along?"

"Very well actually, but it's different from my usual work. As you know, I normally stick to landscapes, but for some reason a figurative piece manifested. I mean, it was just there when I woke up this morning."

"Isn't *that* fascinating?"

"Yes," she said softly. "In a way it is."

"It's also a bit unnerving, isn't it?"

"Very," Mina said, sipping some wine.

"Perhaps your vision has taken a new turn," he said, his slight German accent becoming more obvious at times. "I'd like to think that being here at Crow's Cry has opened your mind and sent you along new corridors that will allow you to further explore your work in deeper and more meaningful ways."

Mina looked down at her food. "I just hope the piece is good enough."

"Don't be silly," Klaus said gently. "I'll bet it's some of your best work."

How the hell does he know that?

"I hope so," she told him.

"I'm sure it's brilliant. I look forward to seeing it when you're ready."

Klaus made Mina feel so wanted, smart, and talented. He made her want to do nothing but paint, to spend her days and nights in that tiny apartment, painting furiously and pouring her soul out across canvas after canvas.

"I won't disappoint you," she heard herself say. "I promise."

Mina was shocked that she'd said that to Klaus just then. She hadn't spoken those words since she was a little girl who still mistakenly believed those responsible for her care actually loved and wanted the best for her. Even more startling, she meant it.

"You won't," Klaus assured her. "You can't."

They ate in silence for several moments, the old house quiet and still. Just when Mina was struggling for something interesting to say, Klaus rescued her by discussing his favorite paintings, many of the places he'd traveled, memories of his native Germany, his time in California, and what it all meant to him.

"My years in California were wonderful, until the accident," he said, gazing into his food. "A terrible fire broke out during one of our…sessions…and a young woman I'd grown quite fond of and was mentoring—among others, of course—was killed. As you can plainly see, I was quite badly burned. I suffered several injuries as well, spent months in the hospital, much of it in a coma, and even longer recovering in a burn unit. Once I was well again, I had to leave there. It was time. I had to put all that had happened behind me and start a new beginning elsewhere. *Here*, as it turned out."

"I'm sorry you had to experience that," Mina said, curious as to what he'd meant by one of their *sessions*. Had they been painting when the fire broke out, is that what he'd meant?

"Thank you, but as they say, everything happens for a reason."

"Yes, it just doesn't always seem like a good reason."

Klaus smiled. "In New York City, at the Museum of Modern Art, there is a triptych by Max Beckmann called *Departure*. He painted those three panels when Hitler had gained power in Germany. He was forced to leave his teaching position in Frankfurt, went on to Berlin, and ultimately had no choice but to move to Amsterdam. Art historians say that the panels express mystical redemption. Beckmann said himself that *Departure* was itself a 'departure from the illusions of life toward the essential realities that lie hidden beyond…'"

Mina had seen *Departure* when she was in art school. "I love the German Expressionists," she said.

"As do I," Klaus agreed.

"Their figurative take on pain is unmatched."

"Perhaps it's more literal than you imagine."

Mina smiled politely. "When Lenny showed me around the gallery earlier, I saw one of your paintings. It really shook me."

"I've only one displayed there, I try to keep that space for others," he said. "But thank you, I'm glad to hear it had such an impact on you."

"Can you tell me more about it?"

"It's quite old. It came to me in my nightmares. My work often did."

Mina hoped her expression didn't give away how shocked she was. "Really?" she said. "My nightmares inspire some of my paintings too. What's the significance of the ship and the night storm at sea?"

Riker watched her a while without answering, his eyes assessing her. "I'm curious, Mina, have you had *similar* dreams?"

A slight tremor moved through her. "I—well—not exactly like your painting, but very similar, yes."

"The synchronicity of souls is an astounding phenomenon," Klaus said. "It seems yours may be on its way to achieving perfect harmony with ours, Mina."

"Maybe so," she said, trying to play it cool but fearful he knew how rattled she suddenly was. He seemed to know everything, much of it even before she did.

"The spirit has no boundaries," Klaus explained. "No sense of time or space. It's transcendent. Only the flesh imprisons us, and most tend to create prisons of their own to compound the problem. It's art that makes us different, Mina. It is *art* that sets us free of those prisons, turns us loose to find those places we were meant to be all along."

"You make it sound so magical."

"Isn't it?" Klaus took a small bite of potato. "How do you feel about magic?"

"I don't know much about it."

"I didn't ask you what you know, Mina. I asked you what you *feel*."

She looked up from her lunch to find his blue eyes boring straight through her. It produced in her a strange feeling somewhere between eroticism and severe anxiety.

"Forgive me if that sounded abrupt or aggressive," Klaus said, wiping his mouth with a cloth napkin then gently pushing his plate away. "As you've no doubt gathered, I can become quite passionate about these subjects."

"I feel like I'm experiencing things here I never have before," Mina admitted.

"And do you view that as a positive development?"

"I think so, but in all honesty, I'm not sure yet."

"Are you *afraid*, Mina?"

"Afraid of what?" she asked.

He stared at her.

"I grew up in foster homes, most of them horrible," Mina told him. "I'm always a little afraid. Fear's a part of me. Has been since I was a very little girl."

Klaus' beautiful eyes filled with sorrow. "I detest deliberate cruelty, especially when it's aimed at the innocent. I'm so very sorry. My heart breaks for that little girl."

"So does mine." Mina cleared her throat awkwardly, steeling herself. "But it's okay, because over the years I learned to control fear and not let it stop me. Sometimes it even motivates me." She wiped her mouth and put her napkin aside. "Why do you ask?"

"I apologize, my dear. I had no right to—"

"No, it's okay. You did nothing wrong. I'm genuinely interested."

Klaus thought about it a moment. "I don't want you to feel as though you have to be, for lack of a better word, *uncertain* when it comes to me, or any of us here. We're all one, Mina. We're artists. It is my utmost wish that you be as comfortable here as possible. I can understand—particularly given your childhood—how trust must be a difficult thing for you, but again, we're not so different, you and I. It takes me a very long time as well. Normally even longer with our visiting artists, yet I feel remarkably comfortable with you. I have from the moment we met."

Mina felt comfortable with him too, but there was something about him that made her uneasy as well. Of all the men she'd encountered in the course of her life, she'd never met anyone quite like Klaus Riker. "You could not have been kinder to me," she said. "I'm just trying to convince myself I deserve to be here and can live up to all the fuss you've made over me."

"No doubt your bleak childhood is also to blame for such unfounded feelings."

"No doubt at all," she said.

"*Deserve* is a strange word, Mina, and an even stranger concept in my opinion, so I can't speak to whether you deserve to be here or not. I suspect you do, but it's really beside the point. This is your destiny. You are here because you belong here, because it's where you were meant to be. If that wasn't the case, we wouldn't have chosen you." Mina watched him, the flames from the candles flickering between them. The dizziness she'd experienced earlier returned, but worse this time, and for a moment she thought she might pass out. Nonchalantly as possible, she gripped the edge of the table, hoping it might steady her, but the dizziness continued, and her vision began to blur.

"And make no mistake, Mina, we chose *you*."

CHAPTER TWELVE

Mina sees only an inky blackness, but hears water moving, running, trickling, and echoing all around her, as if she's been placed in some vast chamber. She senses motion, gentle splashing, and muffled voices saying indecipherable things that sound like they're coming from the far end of a long tunnel.

In her mind she can see herself floating, gliding above the ground as she had in her dream, the tall grass below rushing past as she's swept across an enormous field. The bright sun beats down on her as she approaches the top of the same small hill she's seen before. The tall grass sways back and forth, as if just for her, the squat oak tree with its thick leaves, the forked and gnarled trunk waiting for her just as it had last time.

She knows this place, but where is she?

It's magic. Isn't it?

Black magic, Mina…

As she reaches the hill's summit, her body turns and her bare feet touch the ground. She stands before the old tree, watching it with equal parts awe and dread. On the ground before it are a series of stones that form a large circle. A fire once burned at the center of it, and amidst the ashes scattered about, Mina sees something.

Crouching, she reaches out, pushes ash and dirt aside, and picks up the small object. It disintegrates between her fingers, becomes dust that blows away in the breeze.

It is then that Mina sees another identical object within the circle as well.

She brushes a bit of ash away from it, carefully this time, but doesn't pick it up.

My God…

The woman from Mina's dream, she was kneeling right here as torches burned all around her and figures in hooded robes chanted hideous prayers.

"He takes our eyes…"

Mina vaults back and away from the circle, falling onto her ass in the dirt and kicking frantically with her feet.

"So we can't find our way back…"

It's her eyes. God in Heaven, it's the woman's eyes, they've—

Voices suddenly emerge from the silence.

Are they coming from behind her, perhaps somewhere on the far side of the field?

Mina scrambles back to her feet, looks out across the endless stalks of slowly swaying grass.

No. They're coming from inside her head.

"Come to us, Mina."

She remembers an explosion of fire, and the woman being pulled into it, consumed by flames as sparks flew then fell to the ground in a shower of embers.

As before, Mina feels herself leave the ground and rise into the night sky.

It's not possible.

"Anything is possible in the dark, Mina."

Slowly spinning, her body floats higher. She can do nothing to stop it.

Mina, Hexen können fliegen…

"Mina, witches can fly…"

But I'm not a witch!

"No, you're not. We are."

She wants to scream but can't summon the strength, even as darkness swallows the sunlight. And as the night becomes whole, the field and tree and memories are gone, replaced by sounds of water.

The voices are closer, whispering all around her, accompanied by the strange sense of motion Mina felt before. But there's something else…she can feel it…she can feel them touching her.

"What are you doing to me?" she hears herself ask in a dreamy, singsong voice that sounds as if she's half asleep.

But Mina knows she's not asleep. This is something else, a cross between heavy sedation and the strange chasm that lies between sleep and full consciousness, where all sense of direction and relation to reality is distorted and just beyond the reach of the literal.

As her vision slowly returns to her, everything looks as if she's seeing it through a blurred lens, like someone has smeared Vaseline in her eyes. But she can make out forms, shapes, and the contrasts of dark and light.

Someone touches her forehead, their fingertip moving slowly, drawing symbols before sliding down across her face and neck…

I'm lying on my back—I—what are they doing?

She can smell the strange odors from the canvas Rita gave her wafting about.

And there are others here, lying around her, others standing, moving back and forth between the light and dark and chanting the same muffled prayers she heard in her dream.

The smell of pokeroot and others, both repellent and intoxicating, fill her nostrils.

Mina cannot make out what they're saying, but this time it's because they're not speaking English. And it's not German either, this is something else.

Hands grope her breasts, the palms then fingertips at her nipples, prodding and pulling as spittle and hot breath pulses against her flesh. The hands move over every inch of her body, and as they move between her legs, Mina tries to call out. All she manages is a gurgling groaning sound.

She feels something on her flesh, something left behind by the hands moving over her body. Like some kind of residue...

They're not groping her, she realizes. They're spreading something over every inch of her.

"What are you doing to me?" she says, her words slurred and faraway.

Mina blinks her eyes, tries to clear them, as the prayers grow louder and more adamant, those around her putting words to their ritual. She wants to wipe her eyes but can't raise her arms—is she tied down?—have they restrained her in some way?

Although everything remains blurred, she can make out people in the shadows, completely nude as she is, some of them kneeling around her, their hands moving furiously.

They're covering my body in paint...

Others stand nearby, chanting in what Mina now recognizes as Latin.

"Isa has sacrificed the longest for us," a voice says—Riker? "But soon the horror will end and we will again be one."

"Come to us, Mina," the others chant.

"Help me," she groans.

Another voice, smooth and assured—Rita? "Anoint her with the sacred oils."

More fingers move across her forehead and cheeks, again drawing symbols and strange lines along her flushed skin.

"Cleanse her," the others chant. "Prepare her..."

Mina blinks rapidly, and her vision clears a bit more. She can see them all now. Riker, Jasmin, Maurice, Dave, Rita, Frances, Lenny, and the others from the collective, nude and standing over her, some lying next to her, pressing their bodies against hers, mingling with the paint, their bodies intertwined with her, writhing and sliding, pressing and pushing as if trying to enter her through her flesh.

"I'm dreaming!" Mina screams. "This is only a dream!"

"Paint her," a male voice says, slobbering over her. "Paint the bitch."

Mina's screams echo before being strangled to silence. As the darkness returns, closing in around her, all she can hear are whispers of blasphemous prayers and the feeling of water splashing against her nude body.

* * * *

Pain was the first thing she remembered. Piercing, stabbing pains from behind her eyes fanned out across her cheekbones and down into her jaw.

As she came to, her eyes fluttering open, the pain dissipated along with the darkness and Mina found herself lying on an old Victorian-era sofa in a small room. Heavy curtains on both windows were pulled closed, so the only light came through the open door from an adjacent hallway. Her mouth was sand dry, and she felt weak, as if she hadn't slept in days.

"There is she."

Mina raised a hand to rub her eyes. Her arm felt heavy and weak. "What happened?" she asked in a raspy voice.

"You fainted." Lenny was crouched next to the small couch, her other hand in his. "Are you okay?"

"I don't know, I—yes, I think so." Mina slowly sat up, gently pulling her hand free of Lenny's. She looked around the small room, trying to figure out where she was and if her memories were those from a nightmare or something she'd actually experienced. "Where am I—what's going on?"

"Just one of the bedrooms," Lenny told her, standing. "You fainted and—"

"How did I get here?"

"I carried you." He smiled sheepishly. "I hope you don't mind."

Mina looked at him, then to the doorway, where Klaus stood watching her.

"You gave us quite a scare," the old man said. "I thought it best we make you as comfortable as possible until we knew what was happening."

"I don't..." Mina rubbed the back of her neck; it was stiff and sore. "I remember having lunch and then..."

She was hungover, tired, and stressed, but couldn't recall having fainted before.

"Leonard," Klaus said, stepping into the room, "I think you should drive Mina over to the hospital so a doctor can make sure she's all right."

"No," Mina said, waving at the air. "I'm fine, I don't need to go to the—"

"Are you sure?" Klaus took a small glass of water from a table next to the bed and handed it to her. "The closest hospital is a few towns away, only about a fifteen-minute drive, but I think it best if you went to the ER just to be sure there's nothing—"

"It's okay," Mina said, taking the glass. "I didn't get a lot of sleep last night and was probably dehydrated from drinking, and then the wine and all, it—I'm fine—I—God, I'm so embarrassed, I'm sorry."

"Sorry? Whatever for, Mina? Don't be silly." Klaus smiled warmly.

Mina took a quick sip of water. It was cool and helped with her dry throat. "I ruined our lunch. I'm mortified, I—"

"Nonsense, you did no such thing." Klaus put a hand on her shoulder. "These things happen. I just want to be sure you're all right, that's what's important. You're sure you don't want to go to the hospital just to be sure?"

"I can take you," Lenny said. "It's no problem, Mina, I'm happy to."

Mina shook her head and handed the glass back to Klaus. "I'm okay, really. I think maybe I should just go home and get some rest."

"Of course," Klaus said, turning to Lenny. "When Mina's ready, drive her back to her apartment. Anything else she needs, see that she gets it immediately. Is that understood, Leonard?"

"Yes, sir," he said.

"Again, I'm so sorry, Klaus," Mina said.

"Please stop apologizing," he said, giving her shoulder another pat. "If you need anything—anything at all—you let me know."

Still confused, all Mina wanted was to leave this house and clear her head, get some fresh air and space and try to figure out what the hell was happening to her. So many emotions filled her she couldn't land on one. But fear was certainly among them.

Why was she seeing things? Why was she having these nightmares about people who had done nothing to harm her, who had been nothing but kind and accommodating? Why was she losing time, unable to remember painting or aware of what she'd been doing? Was there something wrong with her? And now she was having fainting spells? She'd never fainted in her life. It was all too much to handle in that moment.

"Thank you for lunch," she said softly. "It was delightful."

"As are you, my dear." Klaus bowed formally. "We shall have to do it again soon. Once you've had some rest, yes?"

Mina smiled awkwardly. "Yes."

"Get some sleep," Klaus told her. "And should your condition change, you let Jasmin or Rita and Dave know and they'll get you to a doctor pronto."

"Thank you, but I don't think that's going to be necessary."

Klaus smiled again, this time the shadows falling across his scarred face like a shroud, and with the limited light from the hallway, in that instant, he looked like something more than a kindly old man. Something in those beautiful blue eyes shifted, and he blinked at her slowly, his gaze no longer warm but cold, reptilian, analytic, like a scientist studying a lab rat recently injected with some harmful agent.

Mina closed her eyes.

Easy, girl, clear your head and look again.

When she did, Klaus had already slipped away into the hallway.

* * * *

It wasn't possible. It simply was not *possible.*

Mina stood in her apartment, the door behind her still open, taking it all in as she began to tremble, tears of frustration and fear filling her eyes.

The painting she'd done was still there, by the windows. But the apartment was clean, the sheets and comforter that had been stained with paint now spotless and the bed made. Nothing was as she'd left it. The place was a mess when she went to have lunch with Klaus, and apparently in her absence, someone had come into her apartment and cleaned it to the point that the only evidence she'd painted so furiously as if possessed the night before was the painting itself.

What the fuck is going on?

Hands shaking, she struggled to light a cigarette. When she finally had it going, she went into the bathroom in search of the clothes she'd had on. The half t-shirt and bikini panties were on the bathroom floor where she'd left them when she changed earlier. The paint smears on both remained, but the apartment was spotless.

Back in the main area, Mina manically smoked her cigarette and tried to hold it together. The three bottles of vodka were lined up neatly on the kitchen counter, two of them empty, the other not yet opened. Her plastic ashtray—empty and clean—sat next to them, the last of the joints Ralph gave her alongside it on the counter.

After a few more quick drags, Mina crushed the cigarette in the ashtray and reached for the full bottle of vodka. Once in hand, she hesitated.

A drink's the last thing I need.

She put it back on the counter and moved to the windows. The courtyard below was empty and still, the large window of the ground-floor apartment dark. With a sigh, Mina wiped the tears from her eyes.

I'm losing my fucking mind. I'm—

A light rapping sound behind her startled Mina back into the moment, and she spun around to find Jasmin standing in the doorway, gently rapping her knuckles against the doorframe.

"Hey, are you okay?" Jasmin asked with a look of genuine concern. "Klaus called and said to check on you, that you fainted at lunch."

"Yeah," Mina said, still unsure of Jasmin, of herself, of everything. "I'm fine."

"You sure?" she asked, stepping into the apartment. "Is there anything I can do?"

"I've got a bad hangover, didn't get much sleep, and I was really dehydrated," Mina explained, hopeful Jasmin wasn't picking up on how shaky her voice suddenly sounded. "I had some wine with lunch and I think that did it. Got lightheaded and I guess I fainted right there at the table. I was so embarrassed."

"Wow, okay. I'm glad you're all right."

"Jasmin," Mina said, moving closer to her, "I need to ask you something."

"Sure, what's up?"

"Did someone come into my apartment while I was gone?"

She frowned, clearly confused. "What do you mean?"

"I mean exactly what I just said. Did someone come into my apartment while I was gone?"

"Who would do that?"

"That's what I want to know."

Jasmin's eyes widened as if a light had suddenly gone off in her head. "Oh shit, you mean somebody broke in?"

"No, there's no damage, nothing's missing and the door was still locked."

"Oh." Again, she looked thoroughly perplexed. "Then why do you think someone came into your apartment?"

Mina felt her anger rising. More frustration and fear, really, but it was coming out as anger, and for a second she feared she might not be able to control it. "Just answer me, please. Did you come in here while I was gone and clean up?"

She cocked her head like a baffled puppy. "What?"

"Stop saying *what* and answer the fucking question!"

Jasmin shrunk a bit, hurt. "I would never come into your place without your permission, Mina. I couldn't even if I wanted to, I don't have a key. There are only two keys to this apartment. You have one, and Frances has the other in case of an emergency. I don't know for sure, but I'd guess she keeps that one somewhere in the office."

"All right, Frances then. Did she come in here?"

"What's this all about? Are you sure you're okay?"

"It's a simple question. Did Frances come in here and clean the place up or not?"

Jasmin glanced around quickly. "You're keeping it pretty clean and neat as it is. It doesn't look like anyone would need to—"

"Jasmin, goddamn it, did she or didn't she?"

"I know Frances can be a drag sometimes, but she doesn't mean anything by it. She's actually got a big heart. She would never just come in here without asking first. None of us would. We respect your privacy. I can't believe you'd think we would—"

"You're sure no one else was in here?"

"I heard you when you went out earlier. The building was quiet until I heard you get back just now."

Mina shook her head in disbelief. "What the hell is going on?"

"I didn't mean to bug you, honest," Jasmin said. "Klaus called and told me what happened and said I should check on you, make sure you were doing okay and see if you needed anything. He's really worried about you."

"Tell him I'm fine."

"Okay." Jasmin hugged herself as if cold. "Mina, if I did something wrong, I'm so sorry, I—"

"No, you didn't," Mina said, feelings of guilt nearly overtaking the fear. "I just—it's been a crazy day and I don't feel well—I should get some rest. I didn't mean to snap at you, I'm sorry."

"Does the apartment look different or something?"

"It's okay, it's just me. I'm out of my head. I need to get some sleep."

Jasmin smiled broadly, as if all was suddenly right with the world. "I'll split then and give you your space." She skipped over to her, planted a kiss on Mina's cheek, then skipped away, back to her usual self. "If you need me I'm right downstairs!"

"Thanks," Mina said, doing her best to smile.

"I'll check on you in the morning." She hesitated in the doorway. "Is that cool?"

"Sure," Mina said.

"Groovy!" With a quick wave, Jasmin left, closing the door behind her.

Head in her hands, Mina sat on the foot of her bed, fearful she might collapse otherwise. How was any of this possible? How had things been cleaned and the apartment straightened up? She *remembered* how the place looked when she left. How could she be mistaken? It didn't seem possible.

Either Jasmin's lying or I'm going crazy.

Even as she flopped back on the bed, her eyes focusing on the tiny cracks in the ceiling, Mina grappled with both possibilities. Though exhausted, it still took several minutes before she eventually began to drift off to sleep. Her mind tried to make sense of things, searched desperately for a third option, some other explanation as to what was taking place here, but she couldn't take any more, be it emotionally or intellectually. Perhaps as a defense mechanism, her body and mind began to shut down.

Sleep seemed the only escape. Not a cure, but Mina hoped for at least a respite, a chance to reset and assess things further with a clear head.

Thankfully, when sleep eventually did arrive, it came with a modicum of peace, as this time, the nightmares left her alone in the dark.

* * * *

A steady buzzing sound awakened Mina as she came up out of a deep sleep, slowly rising toward consciousness the way a diver gradually ascends to the surface of the ocean. A lone light in the darkness surrounding her flashed and held.

Groggily, she lolled her head to the side. Her phone buzzed next to her on the mattress, a phone number she recognized displayed across the lighted screen. She sat up and took hold of the phone. A subtle amount of moonlight seeped through the windows, but otherwise the apartment was dark.

Jesus, how long have I been asleep?

"Ralph?" she said, answering the phone.

"Yes, it is I, his Ralphness."

"Hold on." Quickly pawing the sleep from her eyes, Mina got up, crossed the room, and turned the fluorescents on, filling the apartment with bright light. She took a quick look around to make sure she was alone. Once sure, she glanced at her watch. It was just shy of eight o'clock. She'd been asleep for hours. "Hi, I'm so glad you called. Things are all confused, and I—I'm not sure what's happening."

"You sound half asleep, did I wake you?"

"I took a nap this afternoon and slept longer than I planned to," Mina explained. "I wish you were here, I—"

"Turns out I am."

"What do you mean?"

"I'm in Crow's Cry," Ralph told her. "I just pulled in about three minutes ago. Interesting place, to say the least, it's got a very Daphne du Maurier dark masterpiece sort of vibe going on."

"Are you serious?"

"Darling, have you read du Maurier?"

"I mean about being here."

"I'm parked in front of an establishment called, and I kid you not, TOPSEY TURVEYS. It looks positively atrocious. We need to go there as soon as possible."

Mina immediately felt a sense of relief wash over her. "Oh my God, you really are here. I thought you said you were coming next—"

"I know what I said, but I needed to see you, so I altered my plans."

"Are *you* all right?" she asked, sensing Ralph's tone had turned more serious.

"Peachy, but we need to talk, love."

Mina gave him the address so he could punch it into the GPS on his phone.

"Got it," Ralph said a moment later. "It says it's only about three minutes away."

"The front door should be unlocked. If it isn't, call me when you get here and I'll come down and let you in. Otherwise, I'm on the third floor."

"Excellent. Make me a drink, something insanely large. I'm on my way."

* * * *

Even before he'd made it through the door to her apartment, Mina threw her arms around Ralph and hugged him tighter than she ever had before.

"Easy," he said, hugging her back. "I'm here, doll, I'm here."

When she finally let him go, she ushered him inside, closed and locked the door behind her, then hurried to the kitchen and handed him the drink she'd poured for him.

"Cool setup," Ralph said, taking in the apartment. "Small but cool. Are you sure these lights are bright enough though? Jesus, I don't know if I should thank everyone for coming and belt out of a tune or prepare to be interrogated. Or is there a baseball game breaking out at some point?"

"It's so good to see you," Mina said, nearly in tears.

"Well, fuck me, it's so good to *be* seen." He sipped his drink then noticed the tears in her eyes. "Honey, what is it?"

"It's nice to see a familiar face," she said.

"I've never known you to be sentimental. Tell me what's wrong."

"Why did you change your plans?"

Ralph was about to answer when he noticed Mina's paintings near the windows. The one that held his attention was not the one she'd started and put aside, but the other one she had only partial memories of painting the night before. "Holy shit, did you do that?"

Mina nodded.

He pointed to the finished piece. "This one too?"

"Yes."

"I've never known you to work in that style."

"I don't."

"Maybe you should. Mina, it's astonishing."

"I barely remember painting it."

"Have you been partying too much? You look tired, kid."

"I am tired. Other than that, I'm not sure what's wrong with me."

Ralph put his drink down long enough to take off his pea coat, toss it over the back of the comfortable chair, and straighten his thinning hair with his fingers. Turning his attention from the paintings, he looked out the windows instead. "I take it that's the infamous apartment down there where Mr. Sexy prances about in the wee hours?"

Mina sat at the foot of the bed, sinking down onto it as if she were deflating.

"You're not laughing," Ralph said, moving closer.

"No, I'm not."

"You're also letting me drink alone."

"Ralph, I'm serious, I really do think I might be losing my mind. I don't know who my parents were, I was in foster care from the time I was a baby. Mental illness could run in my family and I wouldn't even know it."

"We've been through this, Mina. You're not mentally ill."

"How do you know?"

"I just do. You're eccentric and flighty and maybe a little nutsy like all artists, but you're not a lunatic. Whatever you're going through has nothing to do with being crazy."

He looks so pale under these fluorescent lights, Mina thought. *I must look even worse, like some wishy-washy bloodless thing.*

Ralph stood there a moment, sipping his drink.

He's putting off telling me something. I know him, I can tell.

"Doll," he finally said, "I need you tell me what else has happened here that's got you so rattled."

Mina did, going over everything she'd experienced, including fainting at lunch and coming back to an apartment she swore was a mess. Ralph drank and listened intently, refraining from interrupting or throwing out any of his usual snarky comments.

"Still think I'm not crazy?" she asked.

Ralph was quiet a moment. He stared down into his drink, swirling what was left of the vodka around in the bottom of his glass.

"Why did you show up here unannounced, Ralph?"

"I wanted to make sure you were all right, that last call worried me to death. I also wanted to talk to you, and I thought it'd be better to do it in person rather than over the phone this time."

"Why?"

"I did some research."

"Okay, and?"

Pacing over by the kitchen area, Ralph sipped his drink. "Robert Sanders, the man that had the residency before you? No one's heard from him since he went back to California to open a gallery."

"Yes, that's what Jasmin said."

"Well, that's because he's been missing for just over a year. He left here and was headed back to California, but apparently never made it. From all accounts, Sanders had a horrible fear of flying, so when he got the residency, he drove here from Los Angeles. When the residency concluded, he drove back across country, but never arrived. No one's seen or heard from him since."

"That's awful," Mina said, shuddering.

"Yes. People disappear all the time, of course, but when it's an adult male the authorities don't exactly go out of their way to find them, particularly if there's no evidence of foul play. Seems Sanders and this fellow he was going to open the gallery with were actually a couple, so he put up quite a stink about no one looking into this in any meaningful way. Poor guy has a website up and everything, hoping to get some information from someone. When I did a little more digging, I found that Sanders had no family. He must've been a change of life baby because he was born to older parents. He had a sister considerably older than he was, but she and both parents have been deceased for nearly a decade. If it weren't for his boyfriend, nobody'd even be looking. I'm not even sure *he* still is."

"Is that all?" Mina asked.

"No, it's not. The person that had the Crow's Cry residency before Sanders was a woman named Audra Marini. She was from Florida."

Mina's heart dropped. "*Was?*"

"After finishing her residency, she returned to her hometown of Venice. She was single and lived alone." Ralph finished his drink in a single gulp. "Within days of returning, she apparently walked down to the beach, took off all her clothes, folded them neatly, and walked out into the ocean. Her clothes were found in the morning, and despite the fact that no trace of her body has ever been found, she's presumed dead. Her death was ruled a probable suicide, due to the fact that she had a history of suicide attempts in high school, and later in art school in New York City. What I gathered from the few articles on her I was able to find, she did this without notifying any of her friends or family she was back yet. So apparently she returned home from Crow's Cry and, within a day, decided to walk out into the ocean and end her life."

Mina couldn't believe what she was hearing. "My God," she said softly. "I never asked about anyone besides Sanders. I remember seeing the other names that had been awarded the residency in the past on the website when I applied, but—"

"Yes, I have them in my notes app." Ralph pulled his phone from his pocket and brought up the information. "Jennifer Williams from Illinois came before Marini. A Steven Johnson from New Jersey came before her. He received the first residency here."

"Are they all right, or did something happen to them too?" Mina asked.

"I don't know." Ralph shrugged, put his phone away. "Those names are so common I couldn't be sure I had the right people. There's a ton of Jennifer Williamses in Illinois and a boatload of Steven Johnsons in New Jersey, so I wasn't able to find any information on any of them being artists specifically. It's possible they were among those names—probable, even—but there were so many it'd take hours to sift through them all."

"So we don't know for sure what happened to them."

"No, we don't," Ralph said. "But I assume they're alive and well."

"Why would you assume that?"

"What are the odds that all four of the artists that came before you have since died or disappeared, all within a five-year period?" Ralph strode to the kitchen and poured himself another drink. "Can I get you one?"

"I don't think so."

Ralph poured two drinks anyway, then walked over to the bed and handed one to Mina. "Take it," he said. "It'll make you feel better, settle your nerves."

"I keep having these horrible dreams," Mina said.

"Yes, so you've said, and they're quite vivid from the sounds." He sniffed the air and looked around. "*What* is that smell I keep getting?"

"The canvas," Mina said, pointing. "Rita, the one who runs the shop, gave it to me. She said she mixed pokeroot in the gesso when she primed it."

"Whatever the hell pokeroot is, it has quite an odor. What's the point?"

"She said it helps to make a connection between the artist and the spirit world."

"Interesting," Ralph said.

"Klaus teaches that those connections are essential. They all believe it. Rita said to look at the treated canvas as an altar, an object of magic that opens your subconscious to creativity and communion with space and time. She said to think of it the same way priests perform rituals on actual altars; the canvas acts that way for the artist."

"Well, I suppose that's not entirely impossible. I've always believed we can—"

"Ralph, I've dreamed they were witches."

He arched an eyebrow. "You mean Rita and Klaus?"

Mina stared at her glass. "I mean all of them."

"A lot of people are witches. It's not that big of a deal."

"I'm not talking about Wiccans."

"As opposed to what, the ones with the pointy black hats that fly across the sky on their brooms? Or are we talking more of an Elizabeth Montgomery, Agnes Moorehead kind of thing? Always been partial to Endora myself, go figure."

Mina glared at him.

"I'm just trying to lighten the mood, kiddo."

"The mood doesn't need lightening. Look at me, I'm a wreck."

"And you think they're doing this to you?"

"I don't know what the fuck they're doing to me."

"But you think they *are* doing something to you."

"I've known you too long, Ralph," Mina told him. "You wouldn't have come here like this if you didn't think something was wrong too."

"You're right," Ralph said. "But it's not them I'm worried about, doll."

Mina swallowed some of her drink. "Even knowing that two of the four people that came before me here are dead?"

"We don't know that Sanders is dead. He's missing. People go missing all the time, Mina. Sometimes people want to disappear, so they do." Ralph took a deep breath. "I think you're confused as to why I felt I needed to come here. I came to check on you, not to warn you about them. Look, we're talking about artists here, okay? Now, maybe Sanders couldn't handle the pressure. How many times have you seen other artists that are right on the cusp of doing something big—like opening their own gallery, as just one example—fold under the pressure and never get it done? Artists from every area of the arts sabotage themselves or buckle under pressure all the time. Most of us don't exactly ooze self-confidence, right? We're insecure. We never think we're good enough or worthy enough, we constantly question our own validity. Maybe Sanders just couldn't handle it and bailed."

"What about Audra Marini?"

"What about her? The poor woman clearly had psychological issues. For her, suicide was the escape. It's tragic, but we know nothing about her other than the basics I learned online, and even that pointed to a deeply troubled soul."

"Maybe they drove them to—"

"Mina, listen to me." Ralph put his drink down, crouched next to the bed, and rested a hand on her knee. "Why would they do such a thing? Why would a small colony of artists offer a residency and then harm those they award with it? For what purpose, are they all a bunch of psychos? I asked you this once before. Have they given you any indication—and I mean *any*—that they want to hurt you in some way?"

Trembling, Mina shook her head no.

"In fact, they've bent over backward to be accommodating and kind, yes?"

"Why did you tell me about Sanders and Marini then?"

"Because I assumed you'd google them yourself eventually and likely use the information you found to further convince yourself that these people were out to get you. Also, they're both good examples of people that got a great opportunity and squandered it. Something I'm trying desperately to convince you *not* to do."

Mina powered down the rest of her drink. "Have you ever known me to see things that weren't there, Ralph? Have I ever struck you as the paranoid type?"

"You told me yourself you've had vivid and often disturbing dreams since you were a very little girl."

"I'm not talking about dreams, goddamn it! Have you ever known me to see things that aren't there when I'm wide fucking awake?"

"Could you be a bit louder? I'm not sure everyone in the Midwest heard you."

"I'm serious!"

"Stop shouting," Ralph said softly. "And no, I've never known you to see things that aren't there when you're wide *fucking* awake."

"Have I ever done anything to make you think I'm paranoid?"

"Not until recently."

"Exactly," Mina said. "Not until now. Not until I came to this place."

Ralph gave her knee a quick pat, then stood up and retrieved his drink from the table in the kitchen. He had a sip, and then another. "All right, what is it you'd like to do? Tell me so I can help."

"When I left the apartment this afternoon to go have lunch with Klaus," Mina said, slowly rising from the bed, "this place was a mess. There was paint everywhere, on the bed linens, the floor. I didn't have time to clean before I left, so I planned to do it when I got back. But when I got here—"

"Yes, I understand, you said everything had been cleaned up."

"Jasmin claims no one else was in here. Now, either she's lying and someone *did* come in here and clean everything up for some reason, or I did it myself and don't realize it because I'm having some sort of mental breakdown. There's no in between, Ralph. I wasn't dreaming, I wasn't hallucinating, and yes I was stoned and drunk last night, but this morning I was stone sober. I had a bad hangover, but those don't make you see things that aren't there, now do they? So either someone cleaned this apartment and they're lying about it, or I'm having some serious issues here. It's one or the other. It *has* to be. Either way, I'm in trouble."

"Couldn't it also be possible that Jasmin is telling the truth and honestly doesn't know that someone else—like one of the others in the group—came in and cleaned up?"

"I think they may be more than what they appear to be."

Ralph let her statement hang in the air between them a while. "I did take a look at the collective, albeit a rather cursory one, and read about Klaus Riker and their history. So he had some weird ideas about art that didn't go over well in Germany, and he and his wife came to the United States. Now, if you look at the commune thing he and his wife had going when they were in California in the 1970s and 80s, you could make the argument it was cult-like for an artist colony, I'll give you that. But it was just a bunch of hippies following around an older German guy and his wife engaged in experimental art. There was the fire at their compound, and a woman was killed, but from all accounts I could find that was nothing more than a horrible accident. There's not even an inkling of evidence that Klaus or anyone he's associated with has ever hurt anyone, certainly not deliberately, or have ever been up to anything truly nefarious. The information's on their own website, for God's sake, they're clearly not interested in hiding it. So they believe they've found a way to connect with the spirit world through their work. They do some unconventional shit in terms of how they produce and experience their art and explore some avenues others don't. Okay, big whoop. Lots of artists of many disciplines believe that there are strong connections between art and spirituality. Actors, writers, dancers, many of them do, not just painters. It's harmless."

"Are you sure?" Mina asked. "In this case—their case—are you sure?"

"Unless I see something that convinces me otherwise, yes," Ralph said.

Mina put her face in her hands. "I'm losing my fucking mind."

"Maybe you need to come home and talk to someone."

"Because I'm crazy," Mina said, tears filling her eyes again.

"Because you're having some trouble, and talking to a professional could help."

Mina shook her head no.

"Do you want to leave here, Mina?"

"Part of me does."

"And the other part wants to stay?"

"The other part's afraid to leave because I might be wrong and just end up blowing this whole thing."

"All right, how about this?" Ralph said. "We'll do some more digging and see if we can find anything else. I promise to take it seriously if we do. But *you* have to promise that if we don't, you'll either start looking for other explanations to all this or come back home with me and make an appointment with a doctor."

Mina thought about it a moment. "Deal."

"How long were you asleep this afternoon?"

"Six hours or so," Mina said, doing the math in her head.

"That's nearly a full night's sleep. You haven't eaten since lunch then, right?"

"No, I haven't."

"Well, I, for one, am starving. How about we run out, get some fresh air, a late dinner and some drinks over at that hideous TOPSEY TURVEY joint? Then we'll come back here, slap on our detective hats, and storm the Internet."

Getting out of the apartment seemed like a good idea, and she didn't realize until then just how hungry she was. "Okay," Mina agreed.

Ralph finished his drink then gave her another hug. She fell into him and held on tight. When he let her go, he gently wiped the tears from her cheeks with his thumb. "Don't cry, love. Ralph's here, and you know me, I only show up when it's time to save the day. It's time you knew for sure. I'm a superhero. Did you think those sequin capes in my closet were just for show?"

Mina laughed lightly. "What would I do without you?"

"A world without Ralph is too awful to even contemplate." Taking Mina's face in his hands, he dramatically planted a kiss on her lips. "Mwah! Now get your coat, darling, it's time to experience some fine dining at the Michelin star culinary gem that *is* TOPSEY TURVEYS!"

CHAPTER THIRTEEN

TOPSEY TURVEYS was nearly empty, except for an elderly waitress with blue-tinted hair, red lipstick, and equally red cheeks. The bartender was a petite young girl with long black hair, heavily made-up eyes, and pale skin. Despite her best attempts at appearing goth and sporting a skull t-shirt and tattoos of ravens on her arms, she retained a look of youthful innocence and couldn't quite pull it off. She chatted softly to a couple old men in their seventies eating burgers and drinking beer at the bar, glancing up only briefly as Mina and Ralph came through the door.

A blonde waitress with green-streaked hair, and clad in a black dress so tight her ribs and bony thighs were evident, motioned to a few tables near the bar. "You guys can sit wherever," she said listlessly, not bothering to stop on her way to the kitchen. "Be with you in a sec."

"Enchanting," Ralph muttered as he and Mina chose a table.

The place was dimly lit, just scones here and there on the walls, flashing neon lights by the bar, announcing local beers and something called the *Crow's Cry Burger*. The tables were draped with black and white checked tablecloths, the walls consisted of 1950s paneling where framed posters of select New England landmarks hung—Town House Square in Salem, Massachusetts; the Block Island ferry dock in Point Judith, Rhode Island; a scene a few miles from there, the wall at Narragansett Pier—all nightscapes where the moon hung in starless skies. The remaining walls were splintered in places, discolored in others, and the floor was an old hardwood, scratched and worn with age. In the windows and above the door, crystals dangled like the ones at Rita's shop.

Ralph quickly brushed his chair off before sitting down. "The splendor that *is* the décor of TOPSEY TURVERYS is evidently matched only by the boundless enthusiasm and relentless charm of its employees. I can't wait to try the food poisoning."

"It is kind of gross in here," Mina said. "Want to go someplace else?"

"I doubt seriously we'll find anything better in these parts, unless of course there's a 7-Eleven with a full array of microwaves nearby." Ralph picked up one of the laminated menus on the table and flipped it open. "I'm tempted to ask for a wine list just to see how many different boxes they offer."

"At least it's relatively clean," Mina said, taking up a menu of her own.

"Call me particular, but I've always been a stickler for *actual* cleanliness."

"You've seen worse."

"Ain't that the truth?" Ralph's gaze scanned the menu. "I'm going to risk it and go for the *Crow's Cry Burger*. From the looks of this place, I'd say there's a good chance it's got actual crow in it."

"Gross," Mina said, giggling.

The waitress emerged from the kitchen and sauntered over to their table. "Decide what you want yet?"

"I'll have the Crow's Cry Burger with fries, please," Ralph said.

She jotted it down on a small pad, then looked at Mina. "And you, hon?"

"I'll have the same."

"And a side of wings, appetizer size," Ralph added.

"Hot or mild?"

"The hotter the better, baby."

The waitress smiled at him, revealing uneven teeth. "And to drink?"

"How about a couple *brewskis*?" Ralph winked at Mina. "When in Rome, eh?"

"Pitcher's cheaper."

"Super." Ralph beamed. "Let's go for a pitcher then."

"Be just a minute." As she darted away, apron strings flapping, her rubber-soled shoes made a squishy sound as she made her way across the floor.

Ralph watched her until she pushed through the kitchen door, then he shook his head. "Poor thing," he said. "She's no spring chicken, how old do you think she is?"

"Probably in her sixties, maybe seventies," Mina said.

"And still has to work. This country is not kind to our elderly population."

"Speaking of which, are you retiring any time soon?"

"How dare you," Ralph said with mock offense. "I'm just barely out of my teens, you vicious sow."

"At least you have your teacher's retirement."

"That and social security, but I'm—why are we talking about retirement again?"

"Because you're old," Mina said with a wink.

"Old*er*, and besides, once my teaching career mercifully comes to an end, I have plans to pursue my dreams of being Rhode Island's preeminent interpretive dancer. What do you think?"

Mina reached across the table and took his hand. "I think I'm really glad you're here."

The server returned with a pitcher of beer and two mugs, slapped them on the table, then moved away. By the time Ralph had poured them each a mug, she was back with a small platter of chicken wings, two plates, and a stack of paper napkins. She left them all in the center of the table and, without a word, returned to the kitchen.

Ralph handed Mina a plate and a couple napkins, then took the same for him as well. "Okay," he said, eyeing the wings. "They don't look too bad, but you first."

"They must be really hot," Mina said, dropping one onto her plate. "They're making my eyes water."

"Good, that ought to kill any bacteria that came along for the ride." Ralph placed one on his plate and immediately took a nibble. "Oh yeah, these'll take the paint off a Buick."

Mina had about half of one then put it aside. Her eyes were watering, her nose was running, and her scalp had begun to sweat. "That's enough for me. If they're this hot going in, I can just imagine how they'll be coming out."

"There's a fun visual, especially while we're eating."

Ralph had put three of them away when the waitress returned with two giant burgers on brioche buns. Dripping grease, oozing with melted cheese, and topped with slices of tomato and onion, they sat atop piles of crispy fries.

"Anything else?" she asked.

"Just call the closest ER and have them ready the paddles, would you?"

"I think we're good, thanks," Mina said before Ralph could say anything more.

As she left them, Ralph popped a fry in his mouth. "Not bad, nice crunch." His eyes darted to the door. "Wow, balls across the nose. Get a load of *this* masterpiece."

Mina turned, saw someone coming through the entrance, and quickly realized it was Maurice making his way to the bar. Just as it registered, he spotted her and gave a quick wave.

Ralph lowered his voice and leaned forward. "An ascot, seriously? And those shoes, fucking penny loafers—pennies and all—he looks like the lovechild of George Hamilton and Maurice Chevalier. Please tell me there's a local theater group putting on a production of *The Merry Widow.*"

"Don't laugh, his name's actually Maurice."

"You *know* that queen?"

"He's one of them, and he's coming over here."

And there he was, decked out as though he truly was about to star in some 1930s musical. "How nice to see you, Mina!" he said, eyes settling on Ralph. For a moment, a look of concern washed over his face, but then he smiled, his thin mustache stretching over his lips. "And I see you have company."

"Maurice, this is my friend Ralph from back in Providence," Mina said. "He's visiting for a day or two, checking up me."

Ralph wiped his hands on a napkin, then slowly stood up and offered his hand. "Ralph Deckard, how are you?"

"Maurice Larocque," Maurice said, accepting his hand. "Rest assured, Mr. Deckard, we're taking very good care of Mina. She's a *marvelous* talent."

"An absolute treasure, isn't she?" Ralph sank back into his chair. "Would you care to join us?"

"That's very kind, thank you, but no, I'm not staying long." Maurice looked to the bar, then back at Mina. "I just stopped in for a quick drink."

"I just bet they have a *nifty* lineup of exotic cocktails here," Ralph said with a subtle smirk.

Maurice continued smiling graciously. "I must admit this place satisfies a guilty pleasure. Now and then I sneak in and have a Budweiser and get one of their club sandwiches to go when no one's looking."

"How scandalous, Maury!" Ralph said, widening his eyes comically. "You rascal, you're a regular outlaw, aren't you? Look out for this one, Mina. He's a wild man, totally out of control."

Mina laughed helplessly, nervously looking from Ralph to Maurice then back again. "Oh, Ralph, you and your sense of humor, it's—"

"Deadly?" Ralph said with a huge grin.

Maurice smiled but was clearly not amused. "Well, it's certainly good to know you have such a nice friend, Mina."

"We look out for each other as best we can," Ralph said. "Someone has to do it."

"At any rate, I'm off to the bar. It was a pleasure meeting you, Mr. Deckard."

"The pleasure's *all* mine." Ralph took a big bite of his burger. "And call me Ralph. All my friends do."

"I see." Maurice narrowed his eyes. "As always, it's delightful to see you, Mina. Please forgive the interruption. You and *Ralph* enjoy your meal. Have a nice evening."

With that, Maurice turned and sauntered over to the bar.

Mina watched him as he sat alone at the end of the bar. The bartender leaned close and they spoke for a second. Her eyes found Mina, then she turned and grabbed a bottle of beer and put it in front of Maurice.

"Jesus, Ralph, why were you such an asshole to him?" Mina said.

"Oh please, he's so full of shit. Budweiser and club sandwiches, my ass." Ralph took another big bite of burger then wiped the grease from his chin with a napkin. "This burger is revoltingly decadent and unnecessarily over-the-top, by the way. I adore it. I may get another one to go."

"Will you stop fucking around?" Mina said, nibbling a fry. "Why were you so rude just now?"

"Because there's something off about her," Ralph said. "Who is she? What does she want? What is she doing here? What does she hope to achieve in this crazy world, with her ascot and penny loafers? One can only hope ole Maury has better fashion sense at home. I'm thinking saddle shoes and a poodle skirt while singing Connie Francis tunes. 'Where the Boys Are' indeed. Not at Maurice's fucking house, I can tell you that. 'Where the Boys *Aren't*,' more likely."

Mina shot him an angry look.

"Fine," he said, "you don't find it strange that he just happened to show up here?"

"Now who's being paranoid?" Mina asked.

"I never said you were paranoid."

"It doesn't matter. No, I don't buy it either."

Ralph finished his burger in another two bites then started back in on the fries. "My God, I'm famished. I'm getting dessert too. Fuck it."

Mina watched Maurice out of the corner of her eye. "Do you think he's following me?"

"I don't know," Ralph said, signaling for the waitress. "But I'd bet my entire Criterion Collection of DVDs that ass only comes to this dump when he has to. Either his whole shtick is bullshit or he's lying."

"The bartender seems to know him."

"Eat your food," Ralph said as the waitress arrived. "Darling, bring me anything chocolate you can find back there, would you?"

"We got Boston cream pie tonight. Slices are huge."

"I've never been much of a size-queen myself, but that sounds perfect, thank you."

"You want one too?" she asked Mina, unfazed.

"I'm all set, thanks," Mina said, and continued devouring her burger and fries.

As the waitress left them, Ralph said, "I don't know for sure what his deal is, and I'm not buying that he just happened to appear here right after we did, but seriously, Mina, you're worried about *that* guy?" He cocked his head in Maurice's direction.

"If he's lying then why shouldn't I be?"

Ralph shrugged. "Maybe they're keeping track of you."

"Yeah, because that's not creepy at all, and besides, why would they do that?"

"I don't know. Maybe they're being overly protective of the investment they've made in you, or they're trying too hard to be solicitous. It is odd, I'll give you that. But look, I'm full of grease. Let me get a sugar high going and add that to the mix, see what I come up with."

Mina tried to smile, but couldn't. Something really was off here, she could feel it. Everything was darker, felt more sinister than any place she'd been before, and she'd lived in some hellholes when she was a kid. This was different, like some sort of evil in the air, in the buildings, the sea, and every person she encountered.

"I'm worried, Ralph. I can't shake the feeling that my whole world is off, like I stepped into another dimension or something."

"We'll put our heads together, do some research, and I'm sure we'll find they're a bunch of eccentrics and nothing more. But we need vodka, and maybe some red wine to get our blood flowing. In a place this bleak, there must be a liquor store on every block."

"I know of one, it's not far," she said, pushing what remained on her plate aside.

After a moment, Ralph caught her subtly watching Maurice, who was huddled with the bartender again and speaking in whispers as if plotting something. "Been a long time since I've seen actual pennies in penny loafers," he said. "Come to think of it, haven't seen penny loafers *without* the pennies in ages either. Remember the old thing when you were a kid? *See a penny, pick it up, and all day you'll have good luck; let it lay, and bad luck you'll have all day.*"

"Sorry, before my time," Mina told him.

"Oh, me too, it just—eh—something I heard. Anyway, kids used to sing it in grammar school every time somebody found a penny on the playground or walking home from school."

"I never sang much when I was a kid."

Ralph's expression darkened. "I know, doll, and I'm sorry. But remember, there's plenty to sing about now."

"Is there?"

"Isn't there?"

"I guess we'll find out," Mina said, sighing and sitting back in her chair a bit. "You think there's something up with those pennies, don't you."

"No, Mina, I don't."

The waitress delivered his pie, cleared the table, and was gone.

"That *is* huge," Ralph said, eyeing it.

"Then why do you keep talking about his penny loafers?"

"I'm making fun of him and just being bitchy for fun, all right? Also, I'm goofing on this entire experience and trying to make you laugh. I'm hoping you'll stop taking all of this quite so seriously."

"What else you got?"

Ralph had a bite of pie and thought about it a moment. "I remember one of my old neighbors, nice little Italian lady, Estelle Palmieri, talking about pennies. She used to say the front and back of a coin represents a paradox of duality—my words—she'd say it in broken English, absolutely adorable. Anyway, two things that make up one thing. Sometimes, she said, the Italian Strega—"

"Witches," Mina said.

"Yes, Italian for witch, exactly," he said, chewing another bite of pie. "She said they used pennies in their magic, and that the coins are a connection to the afterlife because they used to place them on the bodies of the dead to pay for their journey."

"Journey to where, that's the question."

"Oh, you know, the whole crossing the River Styx thing with the Ferryman and all that."

Flashes of her nightmare blinked before her mind's eye. The sea and the boat, the blind ferryman...

"Interesting anecdote," he said. "But just old-world superstition, of course. Don't go thinking Maury over there's holding tickets to the underworld in his *smokin'* loafers."

"At this point, I'd believe almost anything."

"And that, in itself, as I'm sure you can see, is a dangerous state to be in." He quickly finished his pie. "Come on. Let's get out of here before I order something else. I'll go pay the bill, then we'll make a quick booze stop, head back to your place, fire up your laptop, and get this all hashed out."

Mina watched as Ralph got up and went to pay the bill. He and the waitress were chatting near the bar, but she couldn't make out what they were saying. Whatever it was, it made the waitress laugh, but even the laughter sounded far away, because Mina's thoughts had already returned to those terrifying dreams and visions, even as she wondered why Maurice had shown up here. Even Ralph hadn't bought it as a coincidence.

Once more, she looked over at Maurice, who was still engaged in an intense conversation with the bartender.

Ralph returned to the table. "All set, ready?"

"I think the bartender called him and told him we were here," Mina said quietly. "She's got the shiftiest eyes."

"From the looks, that's the least of her issues."

"Maurice has barely touched his beer, and where's the sandwich he was talking about? You're right, he is full of shit. He didn't come here to drink or eat."

"I'm with you there," Ralph said. "I just don't know why yet."

"I bet he follows us out. I think he's spying on me. Maybe they're all spying on me. They probably have cameras hidden in my apartment."

Ralph took her hands in his and helped her to her feet. "Mina, stop it. I'm sure it's nothing as serious as all that. The night's still young, and we've got a lot to do to put your mind—and mine—at ease, yes?"

"Whatever," Mina said, grabbing her jacket and walking past him to the door. "I need a cigarette."

* * * *

Mina and Ralph stood on the sidewalk outside TOPSEY TURVEYS, sharing a cigarette and taking in the night, a night that drifted around them like a dark dream.

"I don't feel safe," Mina said, inhaling the cigarette deeply and then letting out a stream of smoke. "Do you understand? I don't feel *safe*, Ralph."

"Don't freak out, okay?" He took a puff, handed the cigarette back to her. "I'm a firm believer in never freaking out until or unless it's absolutely necessary. And life has taught me it seldom is. Besides, Ralph's here now, and I'm a badass motherfucker when I have to be. Remember those three cretins that jumped me that time back in Warwick?"

"Those assholes beat you unconscious, Ralph."

"True, but trust me when I tell you all three of those hateful pricks knew they'd been in a fight. I didn't just lie down and take it, Mina. I broke at least one of their noses, one lost some teeth, and I'm sure the other one didn't pee right for at least a week."

"Fine, you're Bruce Lee."

"With some Peggy Lee thrown in for good measure," he said, beaming. "But still, no one's going to do anything to you on my watch. I'd die before I let anyone hurt you."

Mina felt her face flush. No one had ever said that to her before. "I love you, Ralph. You make me crazy, but I fucking love you."

"I fucking love you too, you little shit."

"They watched us when we left, you know," Mina said, shuffling her feet against the cold. "Somebody else is probably watching us right now."

"You're relentless," he said with a sigh. "You really believe that?"

"Yeah, I do."

Ralph frowned with concern. "All right, let's go get some vodka and wine and get out of this cold and back to your apartment."

"They're watching, I'm telling you, they're watching us right now."

"Then let them watch. If you're right, we'll know soon enough." He held a hand out for her. "And if you're wrong, we'll know that soon enough too. Okay? *Okay*? Say okay, goddamn it."

Mina took another drag, then flicked the butt into the street. "Okay, goddamn it."

"Just for the record, that did not sound at *all* sincere."

She took Ralph's hand. Together, they walked in silence toward his car, and into the darkest night of Mina's memory.

* * * *

Back at the apartment, they finished off what was left of the vodka Mina had purchased when she'd first arrived at Crow's Cry, then opened one of the new bottles and grabbed Mina's laptop from the kitchen counter. Ralph sat in the comfortable chair, flipped it open, and began to type. "Bringing up the website Sanders' boyfriend made. I remember seeing an email address on there. I think we should contact him."

"Do you think he'll talk to us?"

"I don't see why not, but I think it might be a mistake to mention you're the new resident artist. From the sounds of some of the entries on here, he isn't too thrilled with the whole operation, so I'm going to say you're a reporter for the Providence Sentinel doing a story on the collective and you want to ask him some questions about Robert Sanders' stay here, okay? I'll use a fake name and give him your number. If he calls, put it on speaker so I can listen in."

Mina sat on the arm of the chair so she could look over Ralph's shoulder and see what he was up to. Colin Brewster, Sanders' boyfriend, was listed on the website as the caretaker of the site. "This is a shot in the dark," she said. "His last post is from July. He may have moved on by now, doesn't look like the site's yielded much of anything."

Ralph scrolled down to a photograph of Robert Sanders. "That's him."

Somehow, the photograph made him more real to Mina. She studied it, a shadowy silhouette of a man working at a canvas, several of his finished paintings nearby, all of which were in the abstract style of Pollock.

Scrolling further, the website revealed blog entries about Sanders' work, as well as some on his showings at local galleries in and around Los Angeles, and his partnership both personally and professionally with Colin Brewster. There were also entries about the disappearance. The heartbreak, the endless search for answers, the frustration and anger Colin felt—it was all there—and finally, in a couple of the last entries, the ultimate realization that he might never know what happened to Robert, or ever see his business partner and the love of his life again.

As Mina scanned the entries, her eyes welled with tears. "God, this poor man," she said. "I can't...I just can't."

"It's heartbreaking, isn't it? But we talked about all the reasons why Sanders could have just dropped off the face of the earth."

"It just doesn't seem to me that a guy like that would walk away from his life and a relationship that he and Colin had because of pressure or—"

"Love, he was driving from here to California. Anything could happen to a person on the road. There are a lot of bad people out there. I don't have to tell you that. He could've met with some sort of horrible end, who knows? Point is, even if he did, there's nothing to tie anything like that to the collective." He clicked a link. "Okay, here's the email address where you can contact Colin Brewster."

"All right, go for it."

Ralph typed a quick email. "How's that, look legit?"

"Yeah," Mina said, reading it. "That's good."

"Okay then." He clicked SEND and the box disappeared. "Off you go."

They tapped their glasses together and each took a long sip.

"When I passed out at lunch with Klaus, I had this dream, or something similar to a dream," Mina said. "They were all around me, and marking me, drawing symbols on my forehead and on my body with oils. They kept saying 'anoint her with the sacred oils and—'"

"Kinky!"

"You promised you'd take this seriously."

"Sorry," he said, closing the website and pulling up Google.

"And they were covering me in paint, my whole body, every orifice."

"A rather symbolic dream for a painter, wouldn't you say?"

"Of course, but—"

"Honestly, all joking aside, couldn't it have just been some sort of erotic wet dream?"

"There was nothing pleasurable about it, Ralph," Mina assured him. "It was fucking horrible."

He looked up at her, and Mina could tell by his expression that he knew this was no laughing matter for her. "All right," he said. "I'm sorry, doll."

"Google that stuff," she said softly.

He typed MAGIC SPELLS, ANOINTING WITH SACRED OILS AND SYMBOLS in the search box and hit the ENTER key. "Let's see what comes up."

A few websites that listed online shops selling oils of every name imaginable appeared. Blessing Oil for special ritual purposes…Cherry Blossoms Oil to guarantee a happy spiritual vibration…Evil Eye, urging the buyer to wear a little on each temple to avert the evil eye… Voodoo Oil designed to be placed at your enemy's door at midnight.

"No rituals? Nothing like that?" asked Mina impatiently.

"Hold on. Here's one that has a link under it. Bat's Heart Oil."

Mina hovered over him, one hand holding her drink, the other on his shoulder as she read aloud the caption beneath a bottle made of dark glass, a skeleton's face etched crudely on a faded label. "Very strong oil used to create anxiety and an impending feeling of doom in the life of your target. Pair with Doom Oil and pokeroot to conjure the Devil."

"Interesting," Ralph said, sipping his drink.

"Pokeroot!" she said, slapping his shoulder. "The canvas, Ralph, remember? Rita said it was treated with pokeroot."

"Ouch. Says here pokeroot has dual properties. Healers use it for good, but so-called black magicians use it in *devil work*, whatever the hell that is, pun intended. Creepy shit for sure, but I doubt anyone ever conjured the Devil or caused somebody to lose their mind by dabbing them with this stuff." He clicked another link. "And here's Doom Oil, made from graveyard dirt, red pepper, black pepper, and crushed insects…ants, wasps, spiders, and a few malefic herbs. Well, that sounds delightful and not at all patently absurd." Ralph threw a hand up. "I mean, there's crazy shit like this all over the Internet. It reminds me of Vittorio Magnus, actually."

"Who the fuck is Vittorio Magnus?"

"He wore a turban, a hippie robe, and beads, and made a fortune primarily on naïve young people and superstitious little old ladies back in the day. No Internet back then." Ralph cleared his throat. "Or, so they tell me. Anyway, you'd have to go to a seer's loft in downtown Providence in those days to get a Tarot reading and a mojo bag filled with stuff like this. Supposedly it guaranteed that your enemies would stay away from you. I had a boyfriend at the time that was into this shit, he even had a few of those bags. He swore it kept him safe from most of the assholes that loved to bash gays. There was a whole faction of those tools back then. It can still be dangerous out there, but that kind of thing was a lot more common then. And hardly anyone cared. They'd put nails in our car tires, corner us on dark streets, follow us around and taunt us, assault us, even rob us sometimes. And I'll tell you, Mina, the seer's predictions never came true. That stupid mojo bag didn't help at all. My boyfriend wore it on his belt, until they stole that too."

"Maybe your Providence seer was full of shit."

"I'm relatively sure they're all full of shit, doll." Ralph brought up another website. "Okay, here's a spell for that Doom Oil stuff. It's a soul transfer spell. Oh, good times, girl, *soul transfer*. Sounds like a 70s funk band."

Mina read out loud, her voice trembling. "That says it's even in the Christian Bible, this kind of thing. *Most times a soul can be made to leave the body temporarily...or it can be permanently replaced with the soul of somebody else.* Scroll down a bit. Jesus, they've got the entire ritual on here."

"Makes you wonder who you'd want to trade souls with, doesn't it?" Ralph grinned. "Do you think Cher's available?"

Mina glared at him.

"I'm just saying we all need to start admitting she's immortal at this point."

"It says it can only work for people who are willing to pass over, who are willing to leave their body," Mina said, ignoring him and reading further. "But they have to be weakened first. Most often just long enough for the stronger soul to overpower the weaker one. One needs to intoxicate the target using Bat's Heart Oil, starting by dipping your left index finger in the oil, then making the sign of the cross in reverse on his or her forehead. Anoint every inch of flesh with oil, including the orifices. Draw symbols of Pluto, the God of Death, and Morden, the God of Murder. Your target will feel as though they're floating, that the world around them is fading away. Once that world fades completely, they are ready to move to the next realm. When sufficiently weakened, filled with anxiety, with self-doubt to the point that they can no longer function, then he or she is ready for the final step." Hands shaking, Mina took another sip of her drink. "Jesus Christ, this is insane, I—Ralph—this is what I felt! It was like I was floating away. And now I feel like I'm falling apart. This is—"

"Mina, it was dream."

She reached down and slid a finger over the pad on the laptop, scrolling further so she could read the rest. "It says you use something called Soul of Transfer Oil," she said. "That the Devil appears when you say this shit in Latin and—"

"Okay, maybe that's enough of this site. We can—"

"Leave it," she snapped. "Read the warning, Ralph."

He sighed dramatically, then obliged. "Do not perform the ritual of soul transfer for fun and games. You will never know what world your target will end up in. It could be one you did not intend."

"So in other words, the ritual can switch souls between two people, or send one to another realm. Or even both. That's what it says."

"How I wish Vittorio were here."

"Will you stop with the Vittorio shit?"

"He's dead, you know. Lived to ninety-seven, ripped off people with his scams until the day he passed."

"Unless he's a part of the collective, I don't give a shit."

Ralph finished his drink, then set the glass down on the floor next to the chair. "Mina, please tell me you're not taking this seriously. I believe in the spiritual side of things, sure, but this is some ludicrous shit."

"I'm getting the creeps just looking at this website," she said, popping up off the arm of the chair and pacing near the windows. "Look at all the strange symbols on the site. They all seem familiar somehow, like I've got them painted on my skin, like they scarred me with them."

"The power of suggestion is very—"

"That's not what this is."

"Mina, you've got to talk to somebody. I think I'm serious about that now."

"Maybe so, I don't know." She flopped back down on the arm of the chair, leaned over Ralph, and scrolled to the bottom of the page. "Look, there's more."

"Splendid, of course there is."

"They prepare the target with an initial soul transfer powder, made from insects and graveyard dirt. Says they conduct spells over it using their victim's name, and then it's sprinkled in corners of the target's residence. It says it right there, look."

"For Christ's sake, Mina, I can read." Ralph winced, stood, and placed the laptop on the chair. "How's this for a shocking revelation? My stomach's starting to act up. Who could've seen that coming? Do you have any Tums or something along those lines handy by any chance?"

"I don't, but check the cupboards. They were stocked with some basic shit when I got here. I don't remember seeing any, but you can take a look."

He had just headed into the kitchen when Mina's phone buzzed.

She looked down at the screen. "Unknown number," she said.

"Answer it, could be Colin Brewster calling us back."

Mina looked at him, then back at the screen. What were the odds that he'd call back so quickly, or at all, for that matter?

"*Mina,*" Ralph said. "Answer the phone."

Hand shaking, she pressed accept then put the phone on speaker. "Hello?"

"Is this Ms. Miller?"

"That's the name I left." Ralph nodded, silently mouthing the words.

"Yes, who's calling?"

"Colin Brewster."

"Mr. Brewster, hello," Mina said, trying to keep her voice even. "Thanks for calling me back so quickly. I'm in the middle of doing a story on the artist collective over in Crow's Cry, and I was hoping I might be able to ask you a few questions about Robert Sanders. I know he did a residency there, but I've been unable to find him, and my search eventually led me to your website."

"Then you know he's missing," Brewster said evenly.

"I was actually unaware of that until I saw your site," Mina said, looking to Ralph.

He gave her a thumbs-up.

"Everyone I spoke to from the collective said they hadn't heard from Robert since the residency ended and he left to return to California."

"I see," Brewster said. "When you mentioned in your email you're a reporter I thought you might have some new information. That's why I got back to you so fast."

"I'm so sorry, Mr. Brewster, no."

"Then what is it I can do for you?"

"I take it there haven't been any new leads regarding Robert's disappearance?"

"*New* leads? Try no leads. Bobby's gone. It was like he got in the car and started for home and vanished into thin air. *I* care, of course, but nobody else seems to give a damn. Look, I don't want to be rude, Ms. Miller, but this is a very painful topic for me, as I'm sure you can understand, so unless you know something about Bobby's whereabouts or have some new useful information, I'm really not comfortable indulging you or your story."

"Maybe we could help each other," Mina said carefully.

"It doesn't much sound like it. I've been looking for Bobby for a long time. I even hired a private investigator at one point. Last time anybody saw or heard from Bobby, he was in Crow's Cry."

"Where did he stay when he was there, do you know?"

There was a pause, and all Mina could hear was Brewster breathing.

"Mr. Brewster, are you there?"

"Why do you want to know?" he finally said.

"Well, doesn't a residency include just that, a residence?"

"Obviously. My question was *why* do you want to know?"

Mina drew a deep breath and tried to think on her feet. "Honestly, Mr. Brewster, I started out writing a story on the collective, but when I saw that Bobby was missing I decided to expand the story to include his disappearance. Maybe the story will bring more exposure and someone who knows something might come forward."

More breathing followed.

Ralph bit his lip then held his hands up helplessly.

"Did he stay in the collective's housing when he was there?" Mina pressed.

"Yes, they had an apartment for him for the duration of the residency. Hold on." He seemed to be gone for an inordinate amount of time. When he returned to the phone, the sound of papers shuffling accompanied him. "Here it is," he said. "He was staying at 330 Merchant Place, Apartment One, in Crow's Cry, that's the address he gave me."

Mina motioned to Ralph to jot that down. He quickly typed it into his phone.

"Did he paint while he was there?" Mina asked.

"Supposedly," Brewster said.

"Meaning?"

"Meaning I never saw anything, and nobody at the collective ever provided me with anything he'd painted while he was there. They claimed he'd done some great work, but he took it with him, which is customary. So whatever Bobby painted while he was there disappeared along with him. They've never even found the car." He cleared his throat, fighting back emotion. "I hired a PI from the Boston area to check the place out, but supposedly he didn't find anything more."

"Why do you say *supposedly?*"

"Let's just say I have my doubts."

"Doubts regarding the private detective specifically?"

"I'd rather not discuss that." Brewster sighed as if annoyed with the question. "There was supposed to be a showing at their gallery at the end of his stay there, but he left a few days beforehand. The people from the collective said Bobby left a little ahead of schedule and canceled the public showing because he told them something had come up back home and he needed to leave. They said he never elaborated but that it didn't appear to be anything too serious. They were disappointed but understood. They said they saw him off, and that he drove away in a rental car. And that was that. They told the cops the same thing. Turns out it was the last anybody saw or heard of him."

"Have you actually been to Crow's Cry?" she asked.

"No, I haven't."

"Can I ask why?"

"I'd planned to fly out for his show, but when it was canceled there was no point. Later, after Bobby disappeared I wanted to, but the private detective told me to stay clear, that it was a strange place. Gave him the creeps, he said. I assume you've been there if you're writing a story about it. Tell me, Ms. Miller, did it give you the creeps too?"

Mina hesitated. "It's definitely different."

"Whatever it is you're doing or writing about, you should probably stay away from there too." He paused a moment. "Or are you there right now?" he asked, his voice trembling. "Tell me the truth. You said we could help each other."

"Is going to Crow's Cry dangerous? Is that what you're saying?"

"I'll answer you this way, Ms. Miller. Bobby was pragmatic and not prone to hysteria, didn't believe in ghosts or anything supernatural. He wasn't an atheist exactly, more an agnostic, but he started changing when he got to Crow's Cry. He started calling me at all hours, saying he'd started having strange dreams about people doing some sort of crazy ritualistic shit to him. He said he was seeing things and people that weren't there even when he was awake, and that all of this was not only changing his art, but it was making him feel like he was losing his mind. And before you ask, no, he had no prior history of mental illness and he didn't do drugs. Christ, he barely drank. I told him to come home, but he wanted to stick it out, and he did for as long as he could. He thought it was all in his head—and maybe it was—but *something* happened to him there. Exactly what, I don't know. I'm not sure I ever will."

Mina's hand began to shake so violently that she had to grip the phone tighter to prevent her from dropping it. "Do you believe Bobby was in danger?"

"I think toward the end of his residency *he* believed he was. I also think that band of so-called artists were messing with his head with all their spiritual connections to art horseshit that creepy old fuck that runs the place is all about."

Mina noticed Ralph rummaging through the cabinets in search of antacids, but he was clearly still listening to their conversation. "Do you think they know more than they're saying?" she asked Brewster.

"I honestly don't know."

"Did the private investigator think they knew more?"

"I believe he did. But you'd have to ask him."

"And you have doubts that he told you everything he found out as well?"

There was another long pause before Brewster answered. "Yes, I do."

"Would you be open to sharing his name?"

"Phillip Bergeron. He's out of Revere, Massachusetts."

"Phillip Bergeron," she repeated, waving for Ralph, who stopped what he was doing long enough to enter it into his phone, then give a thumbs-up before resuming his search of the cupboards. "You didn't elaborate before, so do you mind if I ask again why you have those doubts?"

"For lack of a better word, he became *nervous* at one point, which didn't exactly match his demeanor prior. At first he was very aggressive and seemed like the type that didn't scare easily. And then he suddenly seemed hesitant, like he wasn't sure digging any deeper was a good idea. It was as if he'd come across something that made him not want to go any further. That was my feeling, at any rate."

"There's no easy way to ask this, so I'm just going to put it out there," Mina said. "Do you believe the collective had something to do with Bobby's disappearance?"

A brief period of silence followed.

"Mr. Brewster?"

"I'm not prepared to say that," he finally answered. "Because I'm not convinced they did. But whatever happened to Bobby there, whatever they put him through—whatever *he* believed they were putting him through—could very well have had such a negative impact on him that it led to, or contributed to, his disappearance. Maybe it caused him to have some sort of mental or emotional breakdown. Maybe he lost his mind and wandered off somewhere. Maybe he made a bad decision, was afraid and ran and got himself into a situation he couldn't find his way back from. At the end of the day, I just don't know. But what I'm trying to say is this. Even if those people weren't *directly* responsible for Bobby's disappearance, his time there with them and their influence on him certainly impacted the situation and could've help lead to it. That I *do* believe. For me, that's enough to stay away from the place and the people involved. And there's something more. Bergeron told me when he dug a bit deeper he found that another artist, the one that received the Crow's Cry residency *before* Bobby, took her own life once she'd gotten home. As I say, he'd become hesitant by then but was willing to look into the others too."

"And did you have him do that?"

"No. At that point he'd begun to act peculiarly, I'd heard more than enough, and frankly, his services had become so expensive I couldn't afford to continue to employ him. I don't know what's going on there, but whatever it is it's certainly nothing positive, I can tell you that."

"I understand," Mina said, the words catching in her throat.

"Yes, I'm getting the distinct impression you do." Brewster waited as if he expected Mina to respond. When she didn't, he said, "Bobby was a beautiful soul and a very gifted artist. He never hurt anyone, and I see no reason why anyone would ever want to hurt him. But sometimes this is a very dark world, Ms. Miller, *very* dark."

Mina looked to Ralph. Back from his search of the kitchen cabins, he stood staring at her. Gone was the twinkle of mischievous, cutting humor in his eyes, and his fingers were stained with some sort of white powder.

They prepare the target with an initial soul transfer powder...

"Thanks for your time, Mr. Brewster. If I learn anything more, I'll let you know."

"Yeah, you do that."

"I'm very sorry about Bobby, and—"

"Take it for what it's worth," Brewster interrupted. "Whoever you are, and whatever it is you're up to, I'll give you the last piece of advice Bergeron gave me. Stay away from that place and as far away from those people as possible. I heeded that advice. I suggest you do the same, while you still can."

Before Mina could respond, the call was disconnected. She put her phone down on the counter, returning her attention to Ralph. "What the fuck is all over your fingers?"

"I'm not sure," he said, looking at them. "Diatomaceous Earth, maybe? People sprinkle it around their houses to deter roaches and spiders and shit."

"We both know that's not what it is," Mina said, shaking. "It's the powder. They sprinkled it in the cupboards—deep in the corners—just like the website said."

A look of confusion and disbelief mixed with horror slowly spread over his face. "I—Christ, this is all too much, this can't be, I—"

"You just heard what Brewster said, same as I did."

"Mina, what's your apartment number?"

"I'm not sure. It's in the information pack they sent me, but I'd have to—"

"Bring this up on Google Maps." Ralph showed her his phone and the address Brewster had told them was Robert Sanders' while he was there.

She did. "It's not my place. It's not even this building."

"Where is it?" he asked.

"No *fucking* way." Mina looked up from her phone. "It's the building across the courtyard, the apartment on the ground floor where I saw the painter."

Ralph rubbed his white-tipped index finger and thumb together. "Mina," he said, in an uncharacteristically shaky voice. "What the hell is going on?"

CHAPTER FOURTEEN

Mina tossed Ralph a dishcloth she found in one of the kitchen drawers. As he wiped his hands clean of the powder, she saw more of it along the back corners of the cupboard he'd been rummaging through. She'd never looked that closely or deeply into the kitchen cupboards, and had it not been for Ralph, she would've never known it was there. "Go to Brewster's website again," she said, pouring another drink with shaking hands. "I want to check something."

Ralph sat in the chair, and with the same look of horror, confusion, and disbelief on his face, brought the site up. "Okay, now what?" he asked in a distant voice.

Mina looked over his shoulder at the screen. The photo of Bobby Sanders on the main page was difficult to make out detail due to the shadows and the fact that it was mostly in silhouette. "It's a site about a missing person," she said. "There's got to be a clearer photo of Bobby on here."

As Ralph scrolled over to a menu button, Mina realized his hand was shaking too. "Here," he said, clicking on a category labeled PHOTOGRAPHS. "He's posted quite an array of them actually."

"Good, I want a closer look at him."

A series of pictures appeared on the screen, many showing Bobby with Colin Brewster, but even more of Bobby by himself.

Mina backed away from the laptop, her heart smashing her chest. She'd seen all she needed to. "That's him," she said just above a whisper.

"Obviously, who else would it be?"

"No," Mina said, a hand to her mouth. "That's *him*. The painter I saw in the apartment across the courtyard."

"Oh, come on! Are you serious?"

"Do you think I'd be *joking* at this point, Ralph?"

"You're sure? I mean, you're—"

"Yes."

"You're absolutely certain?"

Mina nodded.

"Okay," Ralph said, shaking his head. "Then he's still here somewhere."

"I don't think so."

"I'm trying to understand, but—"

"I was in there, remember? I was *in* that apartment. No one's lived there in a long time, probably not since Bobby Sanders left, if he ever did leave. Some homeless people broke in from time to time and definitely caused some damage, but otherwise that apartment's been left to rot."

"Mina, it's been a stressful evening. You need to be sure about this. One hundred percent certain, follow?"

"It's him."

Ralph rubbed his eyes. "All right, if you saw him down there, he's still here."

"I don't think he is."

"Then you've lost me."

"Maybe it's all part of this." Mina moved away from the windows, not wanting to look out there in the dark or down at the apartment below. "I think they wanted me to see him so I'd feel like I was losing my mind, the same as they did things to him so he'd feel that way too."

"Okay, so what was he, a *ghost?*"

"Not exactly," she managed, the fear rising in her so violently she felt as if she were close to completely losing control. "I think they did something to me, a spell, a ritual—I don't know what—that made me see things that weren't there. Specific things they wanted me to see. Maybe they made me see things that *had* been there at one time but were actually in the past and—"

"Mina, do you hear yourself? People can't do that."

Darkness passed over Mina's face like a cloud slowly drifting across the moon. "What if they're not people?"

"Of course they're people, what else would they be, end tables?" Ralph put the laptop aside, stood up, then began to pace. "All right, all right, let's not go off the rails on the crazy train quite yet. What we need to do is pull ourselves together."

Mina finished the remainder of her drink in a single gulp then placed the glass on the windowsill. "What we need to do is get the hell out of here."

Brow knit, Ralph nodded. "Yes, I—I think you're right. Whatever these people are up to, they—I mean—whether it's nonsense or not, they clearly believe in whatever it is they're doing. The powder, the pokeroot and the rest, no one goes to that much trouble for nothing, and if they've somehow managed to make you see things that weren't there, and to place nightmares in your head, then at least some of what they're doing actually works on some level."

"Black magic," Mina said.

"We're talking about herbs, plants, powders," Ralph insisted. "This is the work of narcotics, not magic. Regardless, it's obviously dangerous. These people are loons."

"We've both had a lot to drink. I'm not sure I can drive, can you?"

"Oh, believe me. I'm suddenly sober as a judge."

"Then let's get in your car and go."

Ralph seemed to think about that longer than was warranted, but Mina knew he was struggling to make sense of things he couldn't resolve in his own mind. "We've still got a lot to figure out," he said. "But you're right, there's no reason to stick around at this point. And if it turns out we're wrong, then you can—"

"We're not wrong."

Beneath the harsh fluorescent lights, Ralph looked deathly pale. "Pack your things," he said gravely. "You're not staying here another moment."

With a quick nod, Mina hurried to the bedroom.

* * * *

Mina opened the door. Rather than step into the hallway, she hesitated and watched the shadowy stairs and darkness below. The building was quiet.

Outside, the winds had calmed. Everything was still.

"What is it?" Ralph whispered from behind her.

"Jasmin lives downstairs," Mina explained, whispering her reply as well. "And Rita and Dave are on the ground floor. They can all hear me whenever I come and go."

"Just go down the stairs like you would any other time. Don't hurry, don't creep, just go as you normally would. That way, if they're listening for you it shouldn't sound unusual or set off any alarms."

Mina stared into the darkness below, her suitcase held by her side. How would she explain having it if Jasmin or the others came out of their apartments before she reached the car? Despite the silence, she pictured them all standing near their doors, listening and waiting for her.

"Honey," Ralph said, gently resting a hand on her shoulder. "It's all right, go."

Slowly, they made their way down the stairs. Mina never realized before just how creaky they were. It seemed like each step was a screech. Once they'd made it to the second floor, Mina hesitated again. The door to Jasmin's apartment remained closed, and no sounds came from within. Maybe she was asleep. Maybe she wasn't even home.

From their position on the second-floor landing, despite the darkness, they could now make out the small first-floor foyer and the front door to the building beyond.

They continued on. More stairs creaked, but they eventually reached the foyer without interruption. Mina glanced at the door to Rita and Dave's apartment, fully expecting one or both of them to open it at any second.

Ralph gave her a gentle nudge in the back. "Scoot," he whispered.

They slid out the front door, onto the steps, and into the cold night.

It was still bitterly cold, even colder than it had been earlier, their breath dancing around them in the night as they hurried across the sidewalk to Ralph's 2008 Toyota Corolla. Although it was an older model, he'd always taken good care of it, and the car looked much newer than it actually was. The red color shone brightly in the otherwise dark night.

Mina stopped, looked down the dark street. Something was wrong.

The streetlights were out, leaving them at the mercy of relatively sparse moonlight. *Strange*, she thought. *It's just after ten, why aren't the streetlights on? They were on when they got back from the bar, why would they be off now?*

Surely they couldn't all be out at the same time.

Ralph opened the driver's side door, the sound bringing her focus back to the car.

"Get in," he said, still whispering, and slid behind the wheel.

Mina hurried around the rear of the car, ignoring the surrounding shadows and darkness, and the empty, skeletal, black buildings that lined either side of the street and loomed over them like phantoms. As she opened the door and tossed her suitcase into the backseat, she looked once more at her building. It was so dark and lifeless it could've passed for being abandoned.

"Come on," Ralph said, his voice louder now. "Let's get this show on the road."

Mina hopped in and quietly closed the door behind her until it caught, then slid a seatbelt on and leaned her head back against the headrest. "Get me out of here, Ralph."

He started the car. It coughed and groaned, then stalled.

"Sonofabitch," Ralph muttered. "You have *got* to be kidding me."

"What's wrong?" Mina asked as any semblance of relief evaporated.

"Hold on, just—just give me a second here." Ralph tried again. This time the engine wouldn't even turn over. He stopped, pumped the gas, then tried a third time. A clicking noise echoed all around them, but the engine was refusing to turn over. "What's with all the clicking? The hell does that mean?"

"How the fuck should I know? I don't know anything about cars."

"Me either." Ralph shook his head then tried again. More clicking, but even that began to fade. "Maybe the battery's dead?"

"Are you serious with this shit?" Mina said, trying to contain her nerves.

"It's not my fault, I don't understand it either. It was running fine before, and the battery's only a couple years old." Ralph ran a hand over his face. "It's like something out of a goddamn movie. What is this, *Night of the Living Clichés?*"

"Would you still have lights if the battery was dead?" Mina asked, indicating the fully lit dashboard and the illuminated headlights.

Ralph shrugged. "I'm not sure."

"What do we do, look under the hood or something?"

"Look under the hood for *what?*"

"They did something to your car," Mina said, hands on either side of her head. "Jesus Christ, they did something to your fucking car!"

"We don't know that for sure. If we're right about *any* of this, wouldn't they want me to leave?"

"Not if I'm with you. They want to keep me here."

"But how could they possibly know you're with me?"

"I don't know, but they obviously do. Maurice probably told them."

"Okay, makes sense, but wouldn't they just assume I was leaving after my visit?"

"Maybe they heard us."

Ralph pinched the bridge of his nose, up high near his eyes. "This just gets better and better, doesn't it? I'm literally getting a headache."

"Maybe they've been listening in on me this whole time, heard everything I've said—*we've* said—and—"

"Let me try this damn thing again." He did. The results were the same. "I don't understand how it could've been running fine and now it's—"

"This is no coincidence, Ralph. *They* did this. They did something so the car wouldn't start and…" Mina fell to silence, staring past Ralph at the building, her mouth open and eyes wide.

Following her gaze, Ralph slowly looked over his left shoulder.

On the sidewalk, partially concealed in shadow and night, Rita, Dave, and Jasmin stood shoulder-to-shoulder watching the car.

* * * *

"Play it cool," Ralph said, lowering his window a couple inches.

As the trio stepped forward, Mina forced a smile and waved, leaning over Ralph so she'd be closer to the window. "Hey, you guys," she said in as innocent and natural a tone as she could muster. "It's me. We're having some car trouble."

"Mina?" Jasmin asked.

"Yes, I—this is Ralph, a friend of mine," she stammered. "He's here for a visit."

Dave moved closer and leaned forward, hands on his thighs. "Can't get the old girl started, huh?" Clad in sweatpants, sneakers, a sweatshirt, and a heavy jacket, he looked like he'd just rolled out of bed and thrown everything on hastily. "We heard the sputtering from inside, figured we'd come out and see what was up."

"It won't start," Mina said. "There's just a clicking noise."

"Want me to take a look?" Dave asked. "I'm not a mechanic or anything, but I know the basics."

Ralph smiled nervously. "I'd sincerely appreciate it."

"Dave McGrady," he said, attempting to get his hand through the narrow opening at the top of the window.

Ralph lowered it enough to accommodate his hand. "Nice to meet you, Dave," he said as they shook. "I'm Ralph."

"Got yourself all worked up there, Ralph." Dave chuckled. "Holy cow, your hand's shaking like a leaf."

"It's just so infuriating." Face flushed, Ralph took his hand back. "It was running fine a little while ago."

"Chill, we'll get it worked out one way or another." Dave straightened up then motioned behind him. "Oh. Yeah. This is my wife Rita and our friend Jasmin."

"Nice to meet you all," Ralph said. "I'm so sorry to have bothered you."

Rita, who was bundled up in a big fluffy coat, her arms hugging herself, smiled slightly. "No bother at all," she said smoothly.

"Yeah," Jasmin chimed in. "Just hope we can help."

"And by 'we' she means me." Dave's glazed and bloodshot eyes had never left Ralph. "Tell you what, chief, you go ahead and pop the hood and I'll take a quick look for you, see if I can spot anything."

"Thanks again," Ralph said, pulling the release.

As Dave sauntered around to the front of the car, Ralph glanced at Mina, who was still leaning across him. "What do you want me to do?" he whispered.

"Just stay put," she mumbled, and then to Rita and Jasmin said, "You guys must be freezing. You don't have to stand out here on our account."

Rita moved a bit closer to the car. "Don't be silly, Mina, we're fine."

"Okay, try it now!" Dave called from beneath the hood.

Ralph turned the key. Even the clicking had ceased.

"Turn it off," Dave instructed. "Give me a sec."

"Where were you headed at this hour?" Rita asked.

Thinking quickly, Mina answered, "I'm low on smokes."

"Awful habit," Rita said. "But there are worse things."

"Okay, try it again," Dave said suddenly.

Ralph did, but the car was dead.

The hood slammed closed. Dave quickly wiped his hands on his sweats then walked back around to the window. "It's most likely the starter, that'd be my guess, but I'm not sure, could be any number of things, really. Whatever it is, trust me, you two aren't going anywhere tonight. At least not in this crate—no offense—she's dead as a doornail. Do you have Triple A?"

"Not anymore," Ralph said. "I keep forgetting to renew the damn thing."

"You can give a call over to Cassidy's Garage in the morning," he said, casually leaning against the driver's side door. "Just Google the number, they're only a few blocks away. They can tow it over there or maybe even figure out what's going on here."

"I don't suppose they have twenty-four-hour service?"

"Nope, you'll have to wait until tomorrow. Think they open around seven."

This time it was Rita that leaned in closer to the window. "Why don't you come inside and get warm? We'll all have some tea and talk awhile."

Mina sat back, trying desperately to think of something to say.

"That's awfully kind of you, and it sounds lovely," Ralph said, rescuing her. "But I've had a *very* long day. Since it looks like I'll be spending the night after all, if you don't mind, I'd really like to get some rest."

Rita's dark eyes fell on him. "Just for a moment then," she said. "I have a wonderful tea that will help relax you so you can get a good night of sleep. Then you can handle your car troubles come morning."

"Come on," Jasmin said from the shadows behind her. "It'll be fun."

155

"Yes, it will," Rita said, turning and gliding back toward the front steps. "Let's get inside."

Ralph rolled up the window. "I suppose buses aren't running this late."

"No," Mina said quietly.

"Look on the Uber app on your phone," he said, removing the key before giving a quick wave to the others. "Do it quickly but discreetly. Are there any drivers nearby?"

Mina stalled getting out on her side, her phone held down in her lap as she quickly tapped the icon and brought the app to life. "There's no Uber service here."

"You mean right this minute?"

"At all," she said. "It's not available in Crow's Cry yet."

"Of course it isn't, how wonderful." Ralph turned the headlights off. "Then I guess it's *fucking* tea-time."

"Ralph—"

"Stay close," he said, opening his door. "It'll be all right."

Mina had no choice but to believe him, though she wished he hadn't opened that door. She wanted to stay in the car, and for Ralph to stay there with her. All night, if need be, because the last thing she wanted was to go with the others back into that building, where anything could happen. But it was too late for that. They were trapped, and Mina was certain her hosts had seen to it. She could tell from Dave's smirk that he knew she knew he was behind this nonsense with Ralph's car, and even Rita had a smug look of control and dominance that was not evident when Mina first met her at the shop. They were two or three steps ahead of her, had been since she first got there. And they were all well aware of it.

Now, Mina was too.

CHAPTER FIFTEEN

"We could run," Mina whispered, her eyes darting over the icy landscape.

"That seems a bit dramatic and premature at this point." Ralph sighed. "Besides, there's nowhere to go. Let's just play it cool and not take any unnecessary chances. I'd rather not do anything that might escalate the situation."

Begrudgingly, Mina agreed. "All right, just remember I wanted to run for it."

"Duly noted," he said quietly as Jasmin, Rita, and Dave hurried ahead, whispering to themselves as they went. "This ought to be interesting. These people are priceless."

Mina took Ralph's hand as they followed the others up the steps. She took a look up, wondering if it would be the last time she'd ever see the night sky. But something else caught her eye. "What the hell?"

The sculpture of a hideous gargoyle leered from the center of the rooftop. Freezing rainwater streamed down its head and onto the ledge at its clawed feet.

"I don't remember seeing that before," Mina said, gazing up at it. "Maybe we should just wait in the car until morning. Fuck them, and fuck Rita's tea."

"Keep it calm, love, and lower your voice." Ralph casually looked up. "Strange. The building isn't a Gothic structure, but there it is, a gargoyle sitting right on top. I hate those things, they've always weirded me out, but Europeans loved them back in the day. Sometimes they included them in architecture here too. Quite a few in Manhattan, lots of older buildings there are littered with them. You see them all over the city if you take the time to look."

"Who gives a shit? Now's not exactly the best time for a lesson in architecture."

"Well, excuse me, Polly Pleasant."

"Sorry, fearing for my life makes me irritable."

"I doubt they're planning a double homicide, Mina. It'll be all right."

Jasmin looked back and waved at them to hurry.

"Maybe all the monsters are revealing themselves now," Mina said softy. "Don't drink that tea or eat anything they offer."

"No worries, doll, I'm with you. Stay close and don't get your panties in a knot."

"I'm not wearing panties."

"You slut, I love it. Me either."

They made their way behind the others as the front door creaked open and they shuffled through the foyer to the apartment. Mina eyed the stairs, and for a second envisioned herself breaking free and darting up to the third floor.

Rita opened her apartment door, and after Jasmin and Dave had entered, she turned and motioned for Mina and Ralph to join them. "Please, come in."

Mina and Ralph stepped inside and directly into a short hallway, both walls covered in black velvet fabric. They hesitated, and Rita slipped by them, her clothing rustling and her jewelry clicking as she went.

"I thought Halloween was in October," Ralph whispered.

The hallway emptied into a large front room, the entryway lined with black vases filled with white lilies. Framed photographs of old graveyards lined the walls, and a tall wooden coatrack stood in the corner.

Continuing on, they were ushered through a kitchen where jars of herbs filled the counters and miniature broomsticks adorned the walls. Finally they reached a living room full of bookcases, one wall lined with a series of strange silver-framed photographs.

Mina scanned the black-and-white images. They were all photographs of celebrities from an earlier era. Had the old Hollywood stars stayed in Crow's Cry at one time or another, or had these photographs been taken in private rooms, backstage in theaters, or out-of-the-way cafés? Whatever the answer, they were rare poses, photos she'd never seen before in old movie magazines or news clips. Marilyn Monroe in a dark cape...Clark Gable posed beside a casket covered with roses...Lucille Ball holding a black cat, a silver pentagram hanging from his collar and catching the light...Errol Flynn in a red suit sitting on a throne that looked to be constructed entirely of bone...Sammy Davis Jr. adorned in jewelry and holding a gold bejeweled chalice...Veronica Lake in a long white gown standing next to a bubbling black cauldron...

They all had a vacant look in their eyes, even the cat.

"Aren't those photos something?" Dave said suddenly. "The photographer was named Randolph Livinsky. He lived here back in the

1950s, but traveled to Hollywood and New York a lot. That's where these were taken."

"And here I thought they were photo-shopped," Ralph quipped, smiling broadly.

"It's actually a very rare collection. Most have never been seen publicly."

"Oh, how fun," Ralph said, looking around without subtlety. "I love your place. Who does your interior design, Vlad the Impaler?"

Dave smiled, but didn't look amused. "Quite the sense of humor you got there."

"Let's make ourselves comfortable," Rita said, gracefully lowering herself into a faded red velvet chair. She waved her hand. Bracelets jingled. "Please, sit."

Mina sat across from her on a small loveseat. Above it hung a Gothic cross and a painting of a woman with such white skin she appeared to be made of porcelain, black holes where her eyes had once been and her mouth wrenched open in a silent scream. Mina glanced at the black candles burning in skull-shaped holders on the coffee table before her, feeling lightheaded once again. Rather than make eye contact with Rita, she let her eyes wander around the room. All the furniture was old and elegant, and heavy, blood-red velvet drapes hung on the opposite wall, drawn shut to conceal glass sliders that led to the courtyard beyond.

"I'll get the tea," Jasmin said happily. "Rita already has some brewed, and she baked some amazing cinnamon rolls. They'll blow your mind!"

With that, Jasmin kicked off her platform shoes and skipped away to the kitchen, the edges of her bell-bottom jeans scraping the floor.

"We're fine, really," Mina said, too late. Her voice was strained, she looked like hell, and she needed sleep. The last thing she planned to do was consume anything Rita had prepared. "But thank you."

"Maybe just some tea," Rita said. "It'll help relax you."

"If I get any more relaxed I'll be asleep."

"Yes, we had a *huge* meal not long ago, and I think we've had our fill to drink," Ralph said, smiling politely before sitting next to Mina on the loveseat. "But by all means, you kids go right ahead and knock yourselves out."

"Come on," Dave said, hovering near Rita's chair. "My wife's tea and pastries are the best, you can make some room."

Rita gave Dave's arm a gentle pat as her eyes found Ralph. "Let me ask you a question." She paused a moment, seemingly lost in thought as she twisted a large ruby ring on her right index finger. "Was this a planned visit?"

"Not exactly," Ralph said. "I'd planned on visiting, just not this soon. But you've all made such an impression on Mina I just *had* to come for a quick visit a little ahead of schedule."

"So it was more a last minute kind of thing then?"

Ralph smiled knowingly. "Of course, I *did* mention to a couple friends that I was coming to see Mina. You know, so they wouldn't worry about where I'd gone. Tell me, Rita, why do you ask?"

Rita watched him, smiling but not answering.

Suddenly the uneasy silence was interrupted by the sound of silverware crashing to the floor in the kitchen.

"That can't be good." Dave chuckled. "Jasmin's a sweet kid but she's klutzy."

Rita calmly waved him away as if shooing a fly. "Go check on her, dear, would you? See if you can lend a hand."

"Sure thing," Dave said, hurrying off to the kitchen.

Once he'd gone, Rita returned her attention to Ralph. "Do you have family back in Providence? Any good friends, or would you say they're really more acquaintances?"

This time it was Ralph who watched her without answering.

"I hope you don't find my questions inappropriate or intrusive," Rita finally said.

"Honestly, Rita, I do find it a rather odd line of questioning." Ralph smiled sweetly. "But I'm happy to say Mina's my best friend. She always has my back and I always have hers. *Always.* That's really all that matters, wouldn't you agree?"

"Absolutely, it's good to have friends. All of us here at the collective, we've always stuck together. We're very particular about who we let into our little circle. We have to be."

Before Ralph could respond, Jasmin scurried into the room carrying a large silver tray, on top of which were five teacups and saucers, a silver teapot, an array of spoons, a bowl of sugar cubes, and a small container of milk. Dave followed behind her carrying a plate of cinnamon rolls and some napkins.

"Go ahead and help yourselves," Jasmin said, hands trembling and causing the tray's contents to rattle and clang. For a moment it looked as though she might drop everything, but she managed to steady herself then set the tray down on the coffee table. She gave an awkward, nervous smile. "I think I had too much wine tonight."

"It happens," Ralph said.

She giggled, raised her hands, then waved them toward her face and took a deep breath. "Oh, far out, doesn't it all smell so groovy?"

Mina caught a scent of lilac, cinnamon, and something else—musty and unappetizing—wafting about. "It does," she said. "But we're good for now."

"So have you painted anything new, Mina?" Dave asked, scooping up a cinnamon roll and popping the entire thing into his mouth. "I heard you were working on a couple new pieces. How's that going?"

Where'd you hear that, Dave? Mina thought.

"Yeah," she said. "It's going well."

"Cool." Dave chewed noisily.

"Yes, it is," Rita agreed, leaning forward to fix a cup of tea. "We have such high hopes for you, Mina. We want you to be prolific while you're here, but to produce work at the level we know you're capable of at the same time."

Mina smiled and nodded. "Thanks."

"What we *don't* want, are unnecessary distractions," Rita said, her gaze still fixed on Ralph as she dropped a cube of sugar into her cup and gently stirred it with a spoon. "Or anything that might cause a shift in focus from the importance of your work."

"I needed a break," Mina told her. "If Ralph's a distraction, he's a welcome one."

Ralph crossed his legs and sat back. "As I said, I just came here to check things out and spend some time with my best friend, who I've missed terribly. I certainly hope I haven't broken any of your rules or regulations by doing so."

"Of course not," Rita said, sipping her tea. "We all need a break now and then."

Jasmin quickly made a cup of tea and held it out for Ralph. He waved a finger and shook his head no. "Not right now, thanks."

With a frown, Jasmin set it aside.

"So, Ralph, will you be leaving once your car is fixed?" Rita asked.

"Now, Rita, my glorious new friend, you're not trying to get rid of me, are you?"

"Of course not, Ralph, why would you think such a thing?"

"Because that's what it sounds like you're trying to do." He grinned defiantly. "And it's absolutely *crushing* my feelings."

"Oh, you're not so easily damaged, Ralph, I can tell. In fact, you're tough as nails." Rita returned his grin with one of her own. "That said, I certainly don't mean to be rude or in any way imply it's my desire to push you away. I'm simply concerned."

"And why is that?" Ralph asked. "Do tell."

"What Rita's trying to say is that Mina was chosen for a specific reason," Dave said. "And we want everything to go good for her. For her and for us too, get it?"

"Dave," Ralph said, placing a hand against his heart. "With that astonishing level of eloquence, how could I not?"

Rita sipped more tea. "We certainly hope you'll attend Mina's show at the end of her residency though. You must come back for that, Ralph."

"I wouldn't miss it for the world."

"It's so groovy you're there for Mina," Jasmin said, nibbling a cinnamon roll.

"Isn't it though? I'd do anything for her." Ralph's eyes never left Rita. "I'd protect her at all costs, and I'm always there to make sure nothing happens to her."

Dave frowned, hands on his hips. "What do you mean by that?"

"What do you imagine I mean, Dave?"

Mina, who had been reeling, forced herself back into the conversation. "I wanted to ask you guys something," she said before Ralph's duel with Rita and Dave could continue. "I was wondering about the artist that was here before me, Robert Sanders. He's gone missing, it's so strange."

"He was a brilliant painter," Dave said. "But the dude had issues."

Jasmin giggled again. "We all do."

"Speak for yourself, space cadet."

"Apparently he suffered from rather severe anxiety," Rita explained. "He'd been diagnosed bipolar, I believe. He'd paint for days, wouldn't eat, barely even took fluids, and he refused to see any of us while he was in that state. I finally insisted he try some of my herbal teas, just to calm him down and help with his anxiety issues. They worked, but he was just so tortured it was only a matter of time before he went down that dark hole again. In the end, I think Bobby just wanted to disappear from the world. He was such a lovely, sensitive soul—too sensitive for this life sometimes—and I think it was all just too painful for him."

"You talk about him as if he were dead," Mina said.

Rita thought about that a moment. "Perhaps in a way he is."

"Someone's either dead or they're not."

"*Parts* of us die all the time. And who should know that better than you, Mina?"

Stunned, Mina froze, unsure of how to answer that. Rita wasn't wrong, but she said it in a way that was so familiar. Too familiar for someone she barely knew, and who barely knew her.

"But we won't have to worry about you," Rita added quickly. "I can tell. You'll do fine. Now, won't you two have some tea? It's such a shame to waste it."

"I'm sorry," Mina said. "I don't drink tea, never been a fan."

Dave cracked his knuckles. "I don't like tea either, but Rita's is good, not like your run-of-the-mill garbage out there."

Everyone remained silent for a while. Jasmin sat on the floor next to Rita's chair with a cup of tea and another cinnamon roll.

Mina looked over at the bookcases laden with old, leather-bound tomes. In the distance, she could've sworn she heard the ocean, and soft classical music playing from another room.

"So you tend to keep to yourselves here, even with your residents," Ralph said. "Is that it?"

"We do," Rita said.

Dave puffed his chest up. "There something wrong with that?"

"Not at all, *Big Dave*! Just asking, hope I'm not being—what was it you said, Rita?—*inappropriate or intrusive?*"

"We believe in many things here others do not." Rita spoke slowly, evenly. "So we must take care, at times, to not only preserve our ways, but to protect ourselves and our residents from those who might *misunderstand* us."

"That's cool," Ralph said. "It's all good. Everyone has their own beliefs. Live and let live, I say. We all need some sort of faith to get by."

"It's about survival," Dave said irritably. "Nothing to do with faith."

"It also has nothing to do with Bobby Sanders and his disappearance," Mina said, ignoring Ralph when he subtly elbowed her.

"Remember that dude that blew through here after Bobby left?" Jasmin chimed in dreamily, flipping her hair over her shoulder. "He was like a cop or a private eye or whatever you call them."

Mina saw a small tattoo of a skull on Jasmin's neck she hadn't noticed before.

"He said a guy fitting Bobby's description kept showing up in gay clubs on Cape Cod and in Boston. Said he was zoned out on drugs, scaring people and acting crazy. He even said he hurt a guy in New Bedford, I think it was. Supposedly goes by Bobby but never uses a last name."

"Yeah, it's probably him," Dave said.

"Interesting, I still go to a lot of clubs in those areas, insane party animal that I am, and move in some of those same circles. Hell, I even hang out with happily married couples throwing barbeques and birthday pool parties for their kids, the types that have good jobs and pay their taxes and mortgages and mow their lawns and join the PTA and everything. Hate to disappoint, but believe it or not, we're not all sex-crazed, drug-fueled, nightclub maniacs. Okay, I am, but I'm a terrible example. Point is, I've never once heard these stories about this mysterious but clearly unforgettable and deranged Bobby person sans a last name."

Dave waved a hand in dismissal then folded his arms across his chest. "You can't know everybody, Ralph."

"Maybe they're just rumors," Jasmin offered in her trippy voice. "Or urban legends, those are so cool! Sometimes I think Elvis isn't really dead and John Lennon's still living at the Dakota and—"

"Jazz," Rita said softly, silencing her before taking another sip of tea.

"Sorry," she said, bowing her head like a scolded child. "I know sometimes I come off like I'm high on shrooms but—"

"Oh, Jasmin," Ralph said with an exaggerated frown. "Only sometimes, honey?"

Jasmin looked at him, her big eyes blinking innocently.

"Mina, I think you're quite *sensitive* yourself," Rita said. "I can feel it. We all felt it the first time we met you. You could say we even knew it before you came here. You have dreams and visions, don't you? You sometimes dream of the dead coming and talking to you."

Mina nodded.

"But you don't believe in magic, do you? Not *real* magic...*dark* magic."

"I'm not sure," she answered softly.

"Sure you are," Jasmin said, smiling up at her from the floor.

Rita placed her tea back on the coffee table. "We believe the universe is filled with magic, and that it exists in this world, but also beyond it. Bobby disappeared. Maybe he's the mysterious Bobby without a last name, maybe he isn't. Who knows? Either way, maybe, just maybe, he's *exactly* where he's supposed to be."

"Meaning what?" Mina asked. "What's his disappearance got to do with magic or dreams or visions—with any of that—are you saying he had these experiences too?"

Behind the red drapes, rain sprayed and drummed against the glass sliders.

"Let me explain something to you two," Dave said, arms still crossed over his chest. "People that are into the black arts conduct their ceremonies carefully and with purpose, okay? They can't be as unorganized in their beliefs as the paintings Bobby made while he was here. Real magic and real ceremonies exist, and some of them can be dangerous and deadly, so you've got to be careful about how you go about it, see? Klaus could tell you about them. He's seen it all."

"What about you, Dave?" Mina asked, though she was certain she already knew the answer. "Are you one of those people? Could you tell us about it too?"

Dave's silence, along with the triumphant look on his face, was unsettling.

"Maybe Bobby was involved in that kind of thing," Ralph said. "Could be he had a whole other life."

"You mean black magic, Ralph?"

"That's what we're talking about, isn't it?"

"Anything's possible," Rita answered for him. She crossed her legs, and a hint of lace stocking and high-heeled boots poked through her long black velvet skirt, a silver anklet of tiny daggers glittering in the candlelight. "Maybe his allegiance is to Satan."

"How 1980s," Ralph scoffed.

Rita smiled slightly. "Of course, we don't know that. We don't even know where he is. Maybe he came back here and is hiding in one of the many deserted buildings in Crow's Cry."

"Maybe he's dead," Mina said, staring right at her.

"It's certainly a possibility, but I don't feel death around him. Not *exactly…*"

A black cat crept into the room. The same cat from Rita's shop, it flicked its tail then crawled onto Jasmin's lap. Green eyes reflected candlelight, the flames dancing.

"Well, hello there," Ralph said. "And who is this magnificent creature?"

The cat looked at him, growled then hissed.

"Oh." Ralph raised his hands like the victim of a robbery. "All right then."

"Shame on you, kitty," Jasmin said as she lovingly stroked the cat's fur.

Without looking at him, Rita said, "Now, now, be nice to our guests, Gemini."

The cat gazed up at Rita then snuggled deeper in Jasmin's lap and began to purr.

"Forgive him," Rita said. "Gemini can be rather *restless* at times."

"*Restless.* I'd have gone with *psychotic*, but sure." Ralph cleared his throat. "And on that note, I think we'd better call it an evening, folks. Mina and I are tired and we'd like to crash until it's time to get my car to the mechanic in the morning. It's been quite interesting, but—"

"Running along so soon?" Rita asked sweetly.

"Yeah, Ralph's right." Mina wanted to stand but was waiting for Ralph to get up first. "We really should get going."

Dave chuckled as if Mina had said something amusing. It sent a shiver through her.

"Rest is vitally important." Rita slowly rose from her chair. "Just one more thing before we let you go."

At that moment, Rita seemed larger than life to Mina, looming over her and Ralph like some ancient goddess. Smells of herbs, both sweet and musty, filled the air.

Ralph uncrossed his legs and sat forward, hands in his lap. "What is it?"

"This." Rita opened her hand and blew on her open palm.

White powder exploded all around them, surging directly into their faces.

Mina heard Ralph gasp, but she was already blinded by the substance, and as she tried to stand, the powder filled her nostrils, eyes, and mouth, burning all three.

Her vision returned, blurred, but the room was tilting and moving and she was certain she'd fall over. From the corner of her eye she saw Ralph slump, slide from the loveseat, and crash face-first to the floor.

Gemini screeched and bolted, a blur of fur and green eyes slashing past.

The candlelight cast soft shadows across Rita's devilishly smiling face. And then Dave and Jasmin were by her side, Jasmin blabbering about how everything would be all right and for Mina to not be afraid.

Mina swung with a clenched fist but came nowhere near them, her body twisting and her knees buckling as the room continued to spin.

From behind Dave's shoulder, through her blurred vision, Mina saw other forms entering the room. Maurice peeked at her, smiling proudly, and there were others, some standing in the corners, others crawling toward her across the floor.

Klaus stepped from behind the red drapes, watching her quietly, emotionlessly.

"What are you doing to me?" Mina screamed, or thought she had, but it came out as a slurred and garbled choking sound that died in the base of her throat.

She tried to run, but fell to the floor in a heap.

Everything went dark.

"All our years of waiting," Rita said in a voice ethereal and musical, like magical chimes disturbed by dark winds. "The offerings, beginning with the first, and now the last, have all led us here, to this. We're so close."

At the very edges of her consciousness, Mina heard Klaus speaking in a weak, labored voice.

"Soon we'll be whole again, my children... *Whole again...*"

CHAPTER SIXTEEN

As the boat rose and fell, jerking about and crashing through walls of violent, enormous waves, the storm raged and lightning split the night sky in a brilliant flash.

Catapulted forward, Mina found herself crashing onto the slick deck. Huge sprays of water exploded from the churning sea, showering down and drenching her with tremendous force. Mina struggled to get back to her feet, but wave after wave slammed the boat, rocking it so fiercely she was hurled across the deck in midair. Smashing into the side of the boat and nearly flipping overboard, Mina managed to grab hold of the railing at the last second.

Hanging on as best she could, she sensed something above her.

Through the darkness Mina saw the grim-faced ferryman from her nightmares. Strapped to the mast with lengths of rope and chain, the long stringy hair framing his ghoulish face flailed about in the heavy winds like snakes, his ivory, all-white eyes bulging with rage and leaking blood that stained his stubble-covered cheeks. His rain slicker and clothes were tattered, his boots gone, and his bare feet, bloody and gnarled, dangled several feet above the deck.

"Who are you?" Mina screamed.

He shrieked at her like a wounded animal, struggled to free himself, and glared at her as if he wanted nothing more than to rip her to pieces.

Unsure of how long the chains and rope would hold him, Mina looked around for somewhere to hide, but with the darkness and constant assault of heavy rain and spray from the ocean, visibility was a challenge.

After a moment, still clutching the railing with all her strength, she was able to make out a small door perhaps twenty feet away. Mina knew if she didn't get to it soon she wouldn't survive. Eventually either the madman strapped to the mast would escape, or the violent motion of the boat and strength of the storm would throw her overboard.

Mina didn't want to let go of the railing, but she had no choice. With the storm pummeling her, she released her grip and vaulted to her feet in a single motion. As she did so, the boat broke over a wave and tilted severely before righting itself.

Feet slipping out from under her, Mina fell flat on her back, landing hard and knocking the wind from her. As she slid across the deck gasping for breath, she saw the ferryman above her, still bound to the mast, growling and thrashing about violently. Twisting her body, she struggled up onto all-fours, pushed hair and rain from her eyes, and found the door through the storm. She was closer now, only a few feet away, but it was only a matter of time before the boat shifted again and sent her sliding away in the opposite direction.

Rather than trying to stand again, Mina crawled until she reached the door. Above her, the dark sky blinked with more lightning strikes, the rain falling so hard it hurt on contact. Her stomach clenched and she thought for a moment she might vomit, but she pushed the nausea away and lunged for the lever on the door.

Grabbing hold of it, she yanked down. The door popped open, but the heavy wind nearly tore it from her grasp, so Mina threw her shoulder against the frame to block the door from closing. Seconds later it slipped from her grip anyway, and the door slammed into her once, and then again. The second time, it hit her in the mouth, splitting her bottom lip, and she immediately tasted blood. When the door swung at her the third time, Mina blocked it with her forearm, then threw herself through the doorway and fell below deck.

She landed hard on her side. The sounds of the storm were still deafening, and in the thick darkness surrounding her, Mina remained disoriented, but she was getting her breath back. With shaking hands, she wiped her eyes then looked around. It was dry here, and protected from the wind, but she couldn't see more than an inch or so in any direction.

Still being bounced around, Mina steadied herself against the side of the hull as best she could. "Ralph? Are you down here?"

Even before she heard the voices murmuring through the pitch-black, Mina knew she wasn't alone. Like a prayer awakened and recited by monotone voices coming at her in the dark, it grew louder and louder.

Ralph, what have they done to you? Where are you?

With vague memories of Rita's apartment filling her head, Mina prepared herself for a fight. Sore and exhausted, her shoulder throbbed from when the door slammed it, and her bottom lip was still bleeding into her mouth, but she was determined none of that was going to stop her.

The horrible chanting continued.

Latin… They're praying in Latin…

As the boat rocked and creaked, groaning against the storm's onslaught, something moved near Mina's feet. She pulled them away, bringing her knees to her chest. "Get away from me!"

Something like cold wet fingers brushed the side of her face.

Mina recoiled, peering into the darkness and frantically trying to see. They were all around her now, closer than before, their chants no longer murmurs but screams. Prayers—or whatever they were—screeched as unseen hands grabbed, tugged, and clawed at her.

"Get the fuck off me!"

Mina began swinging and kicking wildly at the darkness. She didn't connect with anything, but those surrounding her retreated, and she no longer felt their touch.

"Stay away!"

Just then the boat rocked, shifted, and sent her tumbling through darkness right toward those hidden in the hull with her.

"No!"

Countless unseen hands pushed and pulled and scratched and pinned Mina down as excited bursts of hot breath pulsed against her face. She fought to free herself, but it was no use. There were too many of them. She couldn't move.

Hands closed over her eyes, her mouth, and her nose.

I can't breathe, I—

Even as she convulsed, hands clamped down harder still.

I can't breathe, I—I can't breathe!

The darkness became complete, and everything went eerily silent.

Time passed, but nothing seemed connected, as if Mina were free-floating in some dark and empty expanse of outer space. No stars, no light, no sound, no sense of up or down, left or right, only a vague awareness that she still existed in some manner.

Slowly, sound returned.

No more screams or chanting, just the wind. But not like before. Gentle now, and without the accompanying noise of the storm, it was more alluring than frightening.

Smell came to her next.

Mina no longer smelled the ocean or the odd musty stench of the hull. Instead, she inhaled the earthy aroma of grass and dirt and trees, the air fresh and warm.

And it was then that she knew where she was.

Her eyes blinked open.

Light…sunshine…a blue sky gliding overhead. Moving—it was moving—sliding over her. No. Wait. It wasn't moving. *She* was.

Mina felt pressure on her ankles and a scraping sensation along her back.

They're dragging me.

She tried to speak but it came out garbled and slurred. When she tried to move, she couldn't. She wasn't paralyzed—not really—she was just so weak she couldn't muster the energy to pull herself free.

They're dragging me across that field.

The bright sun beat down on her as they reached the top of the same hill from her dreams. The tall grass swayed back and forth, parting to reveal the squat oak tree with its thick leaves and forked, gnarled trunk.

They dragged Mina closer, from the grass to the dirt and stones, to the place where the bonfires were to be set. And the same woman on her knees that Mina had seen before, she was there too, kneeling in the same spot, hands bound before her and head bowed. Her sweatshirt and jeans were worn and spattered with various colors of paint, and as she came into clearer focus, Mina was able to make out her face.

As before, she had no eyes, only raw empty sockets, the lids sliced free. Two swaths of dark dried blood stained her sallow cheeks.

Whoever had been dragging her finally released Mina, and her legs flopped to the ground lifelessly. Again, she tried to move, but couldn't. All she could manage was lolling her head to one side or the other.

"He takes our eyes," the woman said. "So we can't find our way back."

"Who…are…you…?" Mina asked with tremendous effort, her voice weak.

The woman snapped her head in Mina's direction. "I didn't kill myself. I didn't drown. They're lying. I never left Crow's Cry. None of us do."

My God, Mina thought. *It's Audra Marini, the resident before Bobby.*

"We're all there," Audra said, bowing her head again. "All of us."

"Where?" Mina gasped.

"They're doing it to us one by one."

"Doing…what?"

"You're the last one." Audra's body began to buck, as if she were crying with eyes she no longer had. "If you don't stop them, you'll be here too."

"Where…is…*here?*"

"The other place," Audra said. "The still place…"

Suddenly a face appeared over Mina, hovering there and looking down at her angrily. "I told you she was awake. Nobody listens."

"*Frances*," Mina groaned.

"Quiet, you," Frances said, slowly raising a short black club. "We're weakening you, but you're not quite ready yet."

"What...are you...doing to me?"

"It's all a dream, Mina, time to put you back to sleep."

The club came crashing down, and Mina felt tremendous impact above her eyes, followed by a flash of bright white light and a brief moment of excruciating pain.

And then the darkness took her once again.

* * * *

Just minutes from Providence, in Warwick, Rhode Island, several police cruisers and an ambulance blocked a desolate side street, their roof lights flashing. Yellow police tape was strung around the area, and a red 2008 Toyota Corolla, the driver's side door still open, was parked diagonally in the middle of the street, a pair of long black skid marks behind it.

Two police officers, one a man, the other a woman, watched as their sergeant and supervisor arrived, stepped out of his vehicle, and approached them.

"What've we got?" the sergeant asked.

"A woman and her dog were out for an early morning walk," the male officer said, motioning to a woman standing on the far curb speaking with another officer on scene. "She came upon the vehicle, abandoned and still running in the middle of the street, the apparent driver lying unconscious over there."

The sergeant looked to where the officer indicated: a nearby vacant lot.

"From what we've been able to determine," the female officer said. "Looks like the driver sideswiped that telephone pole over there then skidded to a stop, where he then exited the vehicle. He made it as far as the lot and collapsed."

"Injuries?" the sergeant asked.

"Minor," she answered. "Some scrapes and bruises."

"But he reeks of alcohol, and he's definitely doped up," her partner added. "The paramedics were able to bring him around. He's either still high as a kite, crazy, or both. He's been babbling about all kinds of nutty stuff. Hard to understand though, sounds almost like he's had a stroke or something. Probably just the drugs; not sure what he's on, but whatever it is we're talking heavy duty grade."

The sergeant nodded. "ID?"

"Ralph C. Deckard," the male cop said, consulting his notes. "He resides in Providence, employed as a schoolteacher."

"Any warrants?"

"None."

"Priors?"

"Couple misdemeanor drugs charges and one DUI from decades ago, nothing recent." The cop shrugged. "Maybe he had a bad night."

"Or a damn good one, depending on which side of the fence you're on," the sergeant said with a chuckle. "Must've been one hell of a binge, huh?"

As they discussed charges, the female officer drifted away and over to the ambulance. The back door was open, and the medics were trying to calm their patient, who they'd secured and strapped to the gurney since she last saw him.

"He giving you a hard time?" she asked.

One of the paramedics looked up from his chart. "We strapped him for his own safety. He's upset, frightened, and more than a little confused."

"Officer," Ralph said, seeing her, his voice slurred and weak. His mind was working, but when he tried to speak it came out garbled. "Please...listen to...me."

"You're gonna be all right," she told him. "Just do what they tell you, they're here to help you, okay? You're lucky you weren't seriously injured and didn't hurt anyone else."

"I wasn't...driving." Ralph struggled to get the words out, but even speaking a few words was exhausting. Flashes of that powder exploding into his face blinked in his mind, Dave holding him steady while Maurice opened his mouth and emptied a bottle of whiskey down his throat, then poured another all over him.

"Was there someone else in the car with you, sir? Is that what you're saying?"

Ralph nodded. More flashes of being dumped in the backseat of his car while Dave drove. He'd struggled to stay awake or even sit up, but was unable to do either. "Yes," he gasped.

"Who was driving?"

"He was, I...I'm trying to tell you...I was...drugged."

"Who drugged you?"

"They...them...they did."

"By *they* do you mean this other person that was driving?"

Ralph struggled to keep her in focus, but his vision kept blurring. He remembered awakening to a loud scraping sound and the car fishtailing before it came to a screeching halt. "He...one of them, they...they've got...my friend...Mina...they..."

"How many people were in the car, Mr. Deckard?"

"Two." Ralph wanted to get up, he needed to get out of this damn ambulance and back to Crow's Cry. These idiots needed to listen to him. Why were they speaking to him as if he'd done something wrong?

"And what happened to this other man?"

Ralph remembered being carried out into the night and dumped on the ground. Vague memories of a second car came to him, Dave jumping in as it pulled away. "Left, he's...gone."

"How much did you have to drink, Mr. Deckard?"

"There was..." Ralph struggled to form the words. "Another car...he got in and...they...left me here, they...drugged me."

"What sort of drugs did you do?"

Ralph wanted to scream but he didn't have the strength. It was taking everything he had just to remain conscious. "Please...help...my friend...Crow..."

"Crow?"

"Crow's...they...they have her...my friend...Mina...they have her now, they...*witches*...they're all...*witches*...spells...powders...they...black magic, they..."

The paramedics looked at her in unison, as if to say, "See?"

"Witches, huh? Jesus, he's tripping balls. Better get a psych evaluation too."

What was that stupid bitch laughing at? Ralph wanted to strangle her. *Goddamn it, help me!*

"Okay, Mr. Deckard," the cop said. "Just try to relax. You'll be at the hospital in no time. Someone will follow up with you there."

"Don't—please—my friend...she's not...safe."

"Go ahead," the cop said, cocking her head. "Take him."

Mina, I'm sorry!

As the door closed and the ambulance pulled out, Ralph tried to get them to listen, but one of the paramedics clamped something down over his face and nose, and he soon drifted back into oblivion.

CHAPTER SEVENTEEN

Everything was strange, nothing seemed right. Lingering at the very edge of consciousness, Mina felt as if she'd turned into someone else, *something else*—lighter and weightless—like her spirit had been set free from the bondage of her body. Had they given her drugs? Or was it some sort of horrible spell they'd cast? As she slowly rose toward full awareness, again becoming cognizant of her physical self, she noticed her hands and feet were numb and that her body was stiff. In an attempt to alleviate the numbness, Mina clenched and unclenched her hands, then wiggled her toes, but both continued to tingle with pins and needles.

Mina opened her eyes. They were dry, her vision blurred, but very slowly, her surroundings came into better focus.

Where the hell am I?

The place reminded her of a funeral parlor, velvet and silk, smoky and cold like the dead; but the bedsheets were softer, more luxurious than the ones in her apartment, the mattress firmer, more comfortable. Still, every bone in her body ached, and the feeling that she wasn't really there, wasn't really anywhere, continued to plague her.

Am I dead?

Suddenly, she no longer felt alone. Elongated shadows drifted across the bed.

Am I dreaming—just—dreaming?

Slowly, Mina managed to sit up, squinting from a sharp pain pulsing in her left temple.

She took in the room: the bed she'd been sleeping in with its ornate headboard, dark wood, strange faces expertly sculpted within delicate carvings of ivy and oak tree branches. Heavy velvet drapes hung on massive cathedral windows, the top panes stained-glass, stunning, sensual Alphonse Mucha figures posing in fields of flowers, clear shining glass panes beneath them. Mina could hear the sounds of the ocean in the distance, but even it sounded odd, off somehow.

"The fuck's going on?" she said, her voice raspy and slurred.

A red candle burned on a dark nightstand by the bed. Along the edges of the nightstand, cherub faces and roses were carved into the wood. The flame flickered and smoke streamed from it, slowly spiraling toward the high ceiling before vanishing in the dark.

Across from her, a large oval mirror hung over a massive bureau with intricate carvings of the moon, the sun, and the signs of the zodiac etched into its mahogany trim. Mina noticed her reflection, but before she could focus it changed and she found herself looking at someone else.

A woman with black holes for eyes, her mouth torn open into a silent scream, blurred and transformed back into Mina's image.

Shivering, she gazed into her own sallow face, dark bags beneath her eyes and—

What the hell am I wearing?

A white clingy thing of delicate lace with red flowers embroidered around the neck and sleeves, it reminded her of something out of a vampire movie, one where the undead rose from coffins clad in Victorian glad rags.

She slid out of bed. A sudden wave of dizziness rocked her, and as she tried to stand, her legs gave out. Collapsing back onto the bed, Mina sat a moment and looked to the windows and the view of the Atlantic in its wintry fury. The sky looked as if an artist had painted it with long strokes of black, deep blue, and purple, stars twinkling, the moon full and round, shining above and illuminating the frantic sea.

After steadying herself, Mina tried to stand again, this time pushing herself up slowly while clutching the headboard. Once she was sure she could stand on her own and the dizziness had subsided, she took a step, but the bottom of the gown tangled around her ankles, nearly tripping her.

"Sonofabitch," she muttered, hiking it up. "Who dressed me in this shit? Where are my clothes? Fuck is Ralph?"

Carefully, she stepped across the floor, her bare feet cold but still tingling as she made her way to the windows. The beach below the cliffs was empty and dark, and a light snow she hadn't noticed before was falling over the shore.

And then the realization hit her.

I'm in the house, I—I'm in Klaus' house!

A memory drifted through her mind like smoke. Lenny's was the last face she'd seen before she blacked out, creeping toward her slowly with a wicked smile. After that, all was lost, gone like dreams forgotten, like words you want to remember but forget before you can write them down.

He and the others had obviously taken her here from Rita and Dave's apartment, but why?

Still moving awkwardly and with uncertainty, Mina managed to get to the bureau. She opened a few drawers in the hopes she might find her clothes, but instead only came across more red candles, incense sticks, a few lacy nightgowns, and old paperback tomes about magical herbs and candle spell magic, benign and mass market writings that people sold online or in so-called New Age shops. Despite the numbness in her hands, she delicately lifted each candle, book, and nightgown, searching for something—anything—that belonged to her, but there was nothing, no trace of her here.

And beneath all the paraphernalia were dusty remnants of white powder.

In a rush, the memories of the same powder in the kitchen cabinets and Rita blowing it in her face came back to her. Mina shuddered, remembering now how Ralph had tumbled to the floor next to her. She clutched the bureau, her heart pounding.

"Ralph," she whispered. "What did they do to us? Where are you?"

Carefully, Mina made her way to the door, and then, holding her breath, turned the knob until it made a soft clicking sound. Surprised but relieved to find it unlocked, with her legs trembling and head throbbing, she slowly pulled open the door.

What are you running from, Mina?

Creeping out of the smoky room and into a hallway where more elaborate furniture lined the walls and red candles burned in copper holders, smoke and ash spiraling in the dim light, Mina looked to the walls. They were lined with paintings of Victorian-era women hung on burgundy wallpaper, their soulless eyes seeming to follow her as she moved along the hallway. Balancing herself on tables and against curios where miniature portraits of men wearing old-fashioned clothing and women wearing the same lacy gown Mina had on, she came to one in particular covered in black velvet, and on which stones of many colors had been set. Next to them were several decks of Tarot cards and strange pendants of silver and wood covered in glyphs and mystical symbols.

Witches...

The pain in her temple moved to her forehead.

All of them...

She pressed her fingers to her head. "Stop it," she whispered. "Please, stop."

All of us...

Once the pain had subsided a bit, Mina continued on until she came to a staircase. Steadying herself against the banister, she looked down into darkness. All was quiet in the huge old house. All she could hear was the rage of distant ocean and the steady thudding of her heart.

Gingerly, she turned and peered down the remaining length of hallway.

At the far end of it, a door stood open, candlelight glimmering from within.

Mina wasn't sure what to do. She wanted to find a way out of this place, but she also needed to find Ralph. He was likely somewhere in this house, but where? And the others could be waiting for her anywhere, ready to pounce and jump out at her as she searched like ghouls from some demented funhouse.

She looked in both directions. Shadow, candlelight, darkness…

They might even be watching me right now.

"Fuck you," she muttered defiantly.

Hang on, Ralph, I'm coming. I'll find you.

With a newfound resolve, Mina threw back her shoulders and started toward the open door at the end of the hallway.

* * * *

Even before she crossed the threshold, Mina's heart sank. She could see there was no one in the room. As she wondered about Ralph's fate, hoping he was safe, she was greeted by the soft scent of lilac.

A vintage hand mirror, comb, and brush set, silver with lilies engraved on the metal, sat displayed on a gilded dresser against one wall. As she moved closer, Mina saw several bottles of perfume, along with hairpins decorated with gemstones. Silk scarves hung from a wall hook next to it, and within a nearby open closet hung numerous vintage dresses, coats, and shawls, all reminiscent of the 1960s and 70s. A velvet jacket made of patchwork designs of light blues and turquoise against a golden background lay across a chair in the corner, and the bed was similar to the one Mina had woken up in.

On the nightstand next to the bed were several envelopes, letters and cards addressed to Isa Riker, Klaus' wife. But if she was truly so deathly ill—bedridden, as Klaus and the others claimed—wouldn't she be here in what was obviously her bedroom?

If she could get up and move about the house then she wasn't bedridden after all, and if that were the case, why did she have a separate bedroom, apart from her husband? This room looked more like it had been set up in *anticipation* of her arrival, not a place she was currently residing in.

The bed was made and meticulously undisturbed. It looked as if no one had so much as sat on it in ages, much less slept in it or spent their sickly days and nights in it.

Mina's entire body began to tremble.

I need to get the fuck out of this house right now and find help.

On legs still rubbery, she turned and looked directly into the eyes of a beautiful woman.

Though startled, she quickly realized it was just a framed photograph—hung by the door—of the same breathtaking woman with long black hair and startling green eyes she'd seen in the portrait downstairs. In the photo she was wearing the patchwork jacket that now lie across the nearby chair. In one corner of the photograph, someone had written something in dark ink.

Mina moved closer so she could better make it out.

My sweet Klaus—I have loved you in this world with all my heart and will continue to do so in the still place. Until we're together again, my love forever—Isa

A vision of a woman with no eyes, only raw empty sockets, the lids sliced free, flashed through Mina's mind. Two swaths of dark dried blood stained her shallow cheeks.

"The other place... The still place..."

Another framed image next to the photograph caught Mina's eye, a painting of a gnarled oak tree at the end of a huge field of tall grass, stones arranged in a circle at its base. It was all there, just as it was in her dreams, and for a moment, Mina was sure she'd pass out.

Witches can fly, Mina...

She grabbed hold of the doorframe to steady herself, and as she looked to the hallway she realized all the candles had been extinguished there.

The hallway was now draped in total darkness.

"Who's there?" Her voice was stronger than before but still maddeningly weak.

Run, Mina...

She took a tentative step into the hallway. A chill coursed through her. It was colder than before, the temperature had dropped significantly.

Run...

"Hello, Mina," a chorus of voices cackled in unison.

Klaus, Rita, Dave, Jasmin, Maurice, Lenny, Frances, and the others all emerged from the darkness, their faces paler than she remembered and their eyes darker.

Mina screamed as the candlelight returned, the flames licking their hideously grinning faces, some of them perched on the furniture, others crawling up the staircase, all holding red candles and dressed in hooded black robes.

"It's almost time, my dear," Klaus said, his ghoulish scarred face looking disembodied, illuminated with candlelight in the otherwise dark hallway. "A shame, really, you have such *lovely* eyes."

Lenny stepped forward, a long knife in his left hand, a small copper bowl in his right. "It'll be okay," he said. "It really hurts, but it happens faster than you'd think."

"Do the bitch," Dave growled, filled with demonic glee. "Do her!"

Rita materialized from the darkness behind him and took his arm. She was chanting or praying—Mina couldn't be sure which—her voice too low to hear clearly, her eyes wide and wild.

"Come on, do her right now!" Dave said again, panting with excitement.

"No," Klaus said. "The ritual must be followed *precisely*, as it has been each time before. We must not deviate, even in her nightmares."

"Don't worry, Mina," Jasmin said, suddenly there too. "It's just a dream, you don't know where you really are yet, but you will soon and—"

"Shut up, Jasmin," Dave snapped.

"Stop it," Rita said. "There's no need to speak to her like that."

"You've got to split," Jasmin said. Her voice was closer now. "I'll miss you, Mina, honest I will. I wish we had more time, but it's the only way."

"Enough delays," Frances said, stepping forward. "Secure her."

Fear and rage erupted together in a tempest of violence and terror as Mina screamed again and lunged for them, swinging wildly. But she was still too weak, and as she lost her balance and her knees buckled, she collapsed to the cold floor amidst their terrible laughter.

Someone leaned down next to her in the darkness. "Almost time now," the voice said. "The still place waits."

CHAPTER EIGHTEEN

Light...

Mina blinked and tried to focus, but her vision was blurred. Above her, on the ceiling, a series of track lights shone down on her, making it even more difficult to see. She could feel their heat pulsing down on her from above, and as she tried to reach up and rub her eyes, she realized she couldn't move her arm. She tried the other but it wouldn't move either. Something was holding her down, something tight. Her legs wouldn't move either, and she couldn't sit up.

"Try not to struggle," a voice she recognized as Jasmin's whispered. "It just makes the binds tighter."

"My eyes, I—they're blurry," Mina said, her voice weak.

"We had to put something in them," Jasmin whispered. "It helps when they—I don't like to say it, I don't even like to think about it, but— you know."

Mina again tried to move, but all she could do was turn her head in one direction or the other. She did so, trying to focus and see as much as she could. She was on her back, arms straight out and legs together, on foot atop the other. Both her wrists and ankles were bound to whatever she was lying on, which as far as she could tell was some sort of huge canvas. She knew this position they'd placed her in.

It was one of mock crucifixion.

Jasmin began gently rubbing something on Mina's face.

"What is that?" Mina turned her cheek in an attempt to avoid Jasmin's touch, but it did no good. Whatever she was administering felt greasy, and she couldn't see anyone else, but there were other voices nearby quietly chanting.

"It's okay, it's just unguent."

"I don't—I don't know what that is, stop, I—"

"It's an ointment," Jasmin explained. "We're anointing you, Mina."

"Where am I?" Mina blinked rapidly, and her vision began to clear a bit.

"The gallery," Jasmin said, slowly running the unguent over Mina's chin.

"No, I've been to the gallery, this isn't—"

"You're upstairs, silly. You've never been up here before. No one comes here except for when it's time for—"

"That's enough," a gruff voice said. Frances. "Go join the others."

The lights above Mina dimmed, and the chanting grew louder.

A spotlight came to life on the wall before her, illuminating a single old painting there. Mina squinted, trying to bring it into better focus.

"Looks familiar, doesn't it?" Klaus asked, stepping forward. He looked so old and pale, the black robe and hood framing his already pale face making it even more white and ghoulish. "You've been there in your dreams, Mina. We've seen to it."

Mina strained to see more clearly, and though her vision still wasn't right, she was able to make out the field of tall grass, the gnarled tree, and a series of five people standing beneath it, before a circle of stones. Four of the people had black holes where their eyes should've been, blood stains running along their cheeks.

The fifth, a woman, was the only one with eyes.

"Do you recognize her, Mina?" Klaus asked as the others all formed a half circle behind him. "Look closely."

It was the beautiful woman from the portraits in his house. Isa, his wife, was the lone woman with eyes gazing out across the field as if waiting for something or someone to arrive. What in God's name was happening?

"Why are you doing this to me?" Mina said in a loud, desperate whisper.

"You're very special," Klaus said, leaning closer. "We chose you to set my love free. You will be the one, Mina, to take Isa's place."

"Please, whatever you're doing, I—"

"Shhh, my dear," Klaus said, bring an arthritically ravaged finger to his lips. "You don't understand right now, Mina, because you're so very frightened. But you're not only setting my beloved Isa free, we're going to set *you* free as well, just like the others before you. My faithful and longtime friend Frances was part of our original circle all those years ago. She was so young then, just a child in her twenties, and although fate separated us for some time, it also brought us back together when we found each other again. Once together, we began our search for what had been lost—a most special painting—and those that had been lost along with it. It took years, Mina, *years* to find, but I never gave up my search, and once the painting was returned to me I put into motion the plan to reunite those who had since joined us here in Crow's Cry with the others from our beloved clan, our *extraordinary* coven. We had to be so very patient, Mina, bringing about the process slowly, gradually, freeing our tribe one at a time. One each year, and being sure to grant our residency to the right artists, those who would not be missed, those with little or no family or friends—outcasts—those who could serve our purpose without drawing too much attention. And so, once the painting was back in our possession, Frances and I began our rituals of transference. This time, our goal was not to transcend our art and become *one* with it. Rather than perform the rituals necessary, rituals it took years to perfect, rituals that would place them *into* the painting, this time we did the opposite and set them free. But in order to free one soul, it must be replaced by another. So Steven Johnson, our first resident, set Maurice free. Our second resident, Jennifer Williams, set Rita free. Our third, Audra Marini, gave us our sweet Jasmin back. The fourth, Robert Sanders, set Dave free. And now you, Mina, you will set Isa free. Finally, my Isa will join us, and our family will be whole again. And you, Mina, like the others before you, will be free from the bonds of this world and the limitations of this life. You will be immortal, Mina. You will no longer simply be an artist. You will *become* art."

"In the still place," the others said in unison.

"Yes," Klaus hissed demonically. "In the still place…"

"You're insane!" Mina shrieked, struggling again to free herself. "God help me!"

"I am the only god here, child." Klaus gently stroked the side of her face with one hand then swept the other behind him to indicate those standing beneath the painting. "These are my disciples. And you, Mina, *you* are their sacrifice. The lamb led to slaughter for their god, the most noble of positions, for a part of you must die so that another may live. And the payment for your blood, for your martyrdom, is that the part of you that survives will live forever. *Forever*, Mina. Worshipped, revered, studied, discussed, displayed, and loved, as all great art should be."

"Fuck you!"

Klaus cringed. "There's no need for such vulgarities, my dear."

"Let me out of this!" Mina struggled again, but just as Jasmin said, the binds only grew tighter, painfully digging into her flesh. "Goddamn you, let me loose!"

"You know I can't do that, Mina. You represent the end to a lifetime of work and study, of worship, of ritual and sacrifice. If you'll just allow yourself to, you'll realize how deeply beautiful it truly is."

"You're crazy, you're all fucking insane!"

"I've been called that most of my life." Klaus smiled at her with what looked like actual fondness. "And why? Because I believed the connections between the artist and their art went far deeper than any of us imagined they might? Deeper than anyone believed they ever could? My dream, Mina, was one of *transcendence*, do you understand? To use magic not for evil, as many would suggest we do, but to take us to an entirely new level of consciousness. Art can alter reality, literally. It took decades to prove that, but we finally perfected the spells necessary to achieve transference. A miracle really, the idea that flesh and blood could become something inanimate without losing its own identity; *insane*, as you and many others have said over the years. It wasn't without pain, of course, but nothing of value ever is. In California, all those years ago, free from the scrutiny we'd been under in Germany, we flourished, and eventually made real what until then had been nothing more than theory. Mistakes were made. A wonderful young woman who'd joined our coven was killed when a fire accidentally broke out during one of our rituals. As made evident by my scars, I was badly burned. I fell into a coma for several months. Our compound was destroyed, but a few things survived, including a very special painting. It, like most of my other possessions that survived, was lost while I wasted away in the hospital. It changed hands numerous times—none of them knew what they had—and it wound up in various stores and flea markets and thrift shops until it finally came to rest in one particular little antique shop in Manhattan. That's where it was—where *they* were—when I finally found it. And I knew then, Frances and I could begin the process to bring them all back. What I've achieved here will one day be studied and marveled over as it rightfully should be, but by then I'll be on to the next plain of existence, as will some of the others. None of that matters, Mina, because we're all immortal in one way or another. The only thing that changes is the venue. Death is a lie. Now, I know you're frightened, but try to clear your mind and realize you're part of something so much bigger than any of us. You're about to not only experience a miracle, you're about to become one."

"Klaus," Mina said in a voice that had again grown weak, the restraints digging horribly into her wrists and ankles. "Please, let me out of this. I—"

"People fear what they don't understand, and what they choose not to believe. They speak of *reality* and criticize *magical thinking*, when they have no idea how ridiculous they sound, themselves existing in a world that consists almost entirely of magic and living in bodies and minds they have virtually no understanding of, certainly not in terms of capabilities. And why, because some asinine academics wasting away in dusty old rooms somewhere, people who have never actually accomplished anything themselves, swimming in antiquated theories they think they discovered themselves, say so? In fact, these things were given to them by the old world, the world of magic, as a means of survival. But it wasn't *their* survival magic was interested in sustaining, Mina, it was our own. The world of magic has never gone anywhere. It exists right alongside our so-called real one, giving those fools their toys to play with, to keep them occupied. Our world existed long before anything else, and will be here long after all else is gone. Those of us in the shadows laugh at the dupes wandering through their lives out there in the so-called *real world*, thinking they know everything. In fact, they know almost nothing. But it's just as well. Let them play with their phones, listen to their soulless alleged music, watch their reality television programs and asinine movies. Let them drive their fancy cars and wear their designer clothes. Let them worship at their petty altars of lies and deception. Let them wage their wars and destroy themselves with hate and ignorance while we *create*. We know the truth because we've lived it, Mina, we've made it so. We've bled for it. And in doing so, we've come not to fear magic, but to live in wonder and awe of what it makes possible. Now, so will you."

Klaus slowly backed away as Lenny stepped forward, the same copper bowl and large knife clutched in his hands.

"It'll be okay," he said softly. "Try not to think about it, Mina, and I promise it'll be over before you know it."

"Don't do it," Mina said through gritted teeth, her fear turning to rage. "Stop, Lenny. Think. Look what you're about to do to me. You don't want to do this."

Lenny smiled, crouched next to her, and slowly ran the side of the blade along her flushed cheek as the others began to chant. "It only hurts for a little while."

"I'm going to fucking kill every last one of you," Mina said, spitting at him.

"I told you she'd fight right until the end," Frances said from somewhere nearby.

"Yes, and good for her," Mina heard Klaus say. "But even with all the fight left in her, she's been sufficiently weakened. You'll see."

Lenny licked his lips as he slid the blade just below Mina's left eye. "Try to stay still now," he said, breathing heavily. "It makes it easier, less messy."

Screams of rage and terror twisted into begging for mercy, and finally wails of disbelief and agony, while the others chanted, closing the circle in tighter around the canvas, their heads bowed and concealed beneath the black hoods.

And then, through the pain and terror, the world went dark and quiet.

Still. So very horribly *still*.

CHAPTER NINETEEN

The smell of candle wax, herbs, and burning incense permeated the area. Numb, shivering, and frightened beyond comprehension, her body slick with oil, the last thing Mina was able to see was ashes flitting around her in the air like black snowflakes.

"This was meant to be," Klaus whispered. "All of it, from the very moment of your birth. Stars aligned then, a Saturn and Pluto placement in your ninth Astrological house. You'll never know death, Mina, only eternal life."

She could no longer see her tormentors but could hear the sound of them, their voices, their chants, their frenzied breathing. Had her blood sprayed onto their robes, across their hand and faces? "Damn you all to hell," she muttered, her voice so weak she couldn't be sure they'd even heard her.

"Let it all go now," Lenny told her, his grip on Mina's hand loosening, slipping away as she tumbled deeper into the dark.

Moments before, he'd hovered over her, speaking softly, telling her to remain calm, that a new life awaited her. She cried out when the knife point touched her flesh, wailed when she felt blood tricking down her face. Pain assaulted her, sharp, agonizing, before shock took over, and then Lenny told her, "We want you to know all the colors—every brushstroke—they'll all live in that soul of yours. And you, Mina, you will live *within* the canvas. You'll become a part of it, and it a part of you. Forever."

"The still place awaits you," Klaus said. "Go, dear girl. Go to a world where you'll be a queen, just as you've always longed to be."

Mina rose up, floating into what seemed like night, but she couldn't be sure. Time had stopped. Or had it begun again? Like a phantom, she felt her body—her soul—push through the ceiling. She thought she could see, but all the sights, the images, were playing out in her mind. Or were they? Dizziness filled her, pain seared through her, and the sound of hideous laughter erupted below her.

"We've done it!" someone said. Rita?

And in that moment Mina swore she saw her tormenters, the paintings lining white gallery walls, Crow's Cry in all its starkness, the cold sea, the crumbling buildings, a lone girl walking on cracked pavement. Her name was Tiffany...the girl from the market...so small and seemingly insignificant in the vast world unfolding beneath Mina, within her mind.

Other streets, buildings, and cities loomed below, filled with people who would never know this madness or the dark magic that plagued Crow's Cry.

"Ralph!" she cried. "Ralph, where are you?"

No answer came, only the hum of the universe as it stretched out beneath her, around her, above her...*within* her...all of it inside and moving through her as if it had been injected directly into her veins.

That's it. That's how the magic works.

It was all part of her now, paint seeping into canvas, becoming one with her, every image inside her mind—the mind of a painter—conjured by deep and evil black magic.

Mina had the sensation of rising higher, up toward a blue and purple horizon. Exotic birds flew beside her, pecking softly at her cheeks, plucking strands of her hair into their delicate beaks. And all the while, below, like a chaotic song, the coven cried out, their shrieking prayers distant echoes now.

"*Our sacrifice...our imperfect piece of living art...live beyond the confines of Earth...*"

She floated into a moon of impasto yellows and reds, over renderings of cobalt blue mountains, above ancient priestesses dancing around smoldering cauldrons, flames dripping red and yellow. The paint on white robes turning them black as they fluttered in the wind, bony hands clasped in wicked prayer.

Their watery eyes, not quite human, looked to her.

"*Go, Mina, the still place awaits you.*"

Another voice echoed in the blackness, a woman with dark eyes studying her, a pair of sheers in hand, a cigarette dangling from her lips.

Mary Howard, Mina thought, drifting weightlessly.

The last foster mother Mina had, she'd gone to live with her at the age of eleven and stayed with her until she struck out on her own. A plump woman with a teased beehive hairdo who'd encouraged Mina's art and bought her paints and small inexpensive canvases, she was the first person to ever show any interest in Mina's potential as an artist. When

Mina painted crude images of Mickey and Minnie Mouse, Mary told her how much she loved the renderings, and even hung them on the wall in the tiny hair salon she owned in her converted garage. "Put little labels with prices on them, sweetheart," she told her. "I'm sure you'll sell them."

And she had. The old women that went there to have their hair done always fawned over the paintings and encouraged her as well. It changed Mina's life.

That unsure little girl, who couldn't imagine anyone liking anything she'd created, who thought those old women bought her paintings out of pity, soon realized that wasn't the case at all. They saw what Mary had: potential.

And for the first time in her life, so did Mina.

"Besides," Mary had assured her, "those tight old buggers wouldn't spend an extra dime on anything frivolous, trust me."

Trust...

Using a black marker, Mina priced them at twenty-five cents then held her breath each time clients came to see Mary for a perm or a cut, all those older women who liked to gossip and always asked lots of questions about the foster kids Mary cared for. Turned out they loved Mina's Disney characters, paying the twenty-five cents and sometimes even giving her a dollar. Soon she was even getting requests—Donald Duck, Bambi, or Dumbo—and one woman asked her to paint portraits of her cats, offering to pay Mina twenty dollars for each one.

All those tiny canvases tumbled from the darkness...every brushstroke...every color in her palette blending together, and she felt wetness in her eyes—was it blood, tears, or both?—as she remembered that sweet woman, so different than those who hurt and abused her, who kicked her down and held her there. Mary raised her up, and as Mina cherished that memory, the colors all around her fell into place, creating another scene that played out before her.

She walked the streets of Providence, her heart pounding in anticipation, because she'd earned enough money to buy art supplies in the city—fine brushes, paint easier to work with than the cheap brands, strong canvas, an easel. Most of all, she'd gained the confidence to attend the community college, taking art classes, excelling in her studies, then going on to Rhode Island School of Design with a partial scholarship.

Images like camera stills floated above her—Mary smiling proudly with each of Mina's accomplishments, telling her, "Told you so. I knew you could do it."

In an explosion of bright reds and blues, Mary vanished.

Mina stood in front of vast windows overlooking the city. A college art studio where she painted her first large-scale paintings, abstract expressions of the landscape that shined outside the confines of glass. A man stood in front of her, shaggy gray hair, glasses. He smiled, telling her, "You're the best student I've had in twenty years. Keep painting, keep painting."

She drenched her canvas in acrylic washes—blue, orange, white and black. Hues spattered on the windows, the floor, her skin, and she became one with the canvas, shivering as watery shades of sapphire drenched her. The rich blues slowly morphed into an ocean that formed beneath and in front of her.

Fear...

She stood behind the ghostly ferryman from her nightmares as he steered a rickety vessel toward land, where trees swayed and a bright sun beat down. As they reached the shore, the ferryman fastened the vessel to a crumbling dock. Fierce eyes staring at her, he slowly motioned to land.

Mina stepped onto the dock and followed it to shore. When she'd reached ground, she looked back.

The boat and ferryman were gone.

A warm breeze blew past. Mina turned to it, feeling it against her face and neck, in her hair. She walked into it, following the sand up over the dunes and into the tall grass and field from her dreams. Moving steadily, she waded into the grass until she'd reached the end of the field and the stalks finally parted to reveal the squat gnarled oak tree she knew would be there.

The others stood beneath the tree, before the circle of stones, hands reaching for her blindly. Blood streamed across their faces from the black empty sockets where their eyes had once resided.

Only one woman had eyes, and Mina recognized her immediately.

Isa Riker stood before her, even more beautiful than the portraits, her long black hair flowing and dancing in the breeze. "I've waited for you for so long," she said, voice laced with a German accent. "So very long, Mina. So very long. Now you will see, as I have. There must always be a shepherd, Mina, always. My blind little sheep are yours to care for now. The still place is *yours*."

Mina reached for her, but Isa's eyes had already looked to the heavens, as if she'd seen something of huge importance.

Before Mina could reach her, the woman burst into flames, her ashes fluttering in the air before riding the breeze out across the field and disappearing into the tall grass.

"It's all a dream," Mina said, backing away.

No. It never was. It never has been. It never will be. It's your reality now.

The blind, those souls who had come before her—Robert Sanders and the rest—all gathered before her, their mutilated faces searching for her without eyes, trembling hands reaching for her, not to threaten but for reassurance.

My God, she thought. *They want* me *to comfort* them.

As Mina remembered who they were, who they'd once been, she began to cry. Hands shaking, she reached for her cheeks, ran her fingers through the tears, then held her hands out before her.

"I can see," she said, weeping. "They didn't take my eyes!"

The ritual...for me it was only a ritual...

As the others closed around her, their hands touching her, pulling on her desperately, mouths open and working like so many hungry baby birds, their empty eye sockets gruesome and bloody, Mina fell into them.

I'm the shepherd now...

"Mina...Mina...Mina..." they chanted in unison.

They ran their bloody hands over her face, her eyes, nose, lips, and neck, *seeing* her with touch.

Become, Mina. Become art...

And as they clung to her like the mother to them she now was, Mina looked back out across the field, the slowly swaying tall grass, and the world she'd left behind.

CHAPTER TWENTY

Ralph shielded his face from the rain with his hand. The stone gargoyle perched on the rooftop stared down at him, its eyes sculpted into a demonic glare that seemed to mock him. As he stood gazing up at the dark building before him, and the monstrosity atop it, he remembered how Mina hadn't realized the gargoyle was there until the end.

With tired eyes, five o'clock shadow, and having traded his usual stylish look for a wrinkled, ankle-length raincoat, slacks, and a jacket, Ralph looked like a disheveled gumshoe straight out of an old crime noir flick. All that was missing was the fedora. If Mina had seen him like that she'd have teased him, offering some sort of wiseass crack.

Mina, he thought, tears of anguish and rage filling his eyes.

From the moment Ralph got out the hospital—where, against his will, he'd been under observation for thirty days in a psych ward—he started looking for her. Despite his efforts, the authorities made only brief and cursory attempts to locate Mina. They had little interest in what they deemed fantasies conjured in the mind of someone on drugs and alcohol that had also suffered a psychological breakdown. Besides, Mina was a grown woman, someone known to be a regular user, and often an abuser, of drugs and alcohol herself, and other than the wild accusations of a man who had just been released from a psychiatric hospital, there was nothing to indicate she was in any danger.

As for the collective, it no longer existed. They'd shut down while Ralph was in the hospital, apparently, and moved away. Even their website had vanished. There was nothing left but the house on the cliffs, the old apartment buildings they'd inhabited, and the building that had once housed their gallery. All were now abandoned. Two months later, it was as if Klaus and the others had never been there at all.

Ralph watched the first floor as he relived flashes of being in Rita and Dave's apartment, the strange curtains, the smells and sounds, the powder exploding into his face, losing track of Mina as everything went dark.

Shuddering, he moved up the steps and tried the front door. It was locked, so he descended the steps, walked around to the side of the building and into the courtyard. From there he looked up at the windows to what had been Mina's apartment.

Both buildings were dark, the courtyard deserted and even more derelict than before. With a heavy heart, Ralph stuffed his hands into his coat pockets and strode back out into the street. There was no traffic, no signs of life anywhere, the buildings looming all around him dark and deserted, their secrets hidden.

* * * *

The large house before him was as dark and deserted as the apartment buildings. Ralph sat in his car a moment, taking it in, and then stepped out into what had become a misting rain. With its forsaken grounds and nearby cliffs, the ocean beyond and rocky coastline below, the old Victorian looked like a creepy set piece from a classic horror movie of the 1930s.

Eventually, Ralph left his car and approached the front of the house. He knew the front door would be locked, so he stood there a while, watching the old house and listening to the ocean beyond the cliffs and the occasional cries of seabirds. The wind was heavier here, blowing in off the Atlantic, and the smell of saltwater hung in the crisp air.

As he strolled closer to the cliffs, Ralph remembered Phillip Bergeron, the private detective Robert Sanders' boyfriend Colin Brewster had hired.

After several attempts, Ralph finally got Bergeron to agree to a meeting at a beach not far from his office in Revere. A former police detective in Boston who'd retired and opened his own private investigations business a few years prior, Bergeron was a short, pasty, middle-aged balding man in ill-fitting clothes that looked like he'd once been powerfully built but had since become overweight and slovenly. Although he didn't appear to be the easily intimidated type, Bergeron was jittery and paranoid from the start. Despite continually watching the traffic and scanning the beach, even though it was a cold and rainy day and no one else was there, he made it clear from the outset that theirs would be a brief meeting, and that this was the last time he'd see or speak with Ralph.

"Your friend got mixed up with these people, I get it," Bergeron told him. "But there's nothing I can do for you, Deckard. I tried to explain that to you on the phone."

"Her name's Mina," Ralph told him. "And she's missing."

"Yeah, I bet she is."

"They drugged us with this powder, and I—"

"You already told me all this," Bergeron said, waving at the air between them as if to swat the words away. "I saw your police report too. Sometimes it's good to be a former cop, know what I mean? Drunk driving, crashing your vehicle, hallucinogens found in your blood, psychotic behavior. You pulled thirty in a psych ward and your license is suspended. You shouldn't even be driving."

"Does it look to you like I give a shit about a *license?*" Ralph said, struggling to control his rage. "The whole thing was a setup to make me look insane."

"I don't doubt it."

"Then help me. I'm trying to hire you."

Bergeron watched a car slowly pass by on the street that ran parallel to the beach. "You're gonna have your hands full keeping yourself out of jail or the looney bin for the next few months, Deckard. You need a lawyer, not a PI."

"I want you to find Mina."

"Look, I already told you on the phone I wasn't interested." Bergeron fumbled a cigar and a zippo from his jacket pocket. "So if that's all this is about, we can wrap it up right now and—"

"I don't care what it costs. I'm a teacher and an artist, I'm not a wealthy man, but I have savings and a retirement fund. I'm prepared to pay you whatever I have to—"

"Listen to me," Bergeron snapped. "This isn't about the money. I don't care what you pay me. I want nothing to do with those freaks. And trust me, neither do you. Besides, I probably couldn't find them even if I wanted to. They could be anywhere."

"What am I supposed to do?" Ralph asked, voice breaking with emotion. "Just forget about her? Just let it all go?"

Bergeron stabbed the cigar between his lips and snapped open the lighter. "I know it's not what you want to hear, but yeah, that's exactly what you need to do."

"Mina's my best friend, I *have* to find her."

"Just like the rest of them, Deckard, she's gone and not coming back. Sooner you get your head around that, the better off you'll be."

"You worked for Colin Brewster, why not me?"

"I worked for him to a point. Hell, I even kept digging *after* I was working for him, just for my own satisfaction. I told Brewster the same thing I'm telling you. I don't know what the hell they're up to—not exactly—but those people are dangerous, you understand?"

"We were attacked by them, of course I understand they're dangerous," Ralph said, clenching his hands into fists. "So come to the police with me and tell them that. You were a cop once, they'll listen to you."

"They just might," Bergeron agreed. "Until I start talking about the same nutty shit you tried to tell them."

"What have they done to Mina?" Ralph asked desperately. "Is she alive?"

"How the hell should I know?" Bergeron flicked the lighter, cupping the flame with his hands and puffing on the cigar until he got it going. "All I can tell you is that every person that took a residency with them is either missing or presumed dead. Robert Sanders supposedly left in a rental car to head back to California, right? Well, let me tell you something, Deckard. You need a credit card to rent a car in the Commonwealth of Massachusetts. It's a requirement, cut and dry, can't rent a vehicle without one, yet I was never able to come up with any rentals Sanders made, not charged to his card anyway."

"That alone should raise a significant red flag for the police."

"Nobody's ever seen him again, and now Riker and his group are gone too. Who are they supposed to talk to about it? But there's more. You got the woman before Sanders, Audra Marini, out of—"

"Florida. She went home and committed suicide. She drowned herself."

"Did she?" Bergeron exhaled a stream of smoke into the light rain falling all around them. "Nobody saw or spoke to her, and there's no evidence she even made it home. She supposedly left Crow's Cry and drove back to Florida, right? But there's no record of her doing that. No gas receipts, no charges to her debit card or bank accounts. Sure, her car wound up back at her apartment, and a bunch of clothes were found on a nearby beach. So what? Any one of them could've driven her car to Florida, paid cash so there'd be no records, then dumped some of her clothes on the beach and left."

"Do you believe that's what happened?" Ralph asked.

"Yes, I do. Just like I believe Sanders never left there either. Before Audra Marini there was another woman, Jennifer Williams, from Illinois. A loner, no family—like your friend Mina—and she supposedly left after her residency before vanishing in the Midwest. Her car was found broken down and abandoned on a state highway in Indiana. Cops assumed she took a ride from the wrong person and was abducted. No trace of her has ever been found. Before her, the first recipient of the residency was a guy named Steven Johnson, an ex-con that did six and a half years for drugs and a series of robberies. He started painting in prison, apparently got pretty good at it. It ended up changing his life for the better, so he decided to pursue it once he got out. After his residency he supposedly returned to his home state of New Jersey. Took a bus, they said. But guess what? None of the drivers that handle that route could ID him, and nobody in Jersey was able to swear they actually saw or spoke to him after he left for Crow's Cry. Johnson had a history of heroin addiction, and lived in a tough section of Newark. Cops figured he probably fell back into it a few days after he got home, got mixed up in the middle of some drug deal gone wrong, and got iced. Whatever happened, nobody's seen or heard from him in five years."

"And now Riker and his entire crew just conveniently vanish right after Mina goes missing and that doesn't raise any red flags either?"

"You're missing the point. We can raise all the red flags we want. There's nobody left to investigate."

"What about their properties? Surely—"

"Turns out they didn't own any of the real estate they were occupying, not the apartment buildings, not the gallery, not even the old house Riker was living in on the cliffs. They were all rentals." Bergeron shrugged. "Seems they just up and left one night. But hey, people got the right to move whenever they want, Deckard, it's still a free country, more or less. And who's to say your friend's really missing? Could be she just decided to leave with them to wherever they went."

Ralph glared at him.

"I'm not saying I believe that, but it's what the authorities are gonna tell you."

"How is it possible the police aren't interested in any of this?" Ralph shook his head in disbelief. "We're talking about *five* human beings who have all disappeared or supposedly died over a five-year period after coming to Crow's Cry as residents for Klaus Riker's collective. With all that evidence, why wouldn't they—"

"What evidence? You mean *circumstantial* evidence?"

"But there's a mountain of it. People are arrested and convicted on circumstantial evidence all the time. You know that more than most."

"Sure, and I got a couple departments to take a look," Bergeron told him. "It's not like Riker or his people were never questioned, they were. But what do we really have? You've got a group of people telling the same story and a bunch of residents that are all losers or loners—no offense— but the kind of people who tend to be unreliable and statistically prone to having bad things happen to them. And it's not like there was any evidence these things happened in Crow's Cry. The residents come from different states, so these things are spread out all over the country, and that's exactly why Riker picked them. Even if it *did* look suspicious, by the time it did, he and his sideshow would be long gone. End of the day, there isn't enough hard evidence to do anything anyway."

"So they do nothing?"

"Sad to say, but it's the truth. When it comes to people like Mina and the others before her, nobody really gives a shit."

"I do," Ralph said, trembling. "*I* give a shit."

Bergeron bowed his head then looked away, down the beach. "I can't prove it, but you and I both know these people were into a lot of bad shit, black witchcraft and all that. You're an artist, a painter, right?"

Ralph nodded.

"Then maybe you know more about that stuff than I do."

"Are you one of those idiots that think artists of any ilk are all a bunch of closet Satanists?"

Bergeron stared at him a moment, noisily chomping his cigar. "You're accusing me of holding out on you, but you're the one holding out on me. *That's* what I think."

"I'm not holding out on you," Ralph told him. "I'm aware of the same things you've told me so far, nothing more. All I know is that they were conducting strange rituals having to do with soul transference. And I'm not accusing you of anything. For Christ's sake, I'm asking you to help me."

"Whatever they were up to, whatever they've done, Klaus Riker and his followers are long gone, Deckard, and so are all the residents. I don't know where they went or what they did with your friend and the rest of those poor souls, but I can tell you this. Not that I think you'll ever find them or your friend, but you better tread real careful trying to track these people down, or you'll wind up missing—maybe worse—right along with the rest of them. These are not the kind of people you want to be fucking around with. You understand what I'm telling you?"

Ralph flipped up the collar of his coat against the wind. "Yes, I do."

"You're wasting your time," Bergeron said. "Mina's probably dead, I—"

Launching himself at Bergeron, Ralph grabbed him by the lapels of his wrinkled jacket and shook him like a ragdoll. "You watch what the fuck you say to me!"

Sparks from his cigar sprayed the air as Bergeron raised his hands defensively. "Jesus H, take it easy, buddy!"

"*You* take it easy! I need to find Mina!"

"Hands off," Bergeron said in a softer tone than he'd been using previously. "I mean it, Deckard. Get your hands off me—*now*—before this escalates to a point where we can't stop it."

Ralph released him, took a few steps away, and ran a shaking hand through his hair. "I'm sorry, I…"

Bergeron straightened himself up a bit. "Look, I know you think I'm an asshole, but I'm just trying to shoot straight with you here. I'm truly sorry about Mina, okay? I am. But think about what they did to you. They could've killed you. They didn't, but they could've. You push this, even if you get lucky and somehow find these fuckers, next time you won't be so lucky."

"This isn't luck," Ralph told him. "This is torment."

"I wish I could be more help to you," Bergeron said, the cigar smoke circling them. "But there's nothing else I can do."

"You mean there's nothing else you're *willing* to do."

"Have it your way. However you frame it, I'm walking the fuck away. It's the smart move, Deckard. You need to do the same thing."

"I'll never stop looking for her." Ralph gazed out at the ocean. "I *can't*."

"Then I'm truly sorry for you too."

As the private detective's frightened eyes and the memory of that day faded, Ralph found himself back at the edge of the cliffs, gazing out at the ocean, the wind whistling in his ears.

I'll never stop, Mina. I'll never stop looking for you.

Wrestling with the anger rising in him, Ralph kicked a small stone with the toe of his shoe. It broke free of the earth, flew into midair, and seemed to hang there a second before plummeting several hundred feet into the sea.

Where are you?

Ralph waited, as if hoping the ocean might answer him in this strange and dark place of ghosts and whispers. But only nightmares replied, flooding his mind as they had since that night, merciless and unrelenting.

Shaking free of them as best he could, Ralph headed back for his car.

CHAPTER TWENTY-ONE

~Oaxaca, Mexico, 2022~

Largely located along a significant portion of coastline in southwestern Mexico, and known for its biological diversity, indigenous peoples and cultures, pre-Hispanic ruins, churches, monasteries, sandy beaches, and a vibrant art scene, Oaxaca had produced several important painters over the years whose works inspired a movement that resulted in the emergence of numerous local art galleries, schools, and museums. Along with other vibrant arts, such as dance, music, and writing, Oaxaca was not only important culturally, it had become a notable center for the arts and a destination for many tourists as well. Most attractions were located in the city and the Central Valleys region that surrounded it, and included an array of indigenous markets and villages devoted to art and various crafts.

Beneath a gorgeous blue sky, in their khaki shorts, sandals, hats, and sunglasses, a young American couple strolled along a narrow street hand-in-hand. The sun beat down over the city as a gentle breeze blew in off the nearby Pacific, which made for a hot but reasonably comfortable afternoon. Small strips of attached buildings—mostly painted red or blue—lined either side of the street, the tower from an old church atop a hill behind them peeking out over the flat rooftops.

Several vendors had set up shop along the street, selling various arts and crafts, and as the couple strolled on, they occasionally stopped to peruse the merchandise. When they came upon a modest vendor who appeared to be an American or European woman selling paintings, they stopped, more out of curiosity than anything else. The woman, dressed in faded denim shorts, sandals, a peasant blouse, and a floppy hat, looked like a hippie from the 1960s. Most of the paintings were propped against the walls of the building in front of which she stood, others were displayed on a long table or on a series of wooden easels she'd set up. There were also several small sculptures arranged along the ground on a blanket.

GREG F. GIFUNE & SANDY DELUCA

The hippie smiled at the couple dreamily as they approached. "Hi," she said. "Isn't it a groovy day?"

The woman, a blonde, exchanged glances with her husband, a tall man with a goatee, and then smiled politely at the vendor. "Are you an American?"

"I live here now but originally, yeah," the hippie girl said. "You guys too?"

"Yes, we're from Chicago. We're here on vacation."

"Far out, feel free to look around. If you see anything you like, just let me know. I'm Jasmin. Anyway, the paintings and sculptures are by local artists from a nearby artist colony we run, and all prices are negotiable."

"Great, thanks," the woman said, pulling her husband along as she began to take in all the paintings on display.

The couple took their time, considering each piece as they went. But there was one painting in particular that caught the woman's eye.

"Jasmin?" she asked, pointing to one at the outskirts of the vendor's area, leaned against the front of a building and off by itself. "Do you know the story behind this painting? It's so *different*."

Jasmin moved closer. "To be honest, we've had it in our stock for a while now, but we're not exactly sure where it came from. It's not signed so we don't know who the artist was or how old the painting is, but we think it probably came from one of the students from our art classes. They just left it behind or never picked it up for some reason and I guess it wound up in our inventory. It's been with us so long I've become kind of attached to it, for sentimental reasons. It has a certain *magic* to it, but nobody's ever shown any interest until now."

"It's kind of creepy," the woman said, still studying the painting. "Yet there's a strange beauty to it too." She looked to her husband, but he gave a disinterested shrug, so she turned back to Jasmin. "How much do you want for it?"

"It's been sitting here for a few years. How's fifty dollars sound? Just so you know, all proceeds go directly to our artist colony."

The woman grasped the frame and stood up, still mesmerized as she held it out in front of her. "That's a little more than I wanted to spend."

Looking impatient, the man asked, "Sweetie, is this the one you want?"

"I think so. What do you think? Do you like it?"

"I don't—I mean—whatever—if you like it I like it. I'm getting hungry, though, we should grab some lunch soon."

The woman bit her lower lip. "Would you take forty?"

200

Jasmin nodded. "Sure."

The woman thought the hippie girl's reaction odd. It was almost as if she was sad to sell the painting, like she was going to miss it. "Okay then, I'll take it."

As her husband paid for the painting, the woman continued staring at it. Such a wonderfully odd piece, it portrayed a field of tall grass that appeared to be swaying in the wind, which led to a large, gnarled tree and a small circle of stones before it. A group of people knelt before the tree, as if in prayer of some kind.

None of them had eyes.

But it was the main woman in the painting she was drawn to most. The only one with eyes, she stood apart from the others, staring out at her with such a profound expression of horror, desperation, and somehow, acceptance. It was almost as if the subject was looking directly into her soul, trying to tell her something, to communicate something of great importance.

"I'm curious," the woman said. "Does the painting have a name?"

"Not really," Jasmin answered. "But we've always called it The Still Place."

"*The Still Place*," the woman muttered. "I like that."

As Jasmin handed change back to the woman's husband, she reached out and tenderly touched the frame a moment. "Like I said, I got a little attached to it. For a while it almost felt like I was a *part* of it." She laughed lightly, as if to herself. "But I'm glad to see it finally getting a new home. It's time."

The woman smiled. "She looks powerful, the woman staring out."

"Yeah," Jasmin said fondly. "She sure does."

"Well, thank you. Have a great day."

"You guys do the same. And thank *you*."

As the couple moved away, Jasmin adjusted her hat and looked across the street to a small café and a couple sitting at one of the tables. An old man and a strikingly beautiful woman considerably his junior had been watching since the American couple approached. Jasmin gave a slow nod and flashed them a peace sign.

In response, the old man slowly raised a glass of wine he'd been drinking, as if to toast her.

As Jasmin tilted her head back so the sun could hit her face, she remembered the painting, and Mina, one last time.

Keeper of the others...the mother...the shepherd...

Shape...form and color...unable to move...unable to hear...

Able only to see...to comprehend...

Pure...realized...important...horrifying...
From the Still Place, Mina watched with silent defiance.
A beautiful work of art now...
Forever lost in a kingdom of the blind.

ABOUT THE AUTHORS

Greg F. Gifune is a best-selling, internationally-published author of several acclaimed novels, novellas, screenplays, and two short story collections. He has been described as 'The best writer of horror and thrillers at work today' by author Christopher Rice, 'Among the finest dark suspense writers of our time' by author Ed Gorman, and 'One of the best writers of his generation' by author Brian Keene. Legendary author of SIX DAYS OF THE CONDOR, James Grady said of Gifune's work, 'How great it is to be in the hands of a seasoned pro like Gifune.' Working predominantly in the horror and crime genres, Gifune's work has been translated into several languages, including German and Russian, has received starred reviews from Publisher's Weekly, Library Journal and others, and is consistently praised by readers and critics alike. His novel THE BLEEDING SEASON, originally published in 2003, is still in print in several languages, has been hailed as a classic in the horror/suspense genres, and is considered by many, including *Famous Monsters of Filmland*, to be one of the best horror novels of its kind ever written. Gifune also consults on film and TV scripts and is developing several film and television projects based on his own work. For film/TV he is represented by Paradigm Talent Agency, Hollywood. Greg resides in Massachusetts with his wife Carol and their dogs, Dudley and Ozzy. He can be reached online at gfgauthor@verizon.net or on Facebook, Twitter and Instagram.

***

Sandy DeLuca has written novels, several poetry and fiction collections and a few novellas. These include critically acclaimed works such as *Descent* and *Messages from the Dead*.

She was a finalist for the Bram Stoker Award® for poetry in 2001, with *Burial Plot in Sagittarius*; accompanied by her cover art and interior illustrations. A copy is maintained in the Harris Collection of American Poetry and Plays Poetry at Brown University, 1976-2000. She was also nominated once more in 2014, with Marge Simon, for *Dangerous Dreams*.

Her visual art has also been published in books and magazines. It has been exhibited throughout New England and in New York's Hudson Valley.

She lives in Rhode Island with several feline companions, including a black cat named Gypsy and her two sons, Gemini and Leo.

She is currently working on a new novel, poetry and a series of large-scale expressionistic paintings. She spends some of her free time volunteering at a local food pantry, photographing abandoned buildings and perusing secondhand shops.

Printed in the USA
CPSIA information can be obtained
at www.ICGtesting.com
JSHW081107301123
52886JS00005B/96